WITHDRAWN

# The Old Man
# of the Mountain

AND SEVENTEEN OTHER STORIES BY

## Allan Seager

SIMON AND SCHUSTER · 1950

NEW YORK

Acknowledgment is hereby made to *Good House-
keeping, Harper's Bazaar, Vanity Fair, Story, Scrib-
ner's, Foreground,* and *Esquire,* in whose pages
certain of these stories originally appeared.

MANUFACTURED IN THE UNITED STATES OF AMERICA
BY VAIL-BALLOU PRESS, INC., BINGHAMTON, N. Y.

FOR *Mary and Laura*

# TABLE OF CONTENTS

# The Street

**Y**ES, IT'S SPRING all right. That big elm tree is just sprouting leaves. Looks like a green mist over the branches. And that old lady, the hump-backed old lady is digging and raking at that patch of lawn in front of her house."

It was spring. For three months now he had not seen a tree, lying there in the clean bare room. But Whitaker, in the bed by the window, could see the street below. He was always talking, as he was talking now, about the first green shoots and foliage and about the little typist—he said she was a typist and pretty, too—who passed every morning and evening. All day long he lay there, sick and still, staring at the gray wall and listening enviously to Whitaker. A vision of the street he could not see grew like a mosaic on the wall. Every day Whitaker gave him something new, a dogfight, the new milk wagon, or a householder smoking in his back yard. These bright fragments he inserted carefully into the whole and trimmed and polished until the wall before him almost became a window through which he too could see the street.

There was nothing else to do but listen. Books had grown stale and, with his low fever, reading hurt his eyes anyway. When his friends came to visit him they always said the same thing. Of course he was not feeling better. Tuberculosis was not the colic. One didn't get well overnight. The only thing was to lie quiet on the right side so the lesions wouldn't drain, and wonder how the trees looked in the street outside.

He wished he had the bed by the window instead of Whitaker. Then he could look out. He could watch the leaves unfurl and the flowers spring up and the people in the street as well. If he could see them come and go, it would be quite easy for him to feel a part of things again. Besides, he thought Whitaker preened himself on having such a fine place. (Though God knows there was no reason why he should. The doctor had assigned the beds.) And Whitaker had begun to use what seemed a superior tone, as if he were the owner and proprietor of all outdoors, as if one could not understand what a car or hand-organ was, or even a tree. He was certain it was a superior tone. As if one were a child. Yes, it was clear that Whitaker held one end of the thread that led back into what he was coming to call "life." And he was coming to hate

Whitaker because he held it. At first he was astonished at his own baseness. He had always regarded himself as a decent fellow. He did not know that confinement and disease can taint decency. "This is silly. I really ought not to notice it at all. I am thirty years old. People, men, do not . . ." The naïveté of the process disgusted him but he went through it like a rosary every day for a while and sometimes he was polite to Whitaker afterward. As the days went by, each like the last, he hated Whitaker simply, and did not think about the baseness.

Whitaker's heart attacks evened things up. They were the price he paid for the best bed. It was quite reasonable. One could not have everything gratis. Sometimes in the night Whitaker would sit upright in the bed choking and panting. His heart would beat two hundred to the minute then, the doctors said. It was very hard for him to get enough air into his rotting lungs.

At the first movement he would be awake and for thirty or forty seconds he would watch Whitaker's shoulders heave and his head jerk. Then with a feeling of condescension he would press the button to call the night nurse. Usually she could relieve Whitaker but when it was very bad, doctors would be called. They came partly dressed and yawning. They would lean over Whitaker in the dark room and talk in low voices. The paroxysms were dangerous when they went on too long, for both his lungs were partly collapsed and, if his heart were not slowed down, he might die for lack of air. Resting on his elbow in the far bed, he would watch with secret satisfaction as if justice were being done. Even in the night when he was waked from sleep, he was angry with Whitaker.

All through the empty summer, the anger grew and festered in him like a sore he could not leave alone. Remorse was rare and short-lived when it came and his thoughts slid back into his grievance with a maddening gravity. He would recite to himself like a nursery rhyme his winter in Mexico or his battle with the trout, but just as he was ready with the net, had got a firm footing in the swirling water, Whitaker would begin about some children in the street and he would be snatched back to be hot and sick again in this damned narrow room. "He doesn't have to do that," he thought bitterly. He was sure Whitaker knew it hurt, always to hear about the street and never to see it.

At sundown his fever rose and as the room grew dim, his head ached and the daytime clarity of his mind vanished. When he looked at the pale oblong of the window, it seemed to him a gateway and beyond it were all the joys and brightness he had been forced to forsake. If he could only stand at the gate and look out, but no, there was Whitaker like a demon guarding the way. It was the gateway to life, and in the darkness Whitaker's gaunt face began to assume the shape and hollows of a skull. He was Death, of course. The reverend sonorities of the Church arose in his mind, confusing him. Phrases about Death and Life, solemn and distorted, he remembered from hymns and prayer books. If he could vanquish Death, he would be granted everlasting life.

"That little girl just passed, the stenographer. She's got a bouquet."

"And you would kill her if you had the chance, just as you would kill me," he would mutter to himself.

Suddenly one night he saw his course clearly: he would not press the button. When he heard Whitaker begin to twitch and pant, he would not press the button. The nurse would not come and Whitaker would die. Through the steaming days of late summer when the street outside was full of people that he could not see; while Whitaker lay describing with brutal detail these men and women who were well and strong, who could even go on holidays, he stared at the bare gray wall, smiling over his secret. The nurse would find Whitaker when she made her rounds. The doctors would come shaking their heads and clucking. They would wheel him out on a stretcher with a sheet over him. Then he would have the bed by the window. He could look out upon the world again and this would make him well. No, the next time—or the time after —he would not press the button.

So he became slyly polite. There was no more sullen silence before Whitaker's unending chronicle; he made talk, even put questions with a false vivacity. This was difficult, for when he looked toward the other bed, he felt a horrible disgust. The frantic nights of fever had imprinted the image of Death on Whitaker, and though the sun was in the room, he saw the fleshless sockets and the bone. He always thought of Whitaker as "He" now, and in dealing with such an adversary one must be courteous so that He may not suspect anything. By this time he never doubted he was right. He was even righteous.

One evening when the autumn rains had set in and the wind pried at the window, Whitaker lay supported by his pillows, looking out.

"You should see the trees sway and the lights flicker in the street. Winter's coming."

"See Him, see Death," he thought, "high over the city, urging on in His heart the winds and the cold. He wants the year to die also."

If he could watch over the city from that vantage point— it was like a tower—he would bring back the year. Firm on that parapet, he would have the power, somehow, to make this bleak season blossom as the rose. That was it, "blossom as the rose." He would make it warm and pleasant, not cold like the night outside and never so hot as his head felt now, but warm and green with bright flowers, and the people would be happy always. But he must have the tower so he could watch and see that nothing went wrong. Death barred the way and over Him he must gain the victory.

A sigh came from the other bed. Whitaker was asleep.

If it could only happen tonight! Punishment was long delayed. It must happen tonight, for had He not lounged there at His ease contriving evil things in His heart, monstrous things against the year itself? Surely these wicked desires would weigh heavily on His heart and make it beat too fast. This was but just retribution, the wages of sin. Soon.

The wind spat hard raindrops against the window. He turned and twisted, seeking a cool place on the pillow. Suddenly there was a gasp and Whitaker lurched upright in his bed, panting and choking. Dim against the window like a shadow, he could see Him writhe and struggle for air. It sounded like a dog that had run too far. This was the time. Now He would die. He smiled calmly into the darkness and waited for Him to stop heaving and panting and shaking the bed and die. It was very severe this time, and at the end Whitaker broke into long dry sobs. Presently the sobbing stopped and the room was still except for the spatter of the rain on the glass. He looked over cautiously. At last. He was dead. In the morning when the street shone in the sun, he would go to the tower and keep watch over the city.

In the morning the bed next the window was empty. When the house physician made his round, he asked him, "Would it be possible for me to have that bed there?"

The physician wore a white coat. He stood making notes in a book. "Why yes, I think so," he said, and then, looking up,

"Too bad you didn't hear poor Whitaker last night. You might have saved him."

"I save Him?"

"Yes, you could have pressed the call-button for the nurse."

"Yes. I might have."

The doctor went out and the nurses moved him to the bed by the window. Soberly, without haste, he arranged the pillows, making ready to look out as one who had come into a kingdom. But when he looked, it was not into a sunlit street. There were no trees. Below him was a rear courtyard of the hospital, a blank place, and all day long it was empty.

# Quitandínha

To FLY over the mouths of the Amazon had taken them more than half an hour. When Carter estimated that the distance was over a hundred miles, a simple fact he must have learned in geography at school, he was uncomfortable. Memory should have prepared him a little for these vast wild floods of brown water. It was twenty minutes to six when they sat down at Belém, and he began to take the camera out of the case as soon as they got down the steps from the plane. An interpreter, a young girl in a gray uniform, guided them ("Please, please, this way") into a low white building to the end of a corridor where behind a counter stood the Brazilian customs officials and a little doctor in a white coat with a glass jar full of thermometers. The officials looked at the passports and the health certificates and the doctor gave them each a thermometer that tasted strongly of green soap. The procedure took only a few minutes and Carter was just inserting some eight-millimeter film into the camera when the copilot stopped beside him and said pleasantly, "I wouldn't bother. The sun's nearly down. There's no twilight on the equator. It'll be dark in ten minutes." Carter said, "Thanks," and looked up at the sun, still bright, but descending rapidly into the rim of trees across the river. The trees, he had been told, were the jungle.

He put the camera back into the case and went to find his wife and little girl. He found them in the waiting room standing with some of the other passengers in front of a bat mounted on the wall. A little sign in English and Portuguese said that the wingspread was nearly six feet and the species was native to the region. He looked at it silently a moment. It was certainly not a flying mouse. He touched his wife on the arm and they all went into the airport dining room, where they ate filet mignon, French fried potatoes, and wonderful fresh pineapple. The sun still shone on the glasses and the cutlery and he was thinking he could have taken a few feet of the jungle but it was only a dark line of trees not very interesting at this distance and none of its terrors would have shown in the picture. What he had wanted was a short sequence of his wife and daughter standing in the little courtyard on the hand-planted grass among the hibiscus, laughing and talking, their first foreign country. His wife was in white linen and the little girl in a pinafore. The jungle, even at a distance, was not the right background.

Coming into Rio at dawn, looking down on the bays and inlets of the harbor with astonishment and wonder, Carter had the feeling that this was a city he had been promised. It was like the youthful assurance you have at sixteen or seventeen when all cities will be easy to go to (and they all are beautiful then) and wealth and fame will come at the twist of a wrist. Once he had expected this, counted on it, then the expectancy had faded but, suddenly beneath him lay this city, a belated gift.

They landed on the Isla de Gouvernador at a military field and crossed the harbor in a launch through the rising mists. At the Santos Dumont airport, where they disembarked, they were served coffee in a long vine-covered arbor and he took his little daughter to see a cage of blue and red parrots that stood on the lawn for an ornament. "This is the way to enter a city," he said to his wife.

He had trouble getting into a hotel. The city was full of people like the cities in the States. Bland young men in English as good as his own told him there were no rooms in Rio— he had better try Petropolis; there was a very good hotel there, Quitandinha. He had been warned that the thing to do in this situation was to shove a one-hundred-cruzeiro note across the counter and, if that didn't work, another, but he had not foreseen the clerks speaking English so well. He had expected them to be foreigners, grateful, obsequious, and speaking Portuguese. It was hard somehow to bribe a man who spoke your own language but at last he slid the hundred cruzeiros across the desk. The clerk's eyes did not leave his but his hand crumpled the note up smoothly, and instantaneously Carter had a small suite of rooms.

They were on a courtyard and it was noisy. The beds had straw mattresses and were as hard as bricks. (It was only later that he learned that all beds in Rio are hard because it is easier to sleep on them in the heat of December, January, and February.) In the bathroom, there was an old-fashioned gas hot-water heater of the kind he remembered from his boyhood and there was a *bidet*. Long before the war Carter had studied a while at the Beaux Arts in Paris and he was able to tell his wife the purposes of a *bidet*. She laughed about it for twenty minutes and it helped them settle into the rooms.

The beach, the Praia Copacabana, and the view of the harbor more than made up for the rooms. Every morning Carter and his wife and little girl lay on the beach in the sunshine, swimming occasionally and drying off and watching the light change on the mountains around the water. On the near side of the harbor the mountains were like the Sugar Loaf, big humps of smooth rock that jumped down into the sea; on the opposite side in the haze they were broken up, irregular, fantastic like the mountains of the moon. Ships came in from Santos or Buenos Aires and there were always planes in the air to watch.

His little daughter's hair was blond and it made her very popular. He could see the women under the beach umbrellas turn to watch her as they passed. In a few days she was playing eagerly with the Brazilian children, building castles in the sand or looking for shells. When Carter asked her how she got along so well when she didn't speak the language, she said very seriously, "Oh, we just smile at each other." Carter and his wife discussed that the rest of the morning, that is, they began by complimenting themselves on having an intelligent child and went on from there to international relations. The war and the peace worried Carter. Although like most Americans he had never been shot at and he had eaten as well as ever, he had believed for a long time that events were hatching that could threaten his whole life, monstrous things could happen that would leave him all alone in a wilderness of unsafe wreckage. The thought that nothing was secure was embedded in his mind almost like a splinter. In this sunshine he could feel himself begin to relax for the first time in six years. He was a little ashamed of it when he thought of the everyday news, yet more important than the shame was what seemed to him an opportunity. He picked up his camera and began to take pictures of his daughter and the other children, of his wife alone, of his wife and daughter, and his wife took a long sequence of the little girl and her daddy.

In all the pictures someone was smiling. If she was not, Daddy stood on his head or did a silly little dance until one of them began to laugh at him. He was very pleased that they were happy in such beautiful surroundings but there was a sort of desperation in his eagerness to get it on film so that later it could be proved to someone.

## II

AT FIRST when he was a bachelor there were the baskets of eggs and the street lamp in a city square snapped from the third story, a nimbus laced across by a web of shadows from the trees. There had to be trees in it or it was no good. There was the occasional gnarled old man and, if he had met some girl who took his artistic protestations seriously, a nude study on a beach, a fringe of grass waving gently about her bare calves with the camera peeping upward from the sand to make her seem tall, "monumental," he called it.

For three or four years he spent nearly every week-end taking pictures with a miniature camera and the evenings in between developing and mounting them. He read books about photography and properly admired the work of David Octavius Hill, Stieglitz, and Cartier-Bresson. Even at that time he had several commissions to design buildings; he was making good money; and he once paid over five hundred dollars for a Leica lens. Photography took almost as much of his time and money as a wife. He became a fair technician but his results did not satisfy him because he did not quite know what the pictures meant to him or why he was taking them. He never sat down with a print in his hands and asked, "What does this mean? Why have I taken it?" It was not so clear as that. He merely took fewer and fewer pictures and at last he decided that photography was just a hobby. When this was plain to him, he gave it up and got married. This was in 1938.

For the first year or so he did not take any pictures at all. His wife was a very handsome girl, a graduate of Smith College, and he enjoyed showing her off. They gave a lot of cocktail parties for interesting people (and he had special recipes for Martinis, Manhattans, and all the ordinary cocktails) but after a while he found that the parties grew to be much the same, and at each party after about four cocktails, the individual guests grew to be much the same, interesting as they had been when they first came in. He went to a doctor to see if he had been drinking too much but the doctor told him he had not. In fact, he was in fine shape. The afternoon following was Sunday. He and his wife were discussing the increasing monotony of their amusements with the symphony coming in

over the radio. The program was interrupted and the attack on
Pearl Harbor was announced. Almost immediately his wife
said she wanted to have a baby. She was certain he would go
to war and she did not want to be left alone. About a year
later they had the baby, the little girl Cynthia, seven pounds,
three ounces. It was about this time that he bought a small
movie camera and started to take pictures again.

During the next few years he took pictures whenever he
could although he did not have much time for it. He tried to
join the Army, the Navy, and the Marines but a little unsus-
pected heart murmur kept him out of all of them. His firm took
war contracts and he was over a drawing board or out with a
contractor seven days a week and many evenings, but on the
occasions of the first big doll, the visit from the grandparents
and especially on the holidays, Carter would be there with the
camera poised, patient, earnest, almost professional in the
tricks he would use to get a smile from everyone. It surprised
his wife to find him driving forty or fifty miles from some half-
finished tool plant or airstrip to take pictures of the Easter
eggs and the stuffed bunnies for twenty minutes and then
drive all the way back again. He was so determined that he
seemed to have what she could only call "some other purpose"
but she could not discover what it was. Slowly they accumu-
lated a large library of films which he never inflicted on anyone else—if he had a free evening, he would run them off at
home, sitting quietly in the library, seldom smiling, rather
staring with fierce attention at the half-self-conscious antics
of his little family, calm, sunlit, and happy. His wife could
not figure it out, for their own unpictured life was happy
enough, she thought, or would have been if it had not been
for the war.

When the war ended and his work slacked off, the other

members of his firm persuaded Carter to take a summer's vacation. It was not easy to do because he was conscientious but they gave as a reason their interest in Brazilian concrete construction, particularly in apartment houses, and, since most of the apartment houses were in Rio, why, that was the place to go. Carter suspected that the errand was flimsily concocted to hide the kindness but he was tired and he had seen photographs of the beaches. A beach would be a nice place to lie around on for a while and of course he could take some pictures himself. He was also vaguely relieved that it was Brazil they wanted him to visit, not France, not England, no ruins.

Almost before he realized it, his colleagues had bought the plane reservations, badgered him into getting his passport and sent letters to some friends at the Embassy in Rio. When they took off in a big DC-4 from La Guardia Field, he was tormented for an hour by the thought that he had forgotten something or left something undone. Then he remembered what it was—it was his work. After that he felt easier and he began to look forward to the trip.

### III

THE INVESTIGATION of Brazilian concrete construction took him only a few days. He presented his letters at the Embassy. An attaché gave him some introductions to contractors and he drove around the city three afternoons, muttering politenesses out of a dictionary and examining the buildings going up. Finished, they were handsome enough, but Carter thought they did not use enough steel. He saw one or two that had no steel frame holding up the concrete at all. In spite of an obvious pride in their ingenuity, the Brazilians built weak build-

ings and an earthquake, he would have bet money, would
kill all the people on the Beira Mar, Botafogo, and Copacabana. One of his hosts, a Brazilian who spoke English, told
him that an apartment house had already collapsed. "They
are still digging for six people," the man said. Carter wrote
his conclusions earnestly in a notebook with a little chill surprise that human life did not seem to be quite so highly valued
there as it was at home.

As soon as he had finished this little job he rented a car and
a driver and they drove around the city to see the sights.
Sometimes they took their lunch in a wicker basket provided
by the hotel and Carter always wore the camera hung from a
strap around his neck. The driver was full of pride in the
beauty of his city like every *carioca,* and by gentle insistent
domineering he presented each of the well-known tourist
views to them, the Vista Chineza, the Alto da Boa Vista, the
sea from Joá with the marvelous hump-backed island striped
with guano in the distance, and inevitably, Corcovado.

Corcovado is a sheer rock peak two thousand feet high.
From its top, it is obvious that Rio has the most beautiful natural site of any city in the world. All the curves and scallops
of the harbor and the distant beaches can be seen at one turn
of the head, veiled in layers of blue haze, and far below, almost at one's feet lies a scattered heap of colored stones, the
city. To Carter, leaning over a railing, it was like the cities he
had dreamed of as a boy, and without turning his mind to the
thought he knew that the reason for the dreamlike feeling was
not only the beauty but the height—he would only have to
step up on the railing and give a little jump for the falling of a
dream to begin.

He and his wife looked over the railing for maybe ten minutes but it was not this view he photographed. It was so strik-

ing that he could always recall it if he wanted to; it was, in fact, only scenery. Against the base of the gigantic statue of Christ he took pictures of the little girl and his wife. The little girl had teased for a lemon banana from a vendor. And he bought her also a little glass dish backed with azure butterfly wings. The sequence shows Mrs. Carter, smiling; the little girl with the half-peeled banana in her hand, holding the dish up to her eye, staring into the wonderful blue of the butterfly wings as if it were deep, deep, and nowhere is there any gulf of air behind them to show it was taken on a high place. Two priests in flat hats watched him take it, soberly commending the beauty of the *crianca*, the little creature.

After a week of scenery, Mrs. Carter wanted to shop. They drove one day to the Avenida Rio Branca (which Carter did not photograph because for him it resembled many of the tree-lined avenues of Paris). On one of the side streets barely wide enough for a car to go down, Mrs. Carter bought a huge aqua-marine and an alligator handbag. They returned to the Ave-nida to walk down it a little way out of curiosity. The street was full of men at that hour, bareheaded, well-dressed or try-ing to be, sauntering along or sitting over coffee at the side-walk café tables. There was a ring of people blocking the sidewalk at one place and when the little girl started to push in through the legs of the spectators Carter let her go and took up his camera. She wiggled through and got to the center of the ring.

There was a hawker selling little dancing Bahiana dolls. His daughter jumped up and down squealing with pleasure. A murmur of admiration was given by the men in the crowd and one or two of them touched her light hair. With his camera up to his eye, Carter was telling his wife to reach into his breast pocket for his money to buy one of the dolls when he noticed through the camera-sight the hawker's partner, sitting on the sidewalk with a lapful of dolls, a ragged Negro with bare shrunken legs and feet. Two short crutches, irritatingly unnatural, lay beside him. Before his daughter could see the cripple, Carter had taken her by the hand and led her out of the ring of men. Then he went back alone and bought the doll. That night his wife found what she thought was a perfectly good reel of film in the wastebasket in their room. She showed it to Carter but he said it was no good. The little girl had turned on all the faucets in the bathroom—she could hear the rush of water—her attention was distracted and she forgot to ask what was the matter with the film.

At last they took the drive to Petropolis, the little city in the mountains built by the Emperor Pedro Segundo as a summer resort. Everyone they knew had assured them they must see the town if only because of Quitandinha, the magnificent hotel and gambling salon. There was also a cathedral where the bodies of Pedro and Teresa were interred, a summer palace that had been made into a museum full of imperial relics, and a live pretender to the throne, a grandson, Dom Pedro Henrique, still surrounded by a pathetic, fiercely punctilious group of retainers.

It was a two-hour drive through the city to the opposite side of the harbor, across some flat land and up into the mountains. On the flat land, rimmed by a tidal marsh, were suburbs full of poor people. To distract his daughter's gaze and keep her from seeing the frightful squalor, Carter took out his pocketbook and showed her money. It was all he had to amuse her with. The camera was too complicated. She could already recognize the engravings of George Washington on the dollar bills and he taught her to recognize the portrait of Getulio Vargas on the cruzeiro notes. He glanced up occasionally, however, and he would see a hut made of brown banana leaves; a wood fire under a dirty kettle; children ten or eleven years old playing naked; long lines of ragged barefoot people who waited, each carrying a battered tin can, for water from a well. There was a bread shortage in the city and these were the ones who felt it, not the ones on the Copacabana where he was staying. He was relieved when they entered a region of market gardens and orange groves and then began to climb. The road wound around and around the mountains in sharp curves. It was a good concrete highway and there were iron roadmenders' huts every few miles. There were also gasoline and telephone stations. As they rose, the weather grew cooler and there were not so many palm trees.

After sixty miles they came upon Quitandinha. It was a long squat white building about five stories high, and there was some detail on the roof that reminded Carter of Swiss chalets. They had dug a small lake in front of it, full of brown-ish water, but the place did not command any breath-taking view although they had been common on the way up. It was just a big hotel, a little like those in Yellowstone Park.

The promised grandeur began immediately, however. A doorman in an immaculate blue uniform, with clean white gloves, let them out of their car when it stopped under a huge porte-cochère. They entered the lobby and the first chandelier took their eyes. With its branches and foliations it was twenty feet long, made of white plaster with a green design painted on it. It seemed to have been fashioned to pump gasps into people and it did. A clerk in morning coat and gray-striped trousers slid gently across the waxed marble floor. He would, he said in English, be very happy to give them the run of the hotel, such a pity there were so few guests, out of season as it was, they should see it in January in the summer. . . . He and his voice trailed discreetly away and the Carters walked into a vast white hall with a coffered ceiling. Twenty expensive sofas sat against each wall at intervals, each with a low table before it and armchairs flanking it. No one was sitting there and Carter noticed that the ashtrays on the tables were clean and shining.

The hall led into a tall circular room with a skylight in the roof. Beneath the skylight, in the center, a fountain played and surrounding the fountain was a bird cage forty feet high. Red and blue parrots, macaws, doves, and particolored warblers chirped, cawed, and flitted about the plunging spout of water. Even the little girl was silent as she stared.

Past the bird cage fountain was a smaller room into which two curving marble staircases descended. The space between the staircases was occupied by severe "modern" sofas in raspberry-colored leather. Another big chandelier, this one of brass, was suspended above them. Something in the décor seemed familiar to Carter. He had seen something like it before, and suddenly he realized what the scene lacked. It lacked a spotlight and Fred Astaire in it, capering gracefully down the broad steps.

They climbed one of the staircases. The little girl was beginning to whine because she was tired. At the top of the staircase they entered the gambling room. Someone had told them that the dome was bigger than St. Peter's and he believed it. It was a vast, midnight-blue shell, plain, without any ornament. The walls beneath the pilasters that seemed to hold it up were covered with yellow satin. There was one spot where you could stamp your foot and hear seven distinct taps in echo. In rows all around covered with dustcloths bearing the house initial stood roulette and baccarat tables—the new President,

Dutra, had forbidden all gambling except the government lotteries.

Carter's wife took the little girl away to play on the children's playground and Carter was left alone in the room. He stared abstractedly at the curve of the ceiling and drew out a cigarette. Before he could scratch a match, a flunky in a blue uniform appeared with a lighter cocked. Carter could not see where he came from. It made him angry to be watched when he thought he was alone. He accepted the light, murmuring *"Obrigada,"* turned, and walked down the steps. He recognized that he was angry really against the luxury of the place, and it was not the anger he knew he ought to have been feeling, a hatred for such wastefulness only two hours away from the tattered banana-leaf huts and the lines of barefooted people waiting for water. It was rather an anger against these riches, vulgar as they were, because he could not have them, own them, possess them, wallow in them, like the times when, as a boy, he would grow sullen in the Christmas toy displays because he knew he could not have everything in the store and did not dare even to ask.

He looked through a glass door at a marble swimming pool shaped like a kidney, full of still blue water. A restaurant reached to the edge of the pool and the whole thing was indoors. Brazil was a strange far-off country (what it was far from, he did not explain to himself) and Quitandinha was far, too, hidden in the mountains, luxurious, beautiful, and safe. Suddenly he remembered the camera on the leather lanyard over his shoulder. He wanted to hurry to find his wife and daughter and take some pictures of this marvelous place with them in it. He started down a long echoing marble hall. He kept opening doors into dining rooms, all empty of guests, with the napkins done into strange flowerlike shapes on the tables, some rooms blue, some red, some yellow, and one was a children's dining room with a frieze of animals and a puppet show to amuse the children while they ate.

He found his wife in the playground swinging the little girl. He took the camera off his shoulder and started to open the case but he stopped. He decided not to take any pictures because he knew he wanted to put his wife and child inside this luxury, himself also, as if they were in a safe secret cave in a fairy distant country, but the luxury was all inside the hotel where the light was bad—he did not want photographs of a children's playground. He already had some of those.

"We're hungry," his wife said.

He looked at his watch. It was one o'clock. They picked their way through a rock garden and over a little stone bridge to a kind of chalet at the edge of the artificial lake. In it overlooking the brown water was the only restaurant serving meals, the Grill do Lago. The waiters spoke all languages. Their uniforms were impeccable. No money had been spared to make the interior piquantly suggest a rude fisherman's shanty. Even the electric lights were hung from the ceiling by chains of fishhooks. Carter ordered a heavy lunch, totting up a heavy bill for it as he did so.

When the waiter finally brought the hors d'oeuvres, his wife said to the little girl, "Come on, darling. Eat your nice lunch." There was no answer. She was lying down on the cushions of the seat. They thought she was playing and paid no attention at first. Then his wife bent down smiling as if to tickle her. Her face came up serious. "Hadden, she's sick."

"No, I'm not," the child said, sitting up. "I want . . ."

"Look at her eyes," his wife said.

They were already bright and watery. Her face was flushed. "Has she any fever, do you think?" he asked.

His wife was putting on the child's hat and coat. Carter, used to his wife's solicitude about any illness, could see they were leaving. He called for the check, paid it, and went out to find their driver. Brazilians like to drive fast and the driver had a fine time showing off his skill on the hairpin turns of the way back to Rio. The little girl chattered all the time with a bright febrile exhilaration.

## IV

Two SNORES filled the courtyard. One was light, neatly regular, a kind of tenor. The other was a heavy bronchial scuffling.

Carter, holding the telephone well away from him, began slowly in English, "Dr. Ribeiro?"

"Yes."

Carter explained in a loud clear voice that the American Embassy had recommended Dr. Ribeiro, that his daughter had been taken very ill several hours ago, that he himself was an American, Hadden Carter, staying at the Riviera Hotel, and could Dr. Ribeiro come at once? While he was talking, he could hear the little girl gagging and coughing again, and he did not look around at her because he was beginning to be afraid. The doctor said he would come as soon as he could, perhaps at three o'clock.

"At three then," Carter said.

His wife looked up furiously from the bed. "Why can't he come now? What's keeping him? What's he doing?"

Except for the birth of his daughter, there had never been

any crisis in Carter's married life. No one had been seriously
ill before. There had been no real quarrels. He had always had
plenty of money to meet other emergencies, and Carter, perhaps, he thought now, fatuously, had believed he had been
responsible. He had stood guard at the door, fending off evil
possibilities, never letting them break in. Seeing his wife as
angry as she was, knowing it was foolish yet permissible, he
admitted that his defense had been broken through. He could
only do little things hopefully from now on. "He's coming as
soon as he can."

"What's he doing at this time of night?" As if Carter and the
doctor were to blame, she said bitterly, "This is a very sick
child. We've got to stop her vomiting."

The little girl had been throwing up every ten minutes now
in a dreadful cycle. Unlike herself, she was ominously quiet
between the paroxysms. She lay on the hard bed with her
eyes open looking to her father and mother for help.

The phone rang. They both jumped. It was the first time
it had rung since they had been in Rio. It was the doctor. He
had called to recommend a preparation to stop the vomiting,
and casually, as if it were something they had already discussed together, he said that this kind of dysentery was not
usually dangerous. Carter did not repeat the word. He asked
about all-night pharmacies.

"When is he coming?" his wife asked.

"Pretty soon. I've got to go get some medicine. I'll be back
as soon as I can. When he comes, his name is Ribeiro."

"I don't care what his name is if he'll just get here," his wife
said. She was smoothing the little girl's forehead nervously
all the time now. "I've got to have some more towels."

"I'll see if I can get some." He wanted to pat his wife on the
shoulder but he did not. She was using the anger to hide her

fear. If he patted her, it would show that he was not respond-
ing to the anger properly and did not believe in it. He did not
want to leave her alone with the sick child and the fear un-
covered.

In the lobby two porters in white coats were talking and
yawning at the desk. No one else was in sight. They looked up
in surprise. He went up to them. "*A menina e doente*," he said
from his phrase book. "*Farmácia aberta?*"

One of the porters was an Indian. His face looked as if it
had been carved out of stone. He braced himself with both
hands on the edge of the counter and looked at Carter intently.
"I—spik—Inglés—a little," he said, and exhaled. "Your—
babby—is—sick."

"Yes." With equal earnestness Carter leaned across the desk,
staring into the *porteiro's* gray rocklike face. He knew it was
a comic scene and he was embarrassed with himself that he
could even recognize it at such a time. "I—must—get—medicine," he called. "Is there—a—pharmacy—open—now?"

Still braced firmly, the porter replied, "I—will—telephone
—to discover." He relaxed and went to the little switchboard.
Carter heard him dial several numbers while he himself looked
out through the lobby toward the dark ocean. He could just
hear the sound of the waves. He remembered the towels.
"*Toalhas?*" he said to the other porter, whom he had not
looked at because he could not speak to him fluently.

"*Sim*," the other porter said and went to get them.

The Indian came back from the switchboard shaking his
head. Nothing was open. He would keep telephoning. Yes, he
would send the doctor up as soon as he came. He was sorry
about the babby.

Back in the room Carter was shocked. He had been thinking
about his little daughter with aimless tenderness all the while

he had been in the lobby. The picture in his mind was the
happy Cynthia, the healthy little girl of the movies. When he
saw her he could feel it in the pit of his stomach. She was
white. Her lips were losing their color. She looked thinner. A
changeling.

His wife did not even glance up. "Five times while you were
gone."

Carter wanted to look behind him. He was weak and he
could no longer tell what he was feeling. He bent forward to
show the fresh towels to his wife, patting and smoothing them
as if they were particularly fine.

"Put them over there," was all his wife said.

Abruptly the child came upright as if she were jerked. His
wife put a towel before her mouth and when the fit was over
and she had wiped her face, she showed him what was in the
towel. It was blood and a mucous jelly.

"She can't stand this much longer. She'll die," his wife said
with a sigh. He saw that his wife's face had changed also.

He began to telephone again. He had been telephoning
most of the night, it seemed; first, the attaché at the Embassy,
next, the party where the attaché was a guest, then the restaurant where the party had gone, then the doctor. He called
the lobby. The porter had been unable to find a pharmacy still
open in all of Rio. He called the doctor's number again and
while he was holding the receiver with one hand and the
phrase book with the other, trying to say something intelligible to the maid at the other end of the line, there was a knock
at the door and the doctor walked into the bedroom. "Ribeiro," he said, putting out his hand and sitting down on the
chair Mrs. Carter rose from.

"My name is Hadden Carter. This is my wife," Carter said
but it was foolish because the doctor was already absorbed,

examining the little girl. He took her pulse, counted her breathing, and pulled down her eyelid with his forefinger. Suddenly she vomited again. He watched her coolly and stood aside while Mrs. Carter cleaned her up. He was a large plump man about Carter's age. He asked one or two questions.

"What is it, Doctor? What's the matter with her?" Mrs. Carter asked.

"I think, dysentery. Bacillus dysentery. It is quite violent. I will give her something to stop the vomiting and then we may see." He said this in a deprecating manner as if he were discussing a case in Rio Grande do Sul or Bahía or some other distant place.

He gave her half a teaspoon of a liquid from a little glass phial. He took her temperature, holding the end of the thermometer between her slack lips with the tip of his finger. He looked at it, shook it down, and put it back in the little case. Carter was watching his face but it was blank.

"What is it, Doctor?"

The doctor glanced at him as if he were judging whether or not he could be trusted with the information. "Fahrenheit, it is ninety-one degrees."

Neither Carter nor his wife knew quite how low a temperature of ninety-one degrees was. They both stared at his face as if some sign would appear in a wrinkle or an eyebrow. He sat down, opened his bag, and fished around in it. "You have been in Rio long?"

"About three weeks," Carter said.

"And how do you like it?" the doctor said, smiling, as if he expected them to like it very much.

"Very well if it weren't for this . . ."

"How sick is she, Doctor?" Carter's wife said. Like most women, she was more realistic than her husband. She saw that

he had been seduced by the doctor's easy manner, forgave
him for it, and interrupted him.

"I am giving her some sulfa now. That will positively cure
the dysentery. Could I have some water?" the doctor said.

Carter, anxious to be useful, went to the tap in the bathroom and drew a glassful. As he gave it to the doctor, the doctor's eyebrows slid up his forehead as if they had been pulled.
"No. You must give her *agua fervida,* boiléd water. Or you
must give her mineral water in bottles."

"The water isn't safe? That's where she got it, then," Mrs.
Carter said.

The doctor was reaching for the telephone. He spoke to the
Indian in the lobby in Portuguese, and sat back in his chair.
"The vomiting seems to have stopped." He leaned over and
patted the little damp white forehead and brushed away the
curls. "Pretty hair."

The *porteiro* brought in a bottle labeled "Caxambú," a mineral water. The doctor mashed a five-grain pill in the bottom
of a spoon with a spatula, and gave the spoon to Mrs. Carter.
"Give her this. It is sulfaguanadina. One tablet every four
hours." Mrs. Carter held the child's head up, murmuring,
"Here, darling," and the little girl swallowed the medicine and
a gulp of water.

"She takes the water," the doctor said tonelessly.

Mrs. Carter picked this up at once. "She's very sick, isn't
she?"

The doctor took a deep breath, folded his arms, and crossed
his legs. "The sulfa is very effective. Nearly all cases respond."
He sat there in the chair watching the child, his trousers drawn
tight over his plump thighs. No one spoke for ten minutes.
Somewhere, it seemed to Carter, idiotically, a rooster crowed.
"Why is he waiting?" Carter thought. "Why doesn't he go?"

"Give her some of the water," the doctor said. Mrs. Carter gave her a quarter of a glass.

The doctor sat still, pulling at his nose, never taking his eyes off the child. They could all hear someone snoring powerfully, ten groaning grunts and a strangle, then the grunts again—the courtyard magnified all sounds.

Suddenly the doctor stood up. He did not address Carter; he addressed his wife. "She must have water. A little—two, three tablespoonfuls. You understand, she *must* have it every ten minutes. I will give you a prescription, something to put in the water. Get it as soon as you can. I will come again at nine o'clock." He wrote out a prescription on a little pad. "You will not fail to give the water? Every ten minutes." He shook hands formally with each of them and went out.

Carter and his wife sat down again. With all the pharmacies closed, there was nothing for them to do but give the water. The little girl had become frightfully emaciated in these few hours. Her skin was stretched taut over her cheekbones, drawing her mouth open over teeth that were perfectly dry. Her eyes were partly open. The pupils were rolled back. Her skin was as white as paper and her lips and the rims of her eyelids were gray. Her hands were limp instead of fists as they usually were when she was asleep. She looked like a war photograph of a starving child, a child who had been treated cruelly without any pity. Yet he had treated her as kindly as he knew how.

"Would you like some coffee? I think they would make us some downstairs," he asked.

"All right," his wife said.

"Maybe I'd better not telephone again. It might wake her, the clicking of the dial. I'll be back in a minute."

"It won't wake her."

"It might. I'll just . . ."

"Hadden, this isn't sleep. It's coma."

He sat down again. He knew they would not need any coffee to keep them awake now, but he could not sit still and watch this. He stood up again. "Maybe I'd better get some boiled water," he said and went out of the room. In the elevator he studied the door in front of him, even rubbing his hand over the grain of the veneer. Death came after coma. He had accepted that as a possibility by the time he reached the ground floor. He spoke to the Indian about the boiled water. In a few minutes, the other *porteiro* brought him a glass jug of hot water. He went back to the elevator with the jug in his hand.

In the last few years death had been all around him, not much real death but pictures of it in magazines and reports of it over the radio, visions and rumors. Even the death of his parents had been merely a summons by telegram and a quarter-view of the old folks decently arrayed, asleep against a background of crinkled velvet. Death then was a going to sleep after a life expectancy of sixty-eight had expired. That was all he really knew of it, but the pictures and the voices had made him afraid and he had tried to put his best life, his happiness, in a safe place so that death could not touch it. The safe place was eight-millimeter camera film. He had even come to Brazil with a deep secret relief because it was a country the war had not touched, or only lightly, a region exempt somehow, he had felt, and of all the places the one that had excited him the most in Brazil, Quitandinha, distant, secure in its mountains, crammed with luxury, this was the place he had been sure he might have been happiest, and it was also the place where his little girl had sickened.

The elevator had been stopped for several seconds. He went out with the boiled water. As he entered the room, his wife was giving his daughter another drink. He put the water down to cool and went to sit at the bedside. The little girl, the little live creature, was his happiness. Not pictures of her. She was not a symbol of anything. With disgust at his selfishness, he understood at last that, small as she was, she might have a life of her own that was valuable to her, not, as he had thought, a mere reflection of his own solicitude, kindness, and gift-giving.

"How is she?" he asked, to be saying something.

His wife made a gesture he had never seen her make before. She spread her hands wide toward the child.

"Perhaps," he said nervously, "I'd better go see if I can get the prescription filled now."

"All right," his wife said.

He went out again. Downstairs he went into the street and it was beginning to get light.

He had noticed a *farmácia* between a fruit store and a hairdresser's on a street back of the hotel. He did not really expect it to be open this early but he walked around the block to see. It was still shut. He sat down on the curb and lit a cigarette, a Continental, with the gilt letters running slanting across a white package, an imitation of Chesterfields, he thought. Manufactured by the Souza Cruz Companhia, with factories in Rio de Janeiro, São Paulo, Bahía, Belo Horizonte, and Fortaleza. The cigarette made the back of his throat taste as if it were peppered. He threw it away. There was another *farmácia*, he remembered, down the street on the corner of Copacabana and Francisco Sá. He walked down the three blocks. The street grew lighter as the sun crowded up behind the mountains and a mist that had been invisible earlier lifted slowly. No one was on the streets, and when he came to the second *farmácia* it was shut.

For the next two hours he walked slowly back and forth between the pharmacy behind the hotel and the other one down the street. The colored maids began coming to work, some with parcels balanced on their heads. He passed a man carrying two baskets of fresh fish from a wooden yoke around his neck who swung his hips like a heel-and-toe walker. Cars started to go by in the streets, and the loiterers started to gather in the café across from the *farmácia,* poor barefooted men with dirty shirts and carefully combed and oiled hair, to drink coffee and stand leaning there to watch him pass. Once Carter said to himself with astonishment as if he were culpable, "I don't seem to think about her much," and yet he knew as he said it that he had not thought of anything else but the ghastly little head of his daughter.

Shortly after eight o'clock the nearer pharmacy opened up. He got the prescription filled and went back to the room. Nothing had changed. His wife sat just as he had left her and the little girl was quiet. He wanted to say something comforting to his wife. "You go down and get something to eat. I'll give her the water."

Before his wife could answer, the little girl rolled her eyes down to look at him and said, "Where've you been, Daddy?"

"I've just been out to get you some medicine, dear," he said. It cheered them both to hear her speak but at once he began thinking she looked no better. Perhaps it was the last time he would ever hear her speak. He said nothing. They sat beside each other watching the child, giving her the prescription mixed with water every ten minutes. The courtyard magnified the yawns and bathings of the awakening guests.

At nine o'clock the doctor came back again, shaking hands with each of them while looking over his shoulder at the patient. "She is better," he said. She looked no better to Carter but when the doctor pointed out the beginning of a pink flush on her cheek he could see it. "It was the water. She was dehydrated. The sulfa will take care of the dysentery. You have no need to worry."

"But we did have. She nearly died, didn't she?" his wife asked.

Dr. Ribeiro looked her in the eye with a charming smile. "In three days she will be playing on the beach. Little children are like that." He gave them further directions, talked to them about the civic growth of Rio for twenty minutes, shook hands again, and went away.

"Hadden, I want to get out of here. When can we get plane reservations?" his wife said.


A week later Carter had his neck crooked and his face pressed against the plane window looking down fifteen thousand feet to the jungle. As far as he could see there was only a gray-green ripple made by the tops of the trees. There were no breaks, no clearings, no villages, not even any smoke coming up anywhere. Every little while there would be a river, a curlicue of lighter gray. They had been passing over the jungle for an hour.

His wife stood up and began to look through the coats and hats and handbags in the baggage rack above their heads.

"What are you looking for?" he asked.

"You left your camera. I know right where it is. It's on top of the armoire in the hotel. I remember seeing it there."

The little girl began to whimper.

"Why, what's the matter, Cynthie?" his wife asked her.

"I didn't want Daddy to leave his camera. I didn't want him to stop taking pictures of me," she sobbed.

"You stop that bawling or I'll give you something to cry for," Carter said sharply.

"Why, Hadden . . ." his wife said. She had never heard him speak that way to the child before.

"You come sit on my lap and look at the jungle," Carter said.

There were no safe places. You could neither go to them nor construct them artificially. And besides he liked the little girl as she was. He blew her nose and wiped her eyes and told her about the anacondas and the jaguars that were surely lurking beneath those trees so far below even if she couldn't see them.

# Sacrament

MR. TIM MOORE was making a speech. He was thanking all the members of the club for their efforts in the last election.

"And I want to thank all of yez for you co-operation. If the members of the Pondiac Social Club works together every year like we done this year, then our whole ticket of candidates will get elected, and if our whole ticket of candidates get elected, I personally can be in the position to co-operate with yez like I have done so many yizz in the past. . . ."

A young man, Joe Carpenter, sat in the front row, almost under the leader's paunch, thinking of a sacrament. The leader's hoarse words went over his head, unheard. It *was* a sacrament. Everybody told you it was. If you got married and did not have any children, you had not consummated a sacrament. It was a duty and he had not done it, he and Millie, and he didn't see how they ever could. They had been married nine years and Millie's mother had come to live with them a year after they had been to the church. He could just feed three on his pay as a billing clerk. He could feed three, and for eight years the third one had been the old woman, sitting in a rocking chair by the window. She was no good to anyone, a dull deaf old woman, better off dead. Millie knew it but she was the old woman's daughter.

He and Millie had talked about it for years, at night, in bed with the door closed, and the old woman snoring on the couch in the other room, as strong as a horse. She might not die for ten years. One night Joe had dreamed that the old woman was lying in a crib, a crib where his son might lie if he could ever get himself born. She had been lying in the crib like a baby. Well, she might as well be a baby, always rocking back and forth by the window.

He could think of no way to consummate the sacrament. There was one way, of course, but it was murder. He had thought of it often enough at night after Millie had gone to sleep. But murder was forbidden and he knew he could not do it. Confused in his mind with the sacrament, the duty, the word which always made him think of the church darkness and the people kneeling and the words of the Mass resonant among the arches, was his desire for a son but he had thought so long about it and so sternly that the duty had overborne his longing, a duty which he could find no way to perform.

". . . and with the interest of good government at your hearts, I sincerely hope the members of the club will give me your loyal support and work to get the vote out like we done this year. I thank each and every one of yez."

The leader was finished, and he sat down mopping his bald head, while hundreds of palms beat together, stirring the smoke in the hall. The leader was a great man. People said admiringly that he made a hundred thousand a year out of the district. No one could erect a building in it without his approval.

The meeting was over and the crowd stood up to stretch and shake hands with one another. At the meetings, you always shook hands with everyone in sight, as a ritual. Joe got up, shook hands to the right and the left, and, at last, stopped in front of the leader.

"That was nice work you done, Joe, nice work." The leader clapped Joe on the shoulder. "If there's any little thing you want, come up and see me about it: any little thing."

Joe was embarrassed by the great man. He knew that his work in the recent election campaign had been small, climbing stairways over delicatessens and billiard halls to urge frightened Italians to come to the polls. He knew that he could not seriously ask for anything, so he passed it off lightly, smiling.

"Well, Mr. Moore, there's just two things I want, I guess. I'd like somebody to give me a thousand bucks, and I'd like somebody to kidnap my mother-in-law."

The leader had a literal mind. That was the reason he had succeeded as a politician. He said, frowning seriously, "Times are hard, Joe, or maybe I could get you a little dough. Tell me about your mother-in-law."

When he spoke of the mother-in-law, the leader could see Joe's face change, and he said, "Come on into the office, Joe, and tell me about it."

The leader took Joe into the office in the corner of the hall and shut the door.

When Joe got home that night and tiptoed into the bedroom, he took Millie by the shoulder. "It's me, hon. Wake up. I got something to tell you."

Outside the bedroom on the couch lay the old woman snoring, strong as a horse.

Every evening, Millie's mother would sit by the window, rocking and looking placidly down into the street, watching the red and blue signs of the chophouses, just the color of the fireworks Millie had on the Fourth of July when she was a little girl; and the swift orange taxis; and the children batting balls against the brick wall across the street. When she looked down at the fruit stand on the corner, with the red and orange globes in neat pyramids, she hardly saw them as apples and oranges, but quickly her mind turned to all the apple pies she had baked and the marmalade she had put up.

She did not mind when the elevated shook the room as it passed. Her ears had bothered her lately, and she heard the roar only dimly. Millie had once been frightened by a freight train when they had lived near the tracks in Scranton. It was on her eighth birthday. She had run into the house screaming with fear, and whenever she heard the faint roar of the elevated, she remembered Millie's cries and the terrible freight engine. She was seventy-seven years old and Millie was her favorite and only daughter. Her memory, now that she was old, filtered everything she saw or heard and presented it to her in the shapes of the past, so that her life now was only the echo of something else that had happened long ago.

Sometimes she wondered vaguely about Joseph. He and
Millie didn't seem to get along very well. His face was always
strained and white and he flew into tempers easily. At night
when he came home with his arms full of groceries, he went
straight into the little kitchen to talk to Millie, cooking the
dinner. She remembered quite clearly what he had said once,
in a high strident voice through the kitchen door, "Good God,
Millie, how many times do I have to tell you? We ain't got
money enough, see? We just ain't got enough money. Shut up
about it, will you?" He didn't make enough money, that was
plain. *Her* husband had always been a good provider, but
then, Joseph was not like her husband. It was too bad because
she knew Millie liked fine clothes better than anything, and
she hoped Millie wasn't nagging at Joseph to buy her a dress
or a coat with fur on it. She meant to speak to Millie about it
but it had slipped her mind.

At night when the other two had gone to bed, she would
often get up from the couch with a blanket and sit by the
window, rocking, her mind wandering aimlessly through the
past, remembering her marriage and Millie's childhood, an
old woman sitting by a window in the night.

So she received the news quite calmly, without regret,
without thinking much about it at all. Millie said to her one
evening, "Now, Mother, Joe has had to take a pay cut, and
we're going to have to put you in a nice home where you'll be
well taken care of. You'll get good food and we'll come to see
you often."

Millie and Joe both seemed ready to say more, but she said
with mild asperity, "Yes, Millie, I know Joseph doesn't earn
much money. It's very hard on you, I must say. I recall that
little dotted Swiss you used to wear and those lovely hair
ribbons. You were a pretty child, and my, how you loved all

those nice things your father gave you. It's too bad you can't have them now. Yes, you were a pretty child."

Millie suddenly began to cry, and Joe spoke up loudly, "Now, Mom, you sit still, and I'll pack your things and get them all ready for tomorrow."

She watched Millie cry and thought how different she had looked as a little girl. Why, now Millie looked old and thin, almost a stranger. It was pleasanter to remember her playing dolls on the grass beside the house in Scranton.

In the morning an ambulance came and they made her lie down on the little cot in it as if she were sick. Joe and Millie talked and fidgeted every minute, and they kept arranging her pillow, and even making jokes until she wondered what was the matter with them.

After a long ride through the city during which she could look through the ambulance window into taxicabs and the backs of trucks, they went through the gates of a high wall and down a driveway across a lawn, stopping before a big white building. It was a clear day with bright sunshine and the flower beds around the building looked pretty in the sunlight.

"Such pretty flowers, Millie," she said.

"Yes, Mother. They're very pretty."

Joe had already got out of the ambulance and gone ahead to talk to a man who came out of the building.

"Yes. This is the case Tim Moore called you about. He'll send you the papers on it. No, we won't need anyone. She won't make no trouble."

She thought it was strange that Joe and Millie both cried when they left her, especially since they had been so lively in the ambulance on the way.

They put her in a long room with white walls and two rows

of beds, each with a rocking chair and a small table beside it. She liked the rocking chair and the food was good, just as Millie had said it would be, only it was queer that the woman in the next chair had to be fed because she dropped her food all over her dress if she tried to feed herself, and the woman sang all day the same little song. And she was surprised when other women in the ward had screamed and shouted and one of them had thrown her little table right through the window and some men had taken her out.

It was nearly three days before she realized that Joe and Millie had put her in an insane asylum. She was watching the woman next to her singing, and suddenly she saw what the place was and she got up quickly and ran trembling to the door of the ward. The guard stopped her.

"I want to see the superintendent. You can't keep me here. You can't do it. I'm not crazy," she cried. "I'm not crazy."

But the guard led her gently back to her chair and gave her a pencil and paper, telling her to write a letter to her people and explain matters. Day after day, she wrote to Joe and Millie, with shaking hands, clinging to the pencil, writing feverishly, afraid to stop, knowing that if she stopped, she would begin to wonder about herself.

Each day the guard would take the letter she had written and drop it outside the door of the ward in the wastebasket. These nuts were always writing letters. He wrote on his report that she never made any trouble.

# Kobold

THE WHITE HORSE won the race but his wife had taken his winnings. After that he was in Texas a while with the Fire Gods down near the border. In that country the Indians and the Mexicans had buried a lot of treasure, a hell of a lot, long before Davy Crockett or Sam Houston came. There was a lot of dirt in Texas; it was a fine country, green near the Gulf and gray in the south part with plenty of room

for the wind, and there were times when you could be nowhere instead of forty miles from someplace. When the air
was not clear in the west, not misty but still not clear enough
to show the foothills, you could see the mountaintops hanging up like hams and swinging if the weather was hot.

The Fire Gods had a special oil. How to make it was a secret
in their family. They poured the oil on the ground and
touched a match to it and a long flame blazed up, all colors,
and pretty soon it would sort of reach out and point in a
certain direction and you went there and dug and there was
treasure.

But when he was with the Fire Gods, they never found any
treasure. The Head God said the oil lacked some one quality.
He himself had put up three hundred bucks, and the Head
God had sent off to New York. Every day while they were
waiting for the stuff to come, they had played stud poker in
Ma Lindley's hotel in Del Rio and he had taken the Head God
for thirty-three dollars, but when the stuff came, in a package
no bigger'n your thumb, and they mixed it with the oil, that
oil still didn't work.

The Fire Gods had found a lot of treasure, though. The
Head God had showed him a handful of old Spanish gold
pieces he was keeping just as a keepsake. But the oil had that
certain quality, then.

So all he ever got from the Fire Gods was the money he
won playing poker in Del Rio. He had a little streak of lean
luck down there but the big, fat, juicy luck was still on the
hog, he said.

I was listening to this in the "office" of his filling station on
a bright Saturday morning. The sign outside read "Senter
Forepaugh—I Fix Flats." The station was built of white tile
like a shower bath and the attendants wore blue uniforms

and leather puttees. I had never seen Senter Forepaugh before in my life. I was looking, in fact, I had been sent by my
wife to find someone to repair the broken handle of our icebox
door. When I had found all the attendants busy, I had gone
into the "office" and this man had begun to talk at once as if
he had been expecting me. He was a little man about forty
with a thin face weathered red and anxious light blue eyes
like an aviator's.

It was a busy Saturday morning, and his filling station is on
a U.S. highway. Cars drove in to get gas from his pumps; cars
drove in to ask the way upstate; and once a crippled Buick
with the side stove in and the windshield cracked sidled up to
the door but he only said, "Smash-up, see?" and let the attendants handle all the trade. He sat with his feet languidly
cocked up against the Gents' Room door, smoking a cigar,
and he began to tell me about his long efforts to get a lot of
money for his brother. Brother had the keenest legal mind in
the country.

"Where does he practice, Washington?" I asked.

"That's just the trouble. He don't practice. He ain't never
practiced." Forepaugh was just drawing breath to explain
when a dirty, plump, unshaven man with his hair in his eyes
came through the office from the door that led to the Forepaugh house. He walked straight past us and out the front
door without stopping.

Forepaugh jumped up. "Morning, Brother, how you feeling?" he asked solicitously.

"Go to hell," Brother said just before he shut the door.

Forepaugh watched him through the window. "Ain't he
the devil, though? Ain't he the devil?" He turned and faced
me. "He got sober yesterday. He pinched my wife and he
broke his watch, all thumbs on both his hands and mad till

suppertime. It don't do for him to get sobered up by happen-
stance. What he needs is to get sober by a system like they
use at one of these alcoholic institutes. Frets him when he
just runs out of liquor." Forepaugh went over to the window
and stood squinting down the highway. "You know where he's
gone?"

"The Idle Hour, Beer, Wines, & Liquors?"

"Nah, why the Idle Hour ain't open yet. It's too early in the
morning. He's gone down to the A&P to get some of that
almond cake flavoring to hold him till the bars open. He
drinks whisky while they're open and flavoring while they're
shut. Al-ways drinking. It sure is hell on him with that mind
right there in his head. Um-*uh*."

"Hell on you paying for it, too, isn't it?" I ventured.

He looked at me with an innocent candor. "I told you he
had the keenest legal mind in the country, didn't I?" He spoke
as if I had misunderstood something. He was honored to be
allowed to pay for the whisky and the cake flavoring.

He sat down again and heaved his feet against the door. He
looked down at the end of his cigar and flicked the ash off
delicately. "In just a month or two, I'm going to have enough
hard-come money, earned money, that is, to send Brother to
one of these institutes where they reduce the craving and
then I'm going to set him up in the law business."

"Are you going back with the Fire Gods? The oil might be
right, now," I said. Even though I could ask the question, he
did not seem to be a fool or a child.

"I was young then." He turned around and looked me
straight in the eye. He shut one of his and sighted along his
cigar. "I want something better than that. That's why I like
the looks of this new proposition."

"What's the new proposition?"

"Well, last Thursday night I go to a spook house . . ."

"What's that?"

"Place where spirits come. Niggers run it. They're more spiritual than us whites," he explained. "I go to 'em every now and then to see what I can pick up. Sometimes I get something, sometimes I don't. But it's always worth the two dollars."

"Look, you don't believe all that stuff about spooks and spirits, do you?"

He drew his brows together as he looked at me. He seemed annoyed. "A Christian's all you got to be. You don't have to be nothing but a Christian to believe in spirits." He leaned forward and spat on the floor in a manner that conveyed somehow deep reproach. He jumped up and began to pace up and down between the red oil pumps and the candy case. "Why, they used to be a woman right around here. You know where the Quaker church is? You turned right there, third house on the left. She sold old chairs and tables. Antiques. Had a sign out front hanging from an ox yoke. Antiques, it said. But that wasn't what she done. No, sir. She was a dreamer. And lemme tell you, she put in some big nights for me. I used to get me a racing form . . ." He stopped and looked at me. "You know what that is, don't you?"

"Yes." He seemed to indicate that anyone skeptical of spirits might also be ready to deny a racing form or maybe even a tree.

"And I'd take the form and give it to her and say, 'Here's a dollar.' That was all her fee, one dollar. 'You take this and see what you can dream up.' And she put the form under her pillow. I'd come back in the morning. Now, mind you, I ain't claiming she had something for me every single time, no. But when she did, they wasn't place horses and they wasn't show horses. They was winners. Always. Never missed.

"One time they was running over at Windsor. This antique woman had dreamed me four out of six. I had 'em on a piece of paper and I was going to the races. Fifty dollars of hard-come, what I had. But some of my help quit and I had to mind the station. You know Big Ott? Drives the Scheider's beer truck on this route?"

"No."

"I give the money to Ott and I tell him to take the paper and the fifty dollars and make a four-horse parlay."

"Whew!" I said.

Forepaugh looked at me coldly. "I enjoined him to do it. So he went. I listened over the radio. Naturally they all come in, and I started counting my chickens. Come five, come six, come seven, eight, nine o'clock, and no Ott carrying my money. At twenty minutes past nine, a big Packard drove in to the station. Big Ott was at the wheel and they was two women with him, all drunk. He leans out of the Packard and hands me a fifty-dollar bill and says, 'Senter. Here's your fifty. I didn't get there in time to put your money down.'"

I said nothing.

Forepaugh's voice did not change. "So you see. That woman had four winners. It was just human wickedness that I didn't get the money. Ott and I're good friends now because I know he's bad and I know how to steer around the badness. They never had been, I'll bet you they never was a four-horse parlay like that in . . ."

"Here comes your brother," I said.

Forepaugh wheeled around in his chair and got up. Brother was walking slowly across the concrete in front of the gas

pumps. A dozen little bottles stuck out of his coat pockets.
Just outside the door he stopped, drew one of the bottles out,
and drank it empty. Then he took careful aim and threw the
little bottle against one of the gas pumps. It broke all to pieces
and he smiled.

"He likes to break bottles," Forepaugh said. "Always did.
Makes him feel good to hear 'em smash."

Brother came into the office smiling amiably and bringing
with him the soft bland odor of almonds. He passed into the
house without speaking. Forepaugh sat down and put his feet
up again.

"This new proposition—I go into the spook house. It was
late, about four o'clock in the morning, and the spook he was
setting there with a candle, a right nice-looking nigger, and
the minute he sees me he starts to talk. He don't trance or
nothing, because the spirit's with him all the time. He just
starts talking. He says, 'I see a little old man with a long white
beard. He's wearing a big hat, might be a Mexican hat. He's
come to you once but he said you turned him off but he's going to come again and show you a place. It's a place by a big
wide-flowing river, and they's a fence by the riverbank with
a lot of crooked fence posts, and past the fence on the sand,
they's a log laying there with a big old bumpy knot on it. He
going to come and show you. You dig six feet down below
that log and you going to find rubies, emeralds, bags of gold,
everything, whoo-*ee*, you going to be rich as Michael. Two
dollars, *please*.' Sounds pretty good, don't it?"

"Beats horse racing and the Fire Gods," I said.

"It's the break I been waiting for. You remember the spook
said the old man had come to me once. That was when I was
a kid. I was asleep and dreaming and I recall it all. Brother
and me was walking down the street and I saw a little square

box, lying in the dust. I went up and kicked it and a little
stream of water, like a fountain, jumped out about a yard
high, and I went and put my hand into the fountain and down
into the box and it was full of twenty-dollar gold pieces and
fancy diamond rings. I got me a handful and I was just going
to stick 'em in my pocket when this little old man, like the
spook said, with a long, white beard and a sombrero came
buckety-buckety down the street hollering, 'You can't take
that.' And Brother took a stick and whacked him on the head
and says, 'You take that.' Now if this ain't a sign, they ain't a
hound dog in Georgia."

"Oh, it's a sign all right but where's the river? Where's the
log?"

"Texas. That place is right on our ranch, and all the fence
posts are crooked just like he said. As soon as Brother don't
like liquor, we leave, and when we find the knot on that log,
we dig."

Without a sound, Brother appeared in the doorway. He
was drunk, smiling and peaceful. He had not shaved or
combed his hair but he had changed into a pair of dirty white
flannel trousers and he carried a tennis racket and a couple of
old balls.

"Sportsman now," he said and staggered out.

"He's going over to the Muni-cipal Courts to play. I expect
he's about the best tennis player you ever saw," Forepaugh
said genially.

"I saw Vines once and Budge and Jack Kramer," I said
deprecatingly.

"Well, Brother's played all these lions and he's beat most
of 'em. If it wasn't for his drinking, he'd beat 'em all. Got a
power ball."

"Power ball?"

"When he hits it, they don't have time to get their rackets up before the dust is spurting up behind 'em where the ball has already hit. An exceedingly fast ball."

"It must be."

"It is. But I got a snake ball," he said. "When it hits, it don't bounce. It just runs along the ground crooked, leaving a little track, like a snake." He wiggled his hand like a snake. "They can't pick it up."

"Did you ever beat Tilden?"

"Never played him. Tennis is just a game and since I been up North here, all I do is sit and figure ways to make a dollar. But when I was a kid, Brother and me played all the time until nobody would get on the court with either one of us. I could see I was going to have to play Brother. I could see it coming because he couldn't get a game and I couldn't get a game. Sure enough, Brother come one day and asked me to play. I was willing but I says to him, 'Brother, I'll play you but I don't want you to get mad.' Got a terrible temper. I plead with him, 'Now, Brother, please don't get mad.'

"He says he won't, so we start to play about three o'clock in the evening. He lams that power ball by me so fast I can't see it, and my snake ball flattens out in the air until it really looks like an egg, and when he tries to get it, it looks like he was hoeing. Pretty soon both sides of the net are torn up right smart, little smallpox holes on my side and big pits with wavy lines around on his side and quite a cloud of dust. We can't neither one of us win any—he takes one game and I take the next. Sun goes down, lights coming on, ham starts to fry, and we still playing. We played until it was black dark and then quit. It was a draw and it was after this Brother liked me best of all our brothers—we got six.

"We never played again, of course, but it was that game

that decided Brother to come and live with me so as I could be the one that put him on his feet in the law business."

I stood up. "I've got to be getting along," I said.

"You live up on the hill, don't you? Well, you can take that other road to get up there, the one by the Muni-cipal Courts. You just stop by there a minute and watch Brother's power ball. If he ain't too drunk, you'll have a treat."

"I don't know as I'll have time, but I hope you and he find that knot on the log." I started for the door.

"I'm confident we will. And when we get back and you get in trouble, remember Brother's the keenest legal mind in the country."

As I was walking down the main road that led past the tennis courts, I could feel the broken handle of the icebox door still in my pocket, unrepaired, but there had not seemed to be any time to ask about it. I wondered why I was bothering to take the road that went by the Muni-cipal Courts.

When I approached them, there was a large crowd of children screaming with laughter, and three or four grown-ups. There was Brother, lurching, smiling, staggering, covered with dirt and sweat, falling down heavily when he chased his opponent's ball. But when he served, he served the fastest ball I ever saw, faster than Tilden's, faster than Vines', and his man didn't have time to get his racket up before the dust was spurting up behind him where the ball had already hit.

# Pro Arte

M Y LAST porchmate had been a great nuisance, fellow named Porter who cried a little every day because he was sure he was going to die and thought he was too young for it. It made me nervous to watch him, and I was relieved when he did die and was shipped away in a pine box on the nine-fifty train, escorted by a file of weeping kinfolk. Since Porter's translation, I had been quite bored. Under its load of snow, the mountain across the way looked like a bad etching, and at twelve below zero, you cannot try to read or your hands will freeze holding the book. I was ready to talk, and I don't suppose anyone had ever been so glad to see Henry Comstock as I was.

He followed the head nurse out onto the porch and she introduced him. "How do you do?" he said politely and gave me a cigarette. He was over six feet tall, with broad sloping shoulders and blond hair. He wore hard-soled slippers, blue pajamas, and a blue flannel dressing-gown with a monogram on the pocket, the kind given by aunts for Christmas. He carried a copy of Somerset Maugham's *Of Human Bondage.* Evidently he had begun his cure in some hospital because he was already fat, and when he put his head down, a well-shaved roll of flesh protruded beneath his chin, but even fat he was handsome, and, thinner, he would have been the handsomest man I ever saw. He got into bed and began to read with such concentration that I was sure someone had sent him the book as a gift.

As I looked him over, I thought Comstock would do nicely. A little young, perhaps, to be entertaining—he was about thirty—but I did not think he would cry himself to death as Porter had. Also he was well-mannered, and, from his face, he seemed to have a pleasant, youthful candor. But I did not, in spite of my anticipation, rush headlong into conversation.

I knew he was not ready to talk yet. When you first come to a sanatorium from the outside, you do not believe you are quite like the other lungers. They get to be pretty silly from worry and confinement. You will be courteous certainly, but aloof. Then in a couple of weeks you are telling the nearest person the things that trouble you when you are awake at night.

Comstock read until his hands got cold. He put them under the covers and stared out at the mountain gloomily. I decided to wait until the next day before beginning to talk to him but the next day I was balked by his visitors.


## II


I SAW THEM coming up the icy path through the trees, the girl giving little screams and laughing when she slipped. The man carried a package under one arm and he made gestures with the other. The girl's coat was sable. They were probably rich.

They entered the cottage. I heard them laughing on the stairs and then they came out on our porch. Comstock was asleep and the man woke him up, touching him on the shoulder.

Comstock opened his eyes at once. "Hello, Arthur. Hello, Mary. God, I'm glad to see you. How are you?" He raised himself up in bed. "Oh, congratulations. I saw the papers. I knew it would be like that."

"Weren't the papers grand? You should have heard me," the man said. "I've never played better. Never in my life. I was just an instrument for the real Beethoven and the papers could see it for once. You know, Iturbi didn't get any better reviews than mine."

"I liked the *American* best. They called him a 'Titan of the Keyboard.' Can't you see him playing in a leopard skin and open-work shoes like Lionel Strongfort?" the girl asked. She was very blond with brown eyes and obviously proud of her husband. "We sat up all night waiting for the papers and drinking coffee. Arthur couldn't sleep all the next day because of the papers."

"It was because of the coffee," he said. "I bought Mary the fur coat—pose for the gentleman, Mary—and I made her quit her job, and now we're on our way to Montreal, and next year we're going to take a house in Connecticut with a Steinway for the noise and a Bechstein for the pearly tone."

"Concert in Montreal?" Comstock asked. "What are you playing?"

"Bridge. This trip is for fun," the pianist said.

The girl had stopped looking at her husband. She said, "Hush, dear, we're being rude. Here is poor darling Henry practically phosphorescent with decay and you talk about your damned pianos. What do the doctors say, Henry? You look well. I mean, you're not thin at all."

"Oh, it's nothing. Just a few little holes. I'll be out of here in a couple of months," he said confidently.

"But what do you do? Just lie here?"

"Lie here and look at the mountains and think. You can do a lot of thinking here."

"I'll bet you can," said the man. "Thinking about your sins. I'd pray, too, if I were you. I've told you about it, haven't I, Mary? Pure Henry's very first affair—his first sane act after a lifetime of celibacy? How Henry trundled his profile round and round the lobby of that hotel in Switzerland? And there was this charming little *Suisse* who spoke only French? She used to come every morning to hear Milstein and Piaty and me play trios. She was trying to learn something about music, she said. But would the wolf Henry let her improve herself? No, by God. He had to be the pupil. He had to learn French."

I looked at Comstock. He was smiling and fidgeting. Obviously they all knew the story very well, and this was only a joke which Comstock was enjoying.

"And it wasn't long before it became necessary to hold the lessons in Henry's bedroom. '*Voici le lit. Vois-tu le lit?*' Talk some French, Henry; you spent enough time on it. And then, to remove the Swiss flaws from their accent, he must take her to Paris so they could learn together the pure tongue of Île de France, and there they lived, how culturally, talking French like mad, night and day, particularly in the daytime, until Henry began to cough and he couldn't talk any more and he had to come home and lie still. The trick lungs are manifestly your wages from an angry Providence. I hope you see that, Henry. I hope you see it as clearly as I do."

It had all been very funny up to this point. The pianist was happy and talkative because of his success, and Comstock was pleased because this fooling reflected his prowess as a male, but now his face changed.

"I got it from her, you know. The TB, I mean. She had it then. She told me when we got to Paris."

"Oh, I'm terribly sorry, Henry. But you never told us," the man said.

The girl leaned over and kissed Comstock on the forehead and said in a low voice, "Arthur's such a fool when he's played well. Forgive him, darling. He didn't mean anything."

"It's all right. I know you didn't mean anything. It isn't as if I were dying," Comstock said.

"But you are getting along all right, aren't you? I mean, there's no danger of serious complications?"

"No. I'm fine. I'll be back at work in a couple of months." He seemed anxious to cheer things up again. "How are the bookings for next season, now that you're the musical white hope of America?"

"Twenty-two already. One date with the Chicago, and I

may get a concerto date with Ormandy—the Liszt E-flat, maybe. If you need any money, let me know. Seriously, I mean it."

"Darling, we've forgotten Henry's champagne. We left it on the bureau in your room there," said the girl.

"We brought you a couple of bottles because you couldn't celebrate with us. It's Mumm's."

"That's swell," Comstock said. "Let's all have a drink now."

"We can't, Henry. Our train leaves in a few minutes."

"Well, it was grand of you to come and look in, and I can't tell you, Arthur, how much your success means to me. You've worked like hell and you deserve all the honors you get. And you'll get plenty. I know you will." Comstock seemed to be making this moment an occasion as if he wanted the pianist to remember it. "You'll be the greatest pianist in the world."

Comstock had a fine forehead. His eyes were very blue, and as far down as his cheekbones his face was lean, virile, and his expression made it almost heroically earnest. It was like a scene in the movies. I almost expected to see Greer Garson and Clark Gable turn from his bed and sadly leave the porch.

## III

AFTER YOU HAVE visitors, you are depressed, and when you are depressed, you talk. Comstock watched his guests go down the path. Then he turned, probably frightened that he could envy them so much, and began to talk at once.

Had I noticed his two visitors? They were Arthur Corey, the pianist, and his wife. He had just made his debut in New York, and already he was considered one of the finest young American pianists.

He himself was a great friend of Corey's. They had been in college together, where Corey had lived over a garage almost without money, practicing ten hours a day on a rented upright. It was a funny thing: he would strike an octave chord and trill the second and third fingers, and then the third and fourth fingers until he could do it perfectly, sometimes as long as an hour. He had worked incessantly and he deserved all the success, all the honors that came to him, didn't I think? Because, after all, a man should have a reward commensurate to his effort.

Opposite me, I reflected, I have one of America's finest young men, tall, callow, and sincere. The reward, so Henry Comstock believed, was equal to the effort. Santa Claus came if you were a good boy, and when you worked nights at the office, the gods made you president of the company. Maybe the gods had sent him as a messenger to tell me that I was profane and cynical and had better watch out. Yet I wondered, according to his system, how Hermes would explain his own disease—he must have done something pretty bad to be punished with TB.

Had I ever heard Vladimir Horowitz play, he asked. His technique was marvelous. Once in Munich, Horowitz had listened to Corey in a small recital, and, being impressed, he had offered to teach Corey something about technique if he would come to Switzerland in the summer. Horowitz had a chalet on the mountainside near Crans-sur-Sierre. Last summer Corey had gone to Crans and he himself had visited Corey there.

(I remember Horowitz playing the *Suggestions Diaboliques* of Prokofieff, leaning over the keyboard, his eyebrows lifted as if in surprise at the swiftness of his fingers with the applause already mounting nervously around him. I remember

Prokofieff, too. He was bald and looked like a dentist. You can remember practically everything, lying here.)

I was a little impatient. I wanted to hear about the girl, "pure Henry's very first affair."

"And the girl? The girl who came to listen to the trios. The one you took to Paris," I said. "You forget the porch is only twelve feet square. I couldn't help overhearing." I cite my behavior as an example of the callousness you acquire in this place.

Comstock accepted my rudeness without offense. "The girl came every morning. Arthur used to play trios with Piatigorsky, the cellist, and Milstein, the violinist, in the writing room of the hotel. She sat on a chair just inside the door. Every morning. She was in love with Arthur then."

"Maybe she just liked the piano," I offered.

"No. She loved him, all right. Or she wanted to be his mistress anyhow."

"Was she pretty?"

"Beautiful. She was only nineteen, just out of a convent school in Lausanne. I couldn't understand why she was on the make. But you don't have to make a fool of yourself just because they are pretty and want to make love."

"Depends," I said. "After three years here, they would not even have to be pretty, now."

"Well, Arthur made a fool of himself. Evenings, he bought her drinks in the bar and, afternoons, when he was supposed to be working with Horowitz, he was out on the side of some alp, talking to her. The summer before his debut, with one of the greatest pianists in the world helping him gratis, and his wife working in New York to help out with expenses, and he gets sidetracked by a girl. It was wrong. It was wrong because of his career and it was wrong because of Mary."

"Impolitic and wicked," I said.

"I talked to him. I've always tried to keep him straight, but artists are flighty, you know, and he's done this kind of thing before. He just laughed. He said somebody had to make love to her. He said that's what she was living for. I said love was just a nervous habit with him. He laughed some more, so I made love to her myself. I thought he would get to work again if I could draw her away. I couldn't sit by and watch fifteen years of work go to pot, could I?"

"Not as his friend," I answered.

"Arthur Corey is my best friend. That's why I did it."

"For art's sake," I said. "Sorry."

He did not get the pun. "I had never been involved with a woman before and I didn't know how to start, so I asked her to teach me French. I've always been kind of dumb about languages."

She probably thought he was crazy, as handsome as he must have been then.

"She had only given me a couple of lessons before I saw there was going to be trouble. She kept looking at me all the time."

"If they look at you like a shot rabbit, it's always love," I said. "But what kind of girl was she? First she falls for Corey; then she falls for you. Her affections were remarkably flexible."

"She was a nice girl. She used to buy flowers every day when I was gone for the mail and I would find them in my room when I came back."

"She was a wonderful girl." Then I had an idea. "When did she tell you she had TB?"

"It was one night after we got to Paris," he said.

The whole thing was plain now. If she knew that her lungs

were bad; if she knew that in six months she might weigh
perhaps sixty pounds; and on the table beside her bed, there
would lie one of those kidney-shaped hospital bowls filling
slowly, but still too fast with blood and bits of her lung; and
then one day she would see the white screen put up around
the bed and only barely hear the chuckle of the oxygen tanks,
why shouldn't she make love? That really was all she was living for. It was not flexibility. It was desperation. I have seen
it here many times. It is a condition quite accepted by the
authorities.

"When did you decide to take her to Paris?" I asked.

"About the time I saw that I was going to have to do more
than just learn French, if I wanted to keep her away from
Arthur," he said.

When they reached Paris, he was afraid that he might see
American friends if they stayed at a good hotel on the Right
Bank, so he took her over to a quaint little rathole on the Quai
des Grands Augustins which advertised a *Grand Vue de la
Seine*. And the *Vue* was really grand all right, he said. You
could see Notre Dame every time you went out the front door.

"I should think it would have been delightful—lovely girl,
quaint old-world atmosphere, wine cheap and plentiful, and
the cathedral to look at when you got tired. Wasn't it delightful?"

"No. Not to me." He paused as if he sought the reasons why
it wasn't, but the echoes of his mother and his father and his
Sunday-school teacher and his headmaster and all the other
voices of his upbringing were too faint for him to catch. "I
don't know how you feel about women . . ." he began.

"No, but you will, my dear Comstock," I said. "You will if
you stay here long enough. You will know how I feel about
women, men, small children, Russia, interplanetary travel,

oysters, everything. It will take me at least a month to tell you
how I feel about everything, and after I have told you, why,
we are a month to the good."

Comstock sat up in bed suddenly. "Let's have some of the
champagne." We went into his dressing room.

There were two bottles of Mumm's on his bureau. He sat
down on the tin wastebasket with the bottle between his
knees, undoing the wire and the foil, and I sat in the only
chair. We drank from our toothbrush glasses. The wine was
cold, dry, and very good.

With the glass in his hand, Comstock began again, "I'd
never had anything to do with women seriously before. I
never thought why until I was sick. But I know now. When I
was about sixteen, my father was made president of the bank
in our home town. He gave me a Ford roadster. I thought he
was a great man and I believed everything he said. One time
he told me about things. He said, 'Son, keep away from
women until you marry.' He was embarrassed and so was I
but I promised him. I thought he must be right, because of
the Ford, I guess. And then I rowed in college and I never
had time to play around with them."

"You are very handsome," I said politely. "It must have
been hard to elude them."

"No. I knew only the sisters of my friends." He poured out
more champagne, and sat looking down into his glass while
he made the wine go round in it. "But they have caught up
with me now all right."

"*Avec ça?*" I said.

"That's French for 'So what?,' isn't it? If I hadn't learned
French, I wouldn't be in this mess."

"You mean you are worried about the girl?" Then I said
heartily, "Oh, she'll be all right. Very likely your little trip did

her good—travel, change of scene." I did not believe the trip had done her good. Unless she was a light case, the strain might kill her. But I wanted to be comforting.

"I wasn't thinking of the girl. I was thinking of myself."

"Oh," I said. "What's the matter with you?"

"Well, you may laugh, but I've done wrong," he said, still looking into his glass.

"Sinned, you mean?"

"Something like that. I feel as though I'd let myself down and I'll never be able to look my wife in the face."

"Have you got a wife?"

"Not yet. But when I have."

"She'll never find it out unless you tell her. It's not branded on your forehead, you know," I said. I had heard of men like Comstock before but I had never seen one. I tried changing the subject. "Did you ever eat at Rouzier's or La Pérouse? They were both in your neighborhood."

"We had a baked truffle at Rouzier's. I had never eaten truffle before and I didn't like it."

I could see that I was not much help. We finished the champagne and Comstock did not say any more. He seemed to be depressed. We went out on the porch and went to bed. It was snowing hard, and the wind made a lot of noise in the trees. I would have liked to have gone dancing somewhere because of the champagne.

For the next three weeks Comstock and I had no conversation. From the little he said, I gathered that he regarded his shame or his remorse as a problem he could solve if he persisted. He lay with his head propped up, looking out at the mountain, smoking his pipe every minute. Perhaps it could even be totted up and balanced, red against black, and then he would feel all right. As I watched him, I could tell that he was trying to save what he could not call his soul, and he lost just nine pounds doing it, which you may say is quite cheap for a rescue of that magnitude.

I lay six feet away from him, envious of the scenes it hurt him to recall. I did not try to help him because it would have been very hard to do and I was without sympathy anyway. He had had an affair with a beautiful girl in Paris, and if he wanted to absolve himself, he could think of the dark inhabited tissues of his lungs, where, in waxen waistcoats (this information is brought to you through the courtesy of the Rockefeller Institute), untold millions of little creatures, fifty thousand of which could pass, could you persuade them to, through the eye of a needle simultaneously without touching the needle or one another, were gorging themselves on his flesh, unhindered except perhaps by antibodies, although science cannot tell us much about antibodies yet. He could console himself with that. He had "betrayed" the girl and she had given him TB. He was paid if he felt that way about it.

One day he asked me to come into his room. "I think I've got it straightened out," he said. "You see, I went into it to help Arthur. It was wrong but I did it to help him. The girl was willing enough—it isn't as if I'd seduced her. She was willing and this TB is a punishment. It evens up, doesn't it?"

"Seems to," I said, wanting to laugh. "Your good intentions even leave you one up."

"I did wrong to help a friend and now I am paying for it," he said. He looked relieved and cheerful, but I couldn't see just why it had taken him three weeks to find the solution.

"*Nunc dimittis,*" I said.

It is not often you get a chance to watch a man tinker with his conscience. It is very interesting. It would have been more interesting if Comstock had given one minute's thought to the girl. He had told me that once in Paris, about dawn, he woke up and he saw against the window the profile of the girl's body in the early light. She was crying. It was her crying that had wakened him, and, turning from the window, timid, expecting his anger, she told him she was ill.

But in his successful calculations the girl was not included.

## IV

AFTER THIS COMSTOCK improved rapidly. He gained weight. His X-rays turned out well. And he took to playing bridge in the cardroom evenings. If you are strong enough, you are allowed to play cards until nine o'clock. The authorities consider it a beneficial relaxation.

One morning I stopped at the post office for the mail. There was nothing for me but there was a letter and a little package for M. Henri Comstock. The postmark was Davos, Schweiz.

When I got back to the cottage, Comstock was in bed. I gave him the letter and the package. He opened the letter and read it. Then he jumped out of bed, went into his room and began to dress. I could hear him. He left the cottage and walked down the hill at much faster than the approved rate of speed.

I thought the girl had died but I wanted to be sure. So I had no qualms about going into his room to look around. On his bureau was the letter. I picked it up and read it. The Directors of Such-and-such Sanatorium at Davos had, it appeared, the unhappy duty to inform M. Comstock of the death of Mlle. Albertine Bergier, a patient in their establishment. Before her death, Mlle. Bergier had requested the writer to send M. Comstock her ring as a remembrance. The

Directors joined in sending M. Comstock their sincere condolences.

On the bureau in a pile of tissue paper lay a pretty little gold ring set with sapphires.

In a few minutes Comstock returned, still quite agitated. "She's dead," he said.

"Mmm," I said. "Send a cable?"

"Yes, that's all I could do." He began to pace back and forth. "I'll never forgive myself now. This is going to haunt me forever."

I must have shouted. I was pretty mad. "For the love of God, Comstock, don't be a damned fool all your life." He stopped and looked affronted.

"Try to think of the girl for just a minute. Your soul is immortal—it'll keep. She was a young girl from a convent. She knew she was sick," I said patiently. "How long do you think it took her to decide to go to Paris with you, to act like a tart so she could see what love was like just once before she died? Not what love was really—she didn't love you—but just a rehearsal in a twelve-franc hotel bedroom."

"You can't talk to me like this," he said characteristically.

"I am talking to you like this and you'll be expelled if you hit me, so you might as well listen. It might even be for your own good. From my obituary, you may find out something about this girl. You see, she knew what the strain of your little jaunt was going to do to her. If you get drunk once in a beer joint downtown, it sets you back a month, but for a couple of hours you're free. She knew it was going to kill her, but she would be free to find out why she was a woman. And at night when she was frightened by her bargain, she went and stood by the window so she wouldn't wake you crying." Now that I had worked this off, I felt better. "Don't let it worry you, Comstock.

She had the choice of maybe two more years alone, or the trip to Paris. She took the trip and the pine box that went with it. It's not your fault. You had nothing to do with it. You were only the male spider."

He did not say anything for about twenty minutes. Then he said, "I'm sorry I was angry. Thanks for helping me out. I see what you mean now."

After that Comstock never spoke of her again, and I don't think he ever saw what I meant. Instead he talked about the romance of the advertising business and the three years he stroked his college boat at Poughkeepsie. Last week he was allowed to leave the sanatorium. He was very fat, looked enormously healthy, and he was beginning to take on the fat man's readiness to laugh.

On the whole, Comstock was good value. He was much more entertaining and instructive than I deserved, and, since no one has been assigned to his bed, I miss him quite a lot. It is a bore not to have anyone to talk to. I lie here and listen to the tree popping. The bole of the tree, they say, shrinks away from the bark suddenly when it is cold enough, and there is a loud crack. Since the sanatorium is in wooded country, the cracks come about every half-minute in this weather. Last winter, my porchmate and I used to bet on the length of time between cracks and I won eight dollars.

# Flight South

H E HAD been trying for four days to go through a whole day without saying a word to anyone. Home was easy; school was hard but it was drawing time and that little old Miss Hastings didn't ask many questions during drawing time. Questions, talking, came at reading time. He was bent over his drawing on the table. A row of thick hexagonal crayons lay in front of him. There was a white crayon between the

purple and the red, the first white crayon he had ever seen.
He was pleased and he smiled before he thought. He peeped
right, left, and forward to see if anyone had caught him at it.
It sure was the right thing to draw cotton with.

Growing, swelling, fluffing out bigger and bigger under his
hand was a bale of cotton. (He drew it all white without any
burlap around it; only the black bands.) Two heavy black
lines on a slant gave him the bed of a cart. He put a wheel on
it and taking the brown crayon he began, with the tongue
curling in and out of his mouth, the hard part, a mule to pull
the cart. The mule and the load of cotton were being driven
by a yet uncreated nigra who lived, as did all scenes and ob-
jects to be drawn, inside the crayon. He would let him out
presently into the warm sunshine of the Front Street levee.
The river was there inside the brown crayon. A magnolia tree
was rolled up inside the green, and somehow in the gray and
black he would find the bottoms across the river that his daddy
said were Arkansas. Last he would unfurl the sun from the
yellow crayon, a big warm real sun, unlike this weak angry
watery red eye that now had begun to sink beyond the window in a thicket of black branches.

He finished the Negro driver hastily and drew two thick
pointed lines for the mule's flopping ears. He was disappointed
that he knew no way to show the flopping. He paused, excited,
and picked up the yellow crayon. He could tell it was not a
very good drawing of the Front Street levee. There ought to
be sparrows in the magnolia tree but he had made the tree
little and the sparrows would have to be such little bitty old
things, just dots, not birds at all (rustling, shifting, starting
from branch to branch among the thick green shiny leaves
spotted white with their droppings), that it was not worth
while putting them in. He didn't care what Miss Hastings

thought about the picture. He wanted the mule, the cotton, the wide brown winding river only as something for this big yellow sun to shine on. The sun was home. This feisty little Yankee sun was cold. He himself was cold, cold all the time, and the snow did not melt properly away but stayed and stayed like white gravel and the streets were smooth with a dark ice as hard as iron and here they said "throwing stones" instead of chunking rocks, and nobody had ever seen a persimmon tree. The sun grew. The crayon went around and around until the shiny yellow disk was as large as an orange, shedding light and splendor.

"Forrest Kirby!"

Startled, he threw up his head at Miss Hastings, and let it drop furtively again. Perhaps if he did not look at her she would not make him answer. He began to print his name meticulously, bearing down hard in large block letters at the bottom of his picture.

"Forrest, let's show the class *your* picture," Miss Hastings said.

He ducked his head further and tried to shrink himself small. The whole day would be wasted if he spoke now but he could hear her footsteps approaching. He stared miserably at his picture, wishing more than anything in the world he could disappear into it and become a boy walking the Front Street levee in the sunshine beside a mule pulling a bale of cotton. The footsteps stopped just behind him.

"Why, Forrest, that's a lovely picture. Tell me what it's about," she said.

Maybe a smile would do. He lifted the corners of his mouth and let his head fall back a little, looking up at her.

"What's this, a mule?"

He nodded.

"And that's some kind of little wagon, isn't it?"

He nodded again.

"But what's this on the wagon? What's the wagon loaded with? We must make everything as plain as plain, mustn't we, Forrest? Now what is it, a big cake of ice? No-o-o, I don't think it's a cake of ice. Is it something wrapped in white canvas? No? Is it a bale of cotton?"

He nodded coldly. Anybody had eyes could see it was a cotton bale.

"But it isn't quite right, Forrest. Here, let me show you."

He saw her hand reach out in front of him for a crayon. She was about to mark up his picture. He struck her hand away, jumped up and shouted, "You get offa my levee, you damn old Yankee schoolteacher, you!"

After the rest of the second grade had gone home, she made him cry. Grownups could always do that to you. They could pat your shoulder and say things about your mother and daddy and disappointment and love, making a cooing noise like pigeons all the time, and sooner or later you cried. But when he felt his throat sickening and the tears warming his eyes, he crossed the fingers of one hand and whispered, "Presto, chango, deveediacum, Joe, Ben, Buck, begone," to himself so the crying wouldn't count. He felt tricked. This wasn't real crying, not like the crying at night in the darkness, and he was not sorry for what he had said. He was only sorry he had spoken at all.

When she said, "Now, Forrest, I want you to tell me you're sorry," and she put both hands on his shoulders and looked him in the eye, he said meekly, "I'm sorry," because he was sorry about something but it wasn't what she thought and having this secret made him feel better.

He hurried out into the corridor so as to keep ahead of Miss

Hastings. He flipped his leather jacket off the hook, snaked his muffler out of one arm and a red stocking cap crammed with his mittens out of the other and put them on. He opened the door and stopped on the top of the steps to look for his sled and while he looked he rubbed the arm of his jacket against the brick of the building to make it look raggedy. He saw his sled hidden under a heap of snow in the yard. *They* had done that. He ran to it, tipped it up, and kicked the snow off it and started down the street looking for anyone who might want to call him Hillbilly.

He had had only one fight. A fourth-grader had called him Hillbilly and he had knocked the fourth-grader down and kicked him in the head. Now he was anxious every afternoon to find someone willing to insult him so he could beat him up. Far down the street he saw some children but when he came up to them, they were just girls petting a big boxer dog. He walked past them looking straight ahead.

He kept walking for fifteen or twenty minutes. He wanted to get to the other side of town where no one knew him or had ever even seen him at all. At last he saw a street he had never been down. He turned into it looking at the sidewalks on both sides to find one that had not been shoveled. He saw a four-bit one a little ahead of him. He stopped and carefully eased a handkerchief out of his pocket. It was rolled up. He unrolled it. In one corner there was a smudge of soot preserved. He had got it off the furnace door. He slipped his hand out of his mitten, touched the soot with two fingers and spread it on his face, rubbing it in lightly here and there. He zipped open his jacket and let his muffler hang loose. Then he started for the house, dirty-faced, in a raggedy-looking old leather jacket unzipped, a poor boy with no one to look after him. All he really needed was seventeen cents.

The house was neat and white with green shutters, set close to the sidewalk. He rang the bell and an old lady in a black dress with three combs in her hair answered the door. There were green diamonds in the combs. With his eyes on the gems, he spoke rapidly in a practiced breathless rush. "Please, ma'am, have y'all got iny old newspapers or magazines or would you like me to shovel off your sidewalk? Ah'm trying to make me enough money to buy my uniform for the Cub Scouts, and I'd sure thank you if . . ."

"You're pretty little to shovel all that snow."

"Oh, no, ma'am. I reckon I got the biggest muscle in my grade at school."

A man's voice called out from inside the house, "How much does he want?"

"How much do you want?" the old lady asked.

"Just whatever you care to pay, ma'am," he said promptly, smiling.

A sour look crossed the lady's face. She resented the appeal to her charity.

"How much did he say?" the man's voice called.

"Whatever you care to pay, please, sir," the boy shouted.

"Oh, the devil. It's not worth but a quarter, but—here's forty cents, Ella."

The boy said, "Yes, sir. Thank you, sir," and the woman took the money from the man and gave it to him. "The shovel's around at the side."

The job took him three-quarters of an hour. He put the shovel back and started home at a dogged, short-legged trot. He had the money inside his mitten where he could make it clink. Panting in the cold air hurt his throat and he slowed down to a fast walk, digging his heels in.

Things at home were just as he had expected to find them.

His brother was not home; basketball practice. His sister was not home. His mother was not home; bridge club. There was a note from his mother on the kitchen table telling his father what was in the refrigerator for supper. As soon as he felt the stillness of the house and was sure there was no one in it but himself, he ran up the stairs to the bedroom where he slept with his brother.

In one corner of his closet, under a permanent heap of dirty T-shirts and jerseys, he found a tin coffee can. It had been heavy. It was now light because there were four dollar bills in it, no longer the mess of pennies, dimes, and nickels he had been saving for so long.

He fished a heap of change out of the pocket of his jeans. On his hands and knees in front of the closet door, he counted out eighty-nine cents. He laid it on the little pile of the four dollar bills and sat back on his heels a moment staring at all that money. He took from the coffee can a piece of paper, an order blank, already filled in with painstaking block printing. He picked up the order blank and the money and went downstairs to his mother's desk in the hall.

He took a square blue envelope from a box of stationery. Then came the question: Should it be addressed in ink or pencil? He could not print small enough with a pen, but if he printed it in pencil maybe they would think it was only a kid that had written it or maybe that someone was playing a joke on them and they would laugh and throw it into the wastepaper basket. He thought a long time, fiddling with a fancy feather pen his mother had stuck in a little glass full of BB shot.

At last he felt the silence of the house. It was so hateful being alone in this house, still strange and new and hateful after seven whole months, that he remembered why he had saved all the money, what he was sending it away for, and he picked up a pencil almost casually and printed the name and address on the envelope. He folded the dollar bills carefully around the coins, thrust in the order blank, and sealed up the envelope. It was lumpy but it looked all right. He took a stamp from a little drawer and stuck it on the letter, jumped up, ran out of the house, and shoved the letter in the mailbox on the corner. He walked back worrying faintly about all the people who had given him old paper or had let him clean off their sidewalks. What if one of them stopped him on the street someday and said, "Where is your Cub Scout uniform?" He could answer that; his Cub Scout uniform would be at home. But what if they said, "Did you ever get that Cub Scout uniform?" He wasn't going to join any damn old Cub Scouts. He would just lie. Lies to Yankees didn't count somehow.

Every day the mailman came about two o'clock in the afternoon while he was at school. If the mailman brought a package for him while he was in school, his mother would find it first. She would ask him what was in it, where he got it, where he got the *money* for it, and everything would be discovered and go smash. He took nearly a week to decide he would have to skip school.

After his letter had been gone seven days, he started for school as usual, walking as he always did, alone. He cut around several blocks until he could come at his house from the rear. He walked quickly through the driveway of the house in back of his, climbed a board fence, and perched warily looking at all the back yards he could see and a long time at his house. Then he ran into his own garage and sat down between an empty steel oil drum and the lawn mower. The garage was empty; he could look straight out and see the mailman when he went to the houses across the street. If he saw him with a big package, that would be the worst time, the daring time. He would have to run out, take the package and hide again until the other kids were coming home from school.

He waited, fearing the truant officer. Nobody had ever told him what the truant officer looked like. It was certain to be a policeman because "officers" were policemen. Maybe there was a court where they tried such as he and the truant officer would take him to it. He could see himself under a bright light being put in the wrong by somber people, unable to answer them in any way that would satisfy them. Perhaps they would throw him in the jailhouse; anyhow there would be trouble, a long coil of tears and reproaches from his parents. He wondered if the truant officer had a mustache. All bad men had mustaches, all robbers, cattle-rustlers and kidnapers in the comic books had mustaches.

He saw the mailman plodding along across the street. He squinted to see him as clearly as he could. He could see no big package. He watched him come across the street to his own house with a sheaf of letters in his hand. The package had not come. He would have to skip school again the next day.

He came to his hiding place the next afternoon and settled down between the oil drum and the lawn mower with his chin on his knees. He had not been there ten minutes when he saw an olive-green U.S. mail truck pull up briskly and stop in front of his house. He was up, running out the driveway toward the truck before he had time to think. It was the package. The man asked him to sign. Panting, he printed his name, grabbed the package and ran as fast as he could toward the garage. He put the package behind him and crouched there, looking and cocking his head to listen. Had anyone seen him? No one called him and he relaxed. He was a fool for not remembering about parcel post.

When he saw other school kids passing on their way home, he got up stiffly, put the package under his arm, and walked toward the back door of his house. He could not be sure just where his mother would be. He turned the doorknob cautiously, opened the door a little and stuck his head through. She was not in the laundry room and he could not hear her moving around in the kitchen. He stepped in and shut the door softly. The back stairway was opposite him ten feet away. He put his head down and glided the ten feet quietly as if he were invisible. He settled his foot on each stair tread before putting his weight on it, missing the fifth one because it squeaked. At the top he listened again. Downstairs in the front of the house he heard the clicking on the dial of the telephone and then his mother's voice. He slipped into the bedroom and laid the package on the floor.

He unwrapped the brown paper stealthily, stopping and raising his head every time the paper crackled, not because the chance of his mother's hearing him made him afraid now, rather he had some doubt that he would actually soar up into the sky from the window ledge. He hated to have any human being aware of him when he failed and there was nothing wrong with his mother's hearing that he knew of.

He raised the cover of the cardboard box gently. A costume of bright blue stockinette with a red flannel cape and a pair of red leatheroid shoes lay in the box. It was a Superman suit. He had worked four months to get it but now that he could see it and feel of it, it did not seem grand enough, somehow. Could it be trusted?

He undressed quickly, tossing a checkered lumberjack shirt and blue jeans in a heap on the floor. He held up the flimsy tights for the Teddy bear to see. It was a small old doll lying covered with a scrap of cloth in a cigar box beside his bed. He had brought it from Home and it had been his silent friend for a long time but he had never expected much of it. He climbed into the suit and pulled on the red boots. He stood before the mirror in the closet door. There was padding at various places inside the suit. He struck out into the air with his fist.

He tiptoed to the window and tried to open it. It was stuck. He put his hands against the top bar of the frame and, arching his back, pushed upward as hard as he could. He did not move it. It always stuck. The one in his mother's bedroom opened easily.

Before he crossed the corridor he stopped at the doorway. His mother was still at the telephone in the front hall downstairs. She might be able to see him as he left his room. He put his head down again and walked quickly across the corridor into his mother's bedroom.

The window was already up a few inches. He raised it silently as far as it would go. He took a Superman pose, his feet apart, his fists on his hips, and looked down on the conquerable world.

He tried to think how the bare trees would look from above. Like hands, claws, trying to snatch him back except that he would be going too fast to notice, his face burning in the rush of air, his shadow flicking across the town. He would have to watch out for the clouds. Inside them it was like fog, they said. He could speed up going through them, faster than a Black Widow or a Shooting Star, and soar out above them, and there it would all be spread out below. The roof of this house would not even be a speck. He could rock back and forth in the wind like a chicken hawk and watch the whole thing: mountains, rivers, cities, even the ocean wheeling beneath him. Then he would point himself South, and zip! he would be Home in the springtime again.

Sometimes they left notes, people going away unexpectedly or those committing suicide. He thought about this a minute, his pose softening. If his mother would come with him, that would be all right, but he knew she would not. "The North is our home now." She had said that and he had not been able to say much to her or his daddy or quite look straight at them ever since she had.

He was sure. He was absolutely sure, he told himself, he would fly once he leaped from the window sill but as he climbed up on the sill and squatted there wretchedly with his chin on his knees, it seemed a long way down into the side yard.

He stood up almost with a jerk, stared up at the high white winter clouds, spread his arms, and jumped. He fell in a slight curve and broke his thighbone when he lit.

As he was coming to, he realized vaguely that his mother was bent over him crying but he did not move or speak because he was beginning to feel the pain and he knew without thinking about it that her crying did not mean she was sorry enough to take him back South. Her sobs seemed to come through a long pipe and he barely heard them because all he was thinking about was his failure. He hadn't done it right. It was only the first time.

# This Town and
# Salamanca

So WHEN HE RETURNED, we asked him why he had gone to live there and he said he'd just heard of it and thought it might be a nice place to live in for a while. He had lived in an old house built around a court. The walls were four feet thick and the windows were larger on the outside than they were on the inside; the sills slanted. They kept goats' milk there on the window sills because the stone made the air cool. You could see the sticks of a hawk's nest hanging over one corner of the roof, and Jesus, the landlady's son—he looked up here to see if we thought it was funny that a man should be named Jesus, but none of us said anything. We read a great deal—he often whistled to it evenings. Yes, the food was good. They had a sausage with tomatoes in it that was very good and the wine was not like French wine, it was heavier and sweeter. And there were no fireplaces for heating but things they called *braseros*. They were big pans like that with his arms stretched and on cold mornings they set it alight and covered the flame with ashes. They would put the *brasero* under a big table. The table had a sort of plush cover to it that hung down to the floor with slits in it. You put your feet through the slits and wrapped the cover around your waist. Then although your feet roasted, you could still see your breath and you couldn't stay in the room long because of the fumes, and sitting by the *brasero* gave you chilblains but they were a common thing and no one minded. Klug asked him about the women. Were they—you know? The women were all right, he said. The peasant girls were very pretty but they faded early and got fat. Yes, but, Klug said impatiently, but he was talking then about the riots, how they used beer bottles full of black powder for bombs and when they bombed the convent, the nuns all ran out crying and waving their arms after the explosion and some fell on their knees and prayed in the midst of the rioters but the bomb had not even chipped the wall, it was four feet thick. All the houses were like that with big thick walls and the streets were narrow and the town was quiet. They could not hang the washing in the courtyards because it was too cool for it to dry, so they spread it on rocks beside the river when they finished. It was a very old town and they lived in the same way year after year. Gordon asked him about the spiritual remnants of medievalism. He answered that the people were very pious and went to the cathedral to pray for everything, even lost articles. The cathedral had small windows and the light was yellow inside, not like the gray light inside the cathedrals in Île de France.

Well, I thought, as they talked on into the evening, it is not anything like that here. You see I remember this particular evening very clearly and all we said because it was the last time John had anything new to tell us, and from that time on, he has lived here with us in this town. We never thought he would settle here. It is a good enough town but nothing to the places he has seen, not even the kind of place you would close your book to watch if you went through on the train. First there are the ball-bearing factory and the electric bell factory, with the other factories hidden behind them; then there are trees hiding the houses with their backs turned toward you; and then you would see the spire, not of a cathedral, but of the Methodist Church, and the town would soon dwindle away into the cornfields and just after that you could look at your watch to see how long before Chicago. It is not like Salamanca, but the four of us were born and grew up here and only John had gone away. And when he came home to see his mother, he would tell us these things that made us seem fools to ourselves for having stayed but we were busy with our work and could not follow him. There are maple trees on both sides of the streets and in summer it is like driving through a tunnel of green leaves.

You see he never answered Gordon's intelligent questions and he always disappointed Klug, who thinks that all the women in foreign countries wait on street corners after dark winking and motioning yonder with their heads. John seldom was an actor in his own play—he merely looked, it seemed,

and told us what he saw. It was the best way, keeping himself
out, but they would not admit it, so they kept on with the
questions. They admitted it to themselves though. Klug said
he talked of the peasant girls with their ankles shining under
their tucked-up skirts doing the washing by the riverbank
when he was scrubbing his hands after taking the cancer out
of Mrs. Gira, the Polish washwoman, and the nurse was counting the used wet sponges and the hospital smell made his
stomach turn. And when the aldermen brought the plans of
the new railroad station back to Gordon and sat down to talk
and object for hours, he saw the smoke drifting from where
the bomb exploded and the nuns praying in the confusion and
one of the aldermen had spots on his waistcoat that he kept
picking at. Though we had nothing but questions when he
came, we all knew that the questions were merely little signs
to show that we too might very well have been there and seen
these things, and that it was nothing more important than
chance that we had stayed here. He talked late and I remember there was a bat lurching to and fro under a light down the
street.

Mrs. Gira got well though and it is a fine new railroad
station.


## II


HE WAS IN an old boathouse whistling. We heard him when
we came down the path. The boathouse was so old the shin-
gles curled and weeds grew on the roof, and we used to tell
him that someday the whole shebang would give way with
him in it and he would have to swim out with the rafters round
his neck. He had borrowed the use of it from Old Man Suggs,

who hadn't kept a boat in years. When we were kids I remember seeing it when we went to the river flats to look for dog-tooth violets. It was a motor launch and he sold it when the tomato cannery started up. Every summer the river is full of blobs of red tomato pulp and no one wants to go out in a boat then. But John was building a sailboat. It was May then and he had worked all his spare time on it since the August before; every Saturday afternoon, and nights after supper he would go down and work by the light of three oil lamps he got from his mother. That was the winter we played so much poker and sometimes we would go to the boathouse at midnight and ask John to take a hand. He was always pleasant about it, without any scruples against gambling, but he never stopped working and we would shout above the hammer blows, "Where do you think you're going in this boat when it's finished? Going to haul tomatoes for the cannery?" He would laugh and say that a good many waters would wet this hull before she was much older. We would laugh because we knew he had got the phrase out of some book, and we would start up the path. The ripples on the water always shone in the lamp-light and we could hear his hammer as far as the dirt road where we turned to Klug's house. Often we played till midnight. I won a lot of money that winter.

When we entered the boathouse we could see it was nearly finished. It looked very big and white and seemed not too much to have put a winter's work into. He was planing some teak for the deck, and when we came near there was the acrid leathery odor of the fresh shavings. We had seen pictures of yachts, and once or twice the ore boats on the big lakes, but the things we saw every day, the houses, trees, and grain elevators, went straight up from the ground. They had roots. If they had not, as they seemed, always been in one place, they always would be. John's boat was a strange shape, curved for the water. Even in the dim boathouse, propped up with blocks, she seemed ready for movement. I looked at John with the handle of the plane easy in his hand, and we were going to be "professional" men, and I knew he would go away. The boat had sprung from some matrix within him that we would never understand, just as he was puzzled when Gordon asked how long she was and how many tons' weight as if she were a heifer fattened for market. When we went out of the boathouse, Klug said, "So long, skipper."

He went away in the boat as I thought he would and after this he never came back for long at a time. God knows how he got the blocks from under her without any help, but one afternoon he launched her all by himself, and in ten days he had her rigged and the galley full of stores. He sailed away without saying anything to anyone, down our little river into the Ohio and then into the Mississippi and out into the Gulf below New Orleans. He was gone all summer into October. I saw him on the street when he returned. He was tanned almost black. We shook hands and I said, "Where did you go? Did you have a good trip?"

He looked at me a moment before answering. "Trip" means a journey you take in a car during your two-weeks vacation in the summer, maybe to Yellowstone or the Grand Canyon or Niagara. It is a relaxation from your work. I could see as I said it that "trip" was the wrong word, but just how far wrong it took me years to find out and then I never was certain. I thought of his boat, a strange and unfamiliar shape, and how he, whom we had seen unsuspectingly every day through his boyhood, had made it.

"Yes, I had a good time."

"Where did you go?"

"Well, down into the Gulf and around."

"Cuba?"

"Yes, I put in at Havana," and then as if he had at last found something he could tell me, "you know, Klug would like that place—they've got a park there where you can get free beer. It's owned by a brewing company and you can go there and drink all you want, free."

"Where else did you go?"

"Oh, the Tortugas, Haiti, Veracruz."

He showed me a gold piece he had got off a pawnbroker in Port-au-Prince. He said it was a moidore. He was nineteen then.

### III

WHEN HE returned next time, he was less reticent. It was not because he was proud of being a traveler but more, I think, that he saw we really wanted to hear about the distant places he had been. When his ship was coming into the harbor of Singapore, he said you could see the junks waiting with their crinkled sails. And when the ship came near, they sailed right in front of the bow as close as they could. Sometimes they didn't make it and they all smashed up and drowned. He said they did it to cut off the devils following behind. The day after he told us that Gordon asked Tom Sing, who runs the chop suey joint, if he believed in devils but Tom only grinned. Gordon said it was the oriental inscrutability. Gordon is quite serious.

During the next ten years John did all the things we said we'd do that time in the apple orchard. He joined the Army to fly and left the Army after a time and went to Italy. I went to his house from the office the day he got home. He was dressed in white, lunging at himself in a long mirror with a foil in his hand. The French held their foils this way with the thumb so, but the Italians that way. After that he was a sailor again on one of the crack clippers that still bring the wheat up from Australia, and from Liverpool I had a postcard with a picture of Aintree racecourse on the back. It said, "Give Gordon my congratulations." Gordon had been elected mayor and we were very proud of him. How John heard of it we couldn't figure out.

One time there was a card from Aden and another from Helsinki. You can see he traveled. No one in the town had ever gone so far and people used to stop his mother on the street to ask where he was then, not that they really cared but because the thread that tied them to him as a local boy tied them also to the strange name his mother answered when they asked.

When he was a sailor in the Pacific, spinal meningitis broke out on board. Eighteen people died and they put the bodies down in the hold. The ship's doctor examined all the crew and said John was the healthiest and the captain ordered him to go below and sew up the bodies in shrouds and heave them overboard.

John got a roll of canvas, a reel of packthread, a leather palm-guard and a needle and went down into the hold. He rigged up an electric light in a wire cage and swung it from a hook over his head. The eighteen lay there in a row. They were quite stiff and, when the ship rolled, sometimes an arm would come up and pause until the ship rolled back. But they were in the shadow and he did not watch them much because the sewing was hard work, about an hour to each one. He jabbed his finger with the needle three or four times and that made it harder. When he got one ready, he would put it over his shoulder and stagger up the companionway to the deck.

High above him beside the funnel, to escape the risk of infection, stood an Anglican parson, one of the passengers. He had an open prayer book and said the service very quickly, the leaves fluttering in the wind. Then John would pick up the corpse again and heave it over the side. Sometimes a shark would rip the shroud almost as it hit the water; others he could see jerked from the ring of foam of their impact and carried quickly below. There were at least a dozen sharks and John said he knew his work was useless and he took bigger and bigger stitches in the canvas. There was quite a wind and John could never hear the whole service because the wind blew the words away but a few snatches would come down to him. He and the parson were all alone, the other people having hidden from fear; and they did not speak to each other. When John brought up the last corpse, it had been a Portuguese merchant from Manila on his way to Goa to see his daughter, the wind stopped suddenly and there was a moment of calm. ". . . to the deep to be turned into corruption," the parson said. John picked up the merchant, balanced him on the rail, shoved him over, and the sharks came.

## IV

"AND ELOISE said it was when she was getting the coffee after dinner. Mr. and Mrs. Booth were setting in the parlor and Mr. Booth was drinking brandy like he always does and the both of them quiet as mutes at a funeral when all at once the doorbell rang and Eloise answered it and there stood John Baldwin. My, I think he's handsome. Oh, he's much better-looking than him. And he asked could he see Mr. Booth and Eloise said he could; he was right in the parlor. So Mr. Baldwin come in but he wouldn't give Eloise his hat. He kep' it and said he was only staying a minute. Well, Eloise said she went to the kitchen to get another cup naturally expecting Mr. Baldwin would have some coffee and when she come back through the dining room she was so surprised she nearly dropped it.

"She said Mr. Baldwin was standing right in front of Mr. Booth and he says, 'Dennis, I've come for your wife.' Just like that. And Mr. Booth says, 'What do you mean—you've come for my wife?' Eloise says she got behind the window drapes so they wouldn't see her and Mr. Baldwin says, 'Frances loves me. I want you to divorce her.' Mr. Booth was drunk on all that brandy and he jumped up and began to shout that it was damned cool and a lot of things about throwing Mr. Baldwin out of the house only Eloise don't think for a minute he could have even if he was sober. Why, John Baldwin's way over six feet and a sailor and always fighting with them little swords and all, but Mr. Booth got white he was so mad, and Mrs. Booth she didn't say anything. She just sat there and looked at them and Eloise said it was like Mr. Baldwin didn't hear a word Mr. Booth said because he was looking at Mrs. Booth all the time and when Mr. Booth stopped talking Mr. Baldwin looked up at him quick like you do when a clock stops. Then he just says, 'Well, Dennis,' and Mr. Booth began to swear something terrible but he didn't try to throw him out, he didn't even come close to him. Then Mr. Baldwin looked at Mrs. Booth and smiled and says, 'Come along, Frances,' and Mrs. Booth smiled back and they walked right out of the house without her even packing any clothes. And that's all there was to it. Eloise says Mrs. Booth walked right out of her house into a new life, never to return. And they say Mrs. Booth has gone to Paris, France, to get a divorce from Mr. Booth. Well, all I got to say is, it serves him right—he was always running around after them dirty little factory girls. Certainly he was. Everybody knows it. Why you know that little Muller girl, the one with the fox fur. Why Eloise says that . . ."

I stopped listening then. I always liked to look at the Italian flags on bottles of olive oil when I was a kid. I had the same feeling then: no one does things like that here, walking into a man's house and taking his wife. If you want a man's wife, you meet her by chance in Chicago and she goes on being his wife afterward. Or maybe it was like the boat. We hadn't lived with him. He was only the things he had done and those at a distance. Now that he had begun his marriage this way I did not think he would change the pattern, but that was before I knew he intended to settle here.

He was, I thought then, rootless and invincible. He didn't seem to want what we had, what we had remained here and worked for. Which comes down to this, I suppose, and little more: the same trees every day when you go to work, in summer hanging over the lawns beside the walks, and bare with snow at the forks of the limbs and the sound of snow shovels scraping the walks; and when you look up, the line of the roof of the house next door against the sky. You could call it peace. It is just peace with no brilliance. I remembered how bright the gold piece was in his hand.

But he didn't go away again. He settled here very quietly and took a nice little house. He and Frances were very happy, and we all used to say how glad we were that they were so happy. We used to say it very loudly to ourselves and sometimes to him, and we put ourselves out to help him meet people. He had been away so long he had forgot or never had known them. We got him into the golf club the first week he was in the bank. Everything we could show him about the town we did gladly.

After he had been married a year, we all came to Gordon's one night to drink beer. Most of the evening we taught John poker, and after that we just sat around and talked. John said, "You know Roy Curtis from out Fruit Ridge way? He came in today and he wanted to borrow the money to buy another hundred acres. That piece by the bridge there. Belongs to Dick Sheppard."

"He'll raise wheat. No money in wheat now."

"That's what I told him but he wants to have a shot at it just the same. Offered to mortgage his place. I don't know, though. What do you think?"

Without saying that we didn't ordinarily do a banker's thinking for him publicly, we told him Roy Curtis was a fool if he thought he could make money in wheat at fifty-six cents a bushel.

"He's got a combine, you know. He says he'll have two hundred acres in wheat and he and his boy can work it all by themselves."

We remembered when he had bought the combine. Two hundred acres is too small for one of those big combines. This isn't Dakota.

"You wouldn't lend him the money, then? He's coming in Thursday. It's good security, a mortgage on his place."

We told him we wouldn't lend the money, but John had drunk a lot of beer. He kept on talking about it.

"He's a smart farmer, Roy. Look at that house he's got there. It's a fine place, as good as any of these here in town. Got a Packard and a big radio. Why, he said he got Rome on that radio the other night. He didn't make his money doing foolish things. I don't know about the loan."

Roy's aunt had left him the money, but that was while John was away. We didn't tell him.

I said, "Do you fence any now, John?"

He got up laughing and went out into the hall and got a mashie out of Gordon's golf bag and came in with it. He began, standing with a bent leg and one hand flung up behind him. He went through the lunges and parries laughing.

"Getting fat," he said. "I can't do 'em any more."

I had to leave then because I had to be at the office early next day. John was still talking about the loan when I left. It had been raining and the wind had blown down leaves from the maples. The evening had been unsatisfactory and I thought about it as I walked along. I was in sight of my house before I thought why, and I stopped to pick off the red leaves stuck to my shoes.

I remembered him in white with his face grave. "You see, the French hold a foil this way. It's not like the Italians. I learned in Marseille." That was the way he used to talk. We know all about loans; we knew all about him now. Of course I could never do more than just remind him of these things because he was so happy. But I did not think he would ever go away again to return and tell us these things, because of his happiness. Suddenly I felt old. It was as if we had trusted him to keep our youth for us and he had let it go. But our youth only.

# Pommery 1921

I T WAS Mr. Peavey's birthday. He was going to celebrate. But he did not whistle or hum little tunes as he took off his office clothes. It was too solemn a festival (for which he had saved twenty-two dollars). He was thinking—*Salons, Ateliers, Matters-de-Hotel, an evening worthy of me at last, among people who will understand me,* and into his mind came vivid pictures of young men with cold proud faces in the light before theaters waiting for limousines with women in evening gowns. These were the people who would understand him.

Mr. Peavey really lived only in the drawing rooms, grouse moors, and paddocks of the illustrated magazines. He inhabited a hall bedroom with bureau, bed, and a curtained corner. On the bureau were three tattered books from the Public Library, a bottle of hair grease, and a birthday card which bore the inscription *Happy Birthday from Mother* with a picture of two doves carrying a red ribbon in their mouths. Behind him—he was looking in the mirror—there was a picture on the wall, a Maxfield Parrish print with a beautiful blue sky, and when it caught his eye as it always did, he thought *Mediterranean someday, Cap Ferrat, Eden Roc,* and like little twittering echoes, very accurate memories of photographs glanced and fluttered in his head.

He dressed according to a ritual he had prepared while coming home on the subway. The clothes lay in a neat row on the bed. The discovery that the dress shirt opened at the back surprised and troubled him. He tied his white tie four times *genteel nonchalance as if I didn't care how it looked.*

He gave his black shoes another wipe with a dirty sock until they shone almost like patent leather. Then he lifted from the bed and drew carefully up his legs the creased trousers and pulled the braces over his shoulders. *Braces, not suspenders.* He put on the coat anxiously and shot his cuffs *it fits O.K.* And in the breast pocket he thrust a white silk handkerchief with genteel nonchalance. Facing the mirror complacently he drew his face into an expression he did not recognize as bored. *Not so bad. If I should meet Hazel in front of the place, suppose she should be walking along there, "I'm sorry, Miss Applegate, I'm meeting some people here."*

He ran a frizzy comb through his hair one last time and took
from the top drawer of the bureau a little book with *Connois-
seur's Guide to Wines* on the front of it. He opened it and
studied it for a moment. *A bottle of Pommery 1921. They
couldn't misunderstand that—Voov Clickott, No. Mote ett
Chandun, too tough to say. Gotta be Pommery. 1921's the
best year.* He settled his tie again, switched off the swinging
light, and went out, feeling choked inside with excitement.

He walked slowly down the dark stairs. Three little girls
playing hopscotch under the light stopped and stared while he
hailed a taxi. "Alberto's," he said and got in.

"Where you want to go?" asked the taxi driver.

"Alberto's. Don't you know where that is? It's a restaurant.
It's on Fifty-fourth Street east of Fifth."

"Fifty-fourt' Street, east of Fift'. O.K."

When the taxi stopped at red lights and people crossing the
street eddied about it, he gazed out with his face tense and
expressionless like the faces of the young men at the theater
hour. He hoped these hurrying cattle would think of him *lol-
ling gracefully* on the seat as he thought of those rich young
men.

The cab stopped before the restaurant, a neat doorway with
little green trees in tubs, clipped and tended, and the light
from within shining through lace curtains. Mr. Peavey paid
the driver, tipping him half a dollar and *strode* inside. He had
thought of himself *striding* across the sidewalk all last week
as he hung from a subway strap.

A page-boy opened the door. "Good evening, sir." Mr.
Peavey nodded *absently,* and walked very slowly over the
thick carpet. *Do I go in now or wait for the Matter-De-
Hotel?* he worried. At last the headwaiter came—"Good
evening, sir"—and led him in. He was so relieved he nearly

forgot to say, "A table by the window, please." *No use knuck-
ling under to these fellows.*

As he walked down the aisle between the tables, he glanced
around the restaurant. *I'm early. Too early. Nobody here.*
Then—*Nobody dines at this hour.* He had expected a crowd
of people, men like himself severe in black and white and the
shoulders of women *gleaming softly in the dim light.* He
saw no one but two people talking eagerly to one another. The
woman even wore a hat.

When they reached the table by the window, the waiter
held a chair with smooth civility. "Oh, waiter," he said loudly,
"has a party called for Mr. Peavey? Well, if they do, show them
to this table." He looked at the lone couple two tables away.
To say he expected someone to call gave him, he felt obscurely,
a certain standing with the waiter, and to say it loudly might
have brought into the mind of the woman two tables away a
picture of himself as he wished to seem that night. It might
have made her look up anyway.

A second waiter came up. "Good evening, sir." For the first
time he noticed the deference of these people. It warmed him
and he took the menu confidently. He looked it over casually
and returned it. "No. Nothing to eat just now. Perhaps later.
The wine list, please." That had the right tone. He could eat
if he wished but he preferred not to. He scanned the wine list
a long time and pulled at his lower lip as if he could not decide.
Then he said, "A bottle of *Pommery, 1921.*" The waiter said,
Yes, sir," and went to fetch it.

Soon the waiter returned and thrust the thick, green bottle
across the table, butt-end first. *"Pommery, 1921, sir."* Panic
roared in his head. What was he supposed to do, take it? But
the waiter put it in a silvery bucket full of cracked ice, twirled
it around, and went away again. He came back presently,

twirled the bottle again, and opened it with sleek professional gestures. The cork popped. The waiter filled Mr. Peavey's glass and departed.

Watching the thread of bubbles from the bottom of the glass, he raised it to the level of his nose and muttered, "To myself and the coming year." *Yes, Hazel, for years it's been my custom to go quietly away and take stock of myself, and when I have chosen my direction for the coming year, to pledge myself in good wine. Last night—yes, it was my birthday—it was champagne, Pommery 1921, a very good year, I believe. Deuced—no, can't say that, she'd laugh—damned queer stuff, champagne.*

He would say this by the water cooler, getting a drink. It was near her desk. *You know, the Crown Prince of Denmark says the taste is like licking dirty windowpanes.* What did it taste like? He sipped and was disappointed. *Sour. Sour and prickly.* What a fool he was, throwing away his dough like this. Still, *The Crown Prince of Denmark says . . .*

He sipped the champagne, catching the dull reflection of the light in the polished panels of the wall and staring at the chandelier itself with its smooth little globes of colored glass like bunches of grapes. The restaurant was beginning to fill up. A girl entered in a gold lamé gown. She had shining yellow hair and earrings that sparkled. *Beautiful. A deb, probably.* With her was the kind of man he had always thought of as a British major, patch of gray at the temple, a neat mustache, and a gaunt, haggard face—*Wounded in Africa. El Alamein.* He watched them approach from the doorway. Where would they sit? Near him? *Turn, damn you, turn this way.* His luck seemed almost audible as they were put at the table next his own, the girl facing him.

*It's a sign. Maybe I'll meet them somehow.* At once he saw

himself in a *motor, a Rolls* and the major was saying *Ah, Peavey, I'm getting old. Can't stand this all-night merriment. My niece is too much for me. Suppose you take her on to the Plaza from here. You can drop me at my place on the way like a good chap.* And he was replying, *Certainly, my dear Major. That is*—turning with courteous deference to the girl—*if Miss*—now what would be her name?—*if Miss Stuyvesant doesn't mind?*

Schemes to meet them occurred to him but none of them had that casual ease *all too daring. Peavey, did you say? Oh, yes, quite, saw you at Saint-Moritz last winter, didn't we?* That was how it ought to be.

He thought about the girl so hard that it seemed as if she must, turned by his effort, look at him. He gulped his glass of champagne and set it down hard on the table. At the noise, the major glanced over at him. *Yes, he's a sad case. Drinking himself to death. See him everywhere alone.* If the major said that to her, perhaps she would come over to the table and plead—but no, *what the hell do you think this is, a funny book?* He looked over at her again and she was clasping the major's hand in a way not like a niece. *Gone now. Whore more'n likely. Might as well get drunk.* He sipped his champagne and waited for the muscles of his face to give the first stiff feeling of drunkenness. He lifted the bottle out of the melting ice. It was nearly empty. He saw the punched-up bottom of the bottle. *Damn gyp, making a bottle like that.* There wasn't enough left to get drunk on. Forgetting that he should let the waiter do it, he poured out the last bit and drank it down.

He looked around him. Now the restaurant was full of people clustered around the tables, nodding and laughing and talking *not to me.* He thought wildly of shouting, making a speech, anything. If only someone would insult him so he could resent it nobly and *in the papers, "Young Society Man Jailed in Restaurant Brawl."* But far within him where, uncontaminated by his loneliness, he kept his own special morsel of truth, he knew that the papers would not say *Young Society Man.* He stared at the empty bottle. There was no way.

Back in his room it seemed as if he had never been away. The same iron bed, the same bureau, the view of the Lundebergs' flat across the air-shaft, Papa Lundeberg reading the paper; Mama Lundeberg sewing; the radio going full blast and the noises from the street. He took off his clothes slowly and went to bed. He was not even drunk. A last bright thought struck him—*tomorrow.*

In the morning he got up and looked in the mirror. He did not look debauched. There were no pouches under his eyes. The image before him was only that of a young man needing a shave. He decided not to shave and quickly, stealthily shaping his decision was the unacknowledged thought that if he did not shave, people, Hazel, would ask him why and then he could say . . .

Deliberately he took a dirty shirt out of his laundry bag under the bed. He put no hair grease on his hair. Carefully folding the dress suit, he put it in its cardboard box and went out with it under his arm. He breakfasted—white tiles, stack of wheats, and coffee in a thick cup—and stopped down the street at Sidney Schaum's, My Tailor, to return the rented suit.

He was five minutes late at the office. He could risk that and they—she—would look up when he entered to see who was late. He entered slowly. She was standing at the file cabinet by the water cooler. He said, " 'Morning, Hazel," and took a drink of ice water. She examined him, thumb keeping the place in the file. "Hello. You look pretty seedy. What's the matter, drunk last night?"

Mr. Peavey answered smoothly, easily, triumphantly, "Oh, no. Not drunk, Hazel. Just a little birthday dinner at Alberto's." *Boy, was it worth it! Look at her eyes when I said Alberto's.* "Major Lawrence, he was wounded at El Alamein, his niece and myself. It's been my custom for years, you know, to go quietly away on my birthday night and pledge myself in good wine. Last night it was *Pommery, 1921,* a very good year, I believe. You know the Crown Prince of Denmark says . . ."

# The Bang on the Head

EGGLESTON was a short man. His head did not stick up over the partition. That was why they did not notice him when they sat down in the next booth. As the place was full of students talking and he himself was intent on the morning paper while he ate his lunch, he did not overhear anything at first.

Then some remark caught his ear. It was Cargill's voice. He

began to listen to it and his first impulse was to stand up, look over the partition and say, "Hello, Ed, where the hell were you?" (He and Cargill always ate lunch together.) Afterward, during the next few days, he could not remember just what it was that had kept him listening, hiding there. It was probably the vivacity in Cargill's voice. It was so unusual and he did remember thinking it sounded as if Cargill had come into money.

Cargill had come into money. He had been given a raise of seventy-five dollars. It took a few minutes for the figures to come out clearly for he was laughing nervously and talking very rapidly but at last the other man, it sounded like Parker, said, "Seventy-five dollars. It's not much but it's better than a bang on the head."

When he heard this Eggleston was overwhelmed. He sat staring at the second half of his tuna-fish sandwich and the inch of coffee in his cup. He could not eat or drink although dimly he knew that he ought to. His own contract had come to him in the morning's mail. It had stayed at the same figure for the last two years and he knew it would continue to stay there until he had finished his thesis. He and Cargill each taught three classes, two of Freshman German, one of Sophomore. Last year and the year before their salaries had been the same. He was certain that Cargill's thesis was no further along than his own because Cargill had discussed every paragraph with him, yet here, in this mysterious unjustifiable way, he had been given a raise of seventy-five dollars.

Once in high school Eggleston had got in a fight with a basketball player, and just before the first blow his stomach had felt as it did then, heavy, burning. He looked wretchedly at the remains of his lunch, wishing he could eat. It was money thrown away to leave so much but he could not touch it. He slumped down in his seat no longer hearing anything, the fear that he had insulted somebody spreading through his body like a chill. It was possible that he had offended some professor, even a dean, but he could not recall the occasion. He had been automatically polite. It was a skill you developed while you were a graduate student, and by the time you were an instructor it was second nature. He was sure, nearly, that his politeness had not failed him recently but he could tell he was excited, therefore confused, and he foresaw that he would not have any peace of mind until he had combed over his behavior for at least the past year.

There was another alternative. If he himself had not offended anyone, Cargill must have done something to ingratiate himself. But what? He could not have entertained the Head of the German Department and his wife in a one-room flat with two electric hot plates and a tiny icebox in the corner. He could not have given him cigarettes during the shortage as Laemmle had (but Laemmle had money of his own) because he was too poor, poor but ingenious. He smoked a pipe in his rooms; yesterday's butts while walking to the campus, saving the fresh whole cigarettes to pull out in his office before his colleagues and the students. It was doubtful if he could have discovered some strange new method of verbal flattery because the Old Man had too smooth and thick a rind to be impressed by it. Still he must have enhanced his prestige somehow. Hardly believing it, tossing it aside as a gambit too unlikely, Eggleston thought, "Perhaps he has written an article."

The possibility that Cargill had written a learned article brought him to his feet with a jerk that knocked over his coffee. He sopped it up mechanically with a paper napkin while the thought lay in his mind, monstrous and shimmering.

He looked around to see if they were still in the next booth.
They were gone. He picked up his check, paid, and went out.
The writing of articles was not encouraged until the doctor's
degree was awarded but he had never heard it was forbidden.
Cargill was intelligent; he had any number of good ideas he
said he was saving, even a new slant on Rilke; he could have
written it but, if he had, he must have written it secretly, without telling anyone. Eggleston felt betrayed.

He began to hurry. It was only twenty minutes to one and
the students dawdled along the sidewalk giving off their usual
chatter. Eggleston brushed by them and climbed the stairs of
the Arts Building to the second floor. He went at once to the
German Reading Room. He did not give his customary nod
to the Librarian. He plunged between the chair backs to the
shelf where the periodicals lay. He wanted to see the latest
issues of the learned journals, the *PMLA, The German Quar-
terly,* and the others. He had leafed through them before but
he was afraid he might have overlooked Cargill's piece somehow. He nearly tore the covers to get at the tables of contents.
He found nothing under Cargill's name. He grew calmer then
(he found himself actually panting) and he was able to think
more clearly, but only to his further distress.

There was, he could see, no reason why he should find Cargill's piece in any of the current issues. Very likely it had been
finished only a few weeks before, shown to the Head, approved, jovially approved, and turned in for publication in a
forthcoming issue. He searched through the magazines again,
going down each table of contents with his forefinger. Again
he found nothing.

He walked slowly down the corridor to teach a class of
freshmen. He set them a paper to write on *Immensee* and sat
with his head in his hands the whole hour staring at a single

page in a grammar. The day was Friday and he had been asked to go to a party at the Brimmers' on Saturday night. Cargill would be there and he would have to congratulate him.

The next morning he made himself a cup of instant coffee on his own hot plate, two pieces of toast, and he boiled an egg. Several years before someone had taken him to lunch at the Faculty Club and there he had seen old Professor Ogilvie, the Shakespeare man, eating a boiled egg in a cup. Professor Ogilvie had taken a degree at Oxford and he whacked the eggshell with the back of a spoon, lifted off the top of the egg, and scooped out the contents. Eggleston had always eaten his morning egg that way ever since without admitting that he felt it made him richer spiritually. Usually the egg gave him a mild exhilaration. On this morning it did not. He was trying to concoct something to say to Cargill.

Saturday was his day for the library. He sat in his carrell with the materials for his thesis spread out on the table before him, one volume open, six or seven volumes shut but stuck with white slips of paper to mark significant passages, and an open notebook at his elbow. He spent most of the day gazing vacantly out of his part of the window where a little poplar shoot stood in a rag of grass in the courtyard putting out leaves.

There was still the chance that he had made an enemy. It would take only one enemy. A remark, a glance, a laugh might have been ill-timed or misinterpreted. Anything a full professor had taken as a slight, any little thing that put him in a bad light, that falsely showed him to be unsound, lazy, or dissipated would be a big enough excuse. He tried to recall the faces of all the big-shots he had ever spoken to, the expressions on them, whether or not they had turned away, and, if they had, abruptly, and what their manners were the next time he had confronted them. Once he bent forward and breathed into his cupped hands to try if there were any odor. In the whole day, he could not recover anything he had done wrong. He had been very careful.

Once or twice a week Cargill had spent an evening with him, talking, and now he could see that Cargill had not gone home to bed but to work. He must have stolen the time. Nearly always they had talked of the future, it seemed quite sincerely, but now it was clear that Cargill had been laughing at him, slipping ahead of him, and laughing at his slowness.

Helplessly all day his thoughts swung like a pendulum between the images of Cargill's faithlessness and the offense he grew surer he had made. Every so often he would try to get to work, to read and take notes, but he was returned forcibly, it seemed, to the seventy-five dollars. He could see the pink university check with the figures shredded into the paper to prevent forgery, the figures with this unjust discrepancy to his own. Seventy-five dollars meant a new suit and topcoat every year. Every single month you could buy a thick book useful in the profession, or two novels, or the records of a symphony or a quartet. Tickets for concerts and plays (that he never went to) could be found in it. It would buy a bottle of whisky or a case of beer. Cargill could smoke cigarettes freely, carelessly now, a pack a day, instead of a pipe at home. With some discretion, a woman could be taken to dinner occasionally although this was dangerous because she might think something was up and seventy-five dollars a year extra would not support a marriage, not very well anyway, not so well as he intended to do it.

At seven o'clock in the evening he snapped out his reading lamp and left the library for a Chinese restaurant where he ate the plain chop suey and rice. He had always liked it very much and he ate it tonight in the hope that it would raise his spirits. It did not stay with you—hunger would come again in an hour. He counted on the Brimmers' setting out peanuts and popcorn at their party.

He went home, changed his shirt, and rubbed a rag over the toes of his shoes. From a closet he took a used brown paper sack and put six empty beer bottles in it. It was a warm spring night and, as he walked along, the prospect of the evening's sociability made him almost forget that he would have to greet and compliment Cargill. He stopped at a supermarket and bought six bottles of beer, turned in the empties and went out again toward the Brimmers' with the full bottles in a fresh paper sack.

He was not prepared for the shock the Brimmers gave him. He was quite willing to acknowledge Henry Brimmer to be intelligent and he seemed to have, well, he guessed it was more energy than himself. Henry had married his wife while they were both seniors in college and they had worn through the first years together pretty well. Dorothy worked as a secretary in Chemistry and their two salaries enabled them to have a slightly larger apartment than the other instructors, with slightly better furniture, a record-player, and bigger Van Gogh and Gauguin reproductions on the walls. By saving their money arduously for three years, they had actually gone to Germany in the summer of 1939. He was the only one of the younger men who had seen, moved, and lived in the country they talked so much about. Of course Henry at thirty-five was four years older than he and had finished his thesis a long time ago.

Eggleston found that he had arrived early and he was greeted by whoops and cries from his hosts. Puzzled, he handed the sack of beer to Dorothy automatically and she took it automatically while she screamed at him joyously. He looked carefully around to see if Cargill were there, his glance picking up a dish of peanuts and twenty-five cents' worth of popcorn in a blue bowl. When he found that Cargill was not yet there, he began to pay some attention to the Brimmers.

They were so foolishly pleased and exuberant that it took him a moment to grasp what they were saying but at last he did. Only that morning Henry had been given his contract by the Head in person, who had told him, in confidence, of course, that he would be promoted Assistant Professor next year.

"And we're going to have a kid!" Henry shouted. "We nearly called off the party so we could get right to work on it."

Eggleston made himself smile and used some of the effort he had been saving for Cargill in getting out his congratulations graciously. Miserable but with a practiced quickness he estimated that Henry would very likely receive twenty-five hundred, hell, he might even get twenty-seven fifty a year. He had this five-room apartment now and in a year there would be a child in it, too, along with the magnificent sunflowers, the pink beaches, and the record-player. "When will you quit your job?" he managed to say to Dorothy.

"That depends, she said coyly," she said. "I talked to the doctor this afternoon and he said, while I'm not too old, conception may not be exactly instantaneous. I can work up to the seventh month, he says. Isn't that lucky?" She took his sack of beer to the kitchen, humming on the way.

"You know what we did? We celebrated. Look." Henry pointed to the record-player. On it lay two volumes of records.

"What are they?" Eggleston asked.

"The *Brandenburg*."

"Wow!"

"I told you. It's a celebration. Sit down. We'll start 'em."

"I'll go get myself a beer. You go ahead." Eggleston started for the kitchen. He had just heard the buzzer and footsteps on the stairs outside. It might be Cargill and he wanted a moment to collect himself. The Brimmers' good luck had struck him with merely the common, the endemic envy and it had not been too difficult to be polite to them. With Cargill it was different. How could he phrase it to suppress this special bitterness that made his stomach heavy and his face hot?

In the kitchen he opened the icebox and took out a bottle of his beer. He wished now that he had been reckless and bought a dozen bottles. He wanted to get drunk. He took the cap off the bottle and drank, listening. It was Cargill, all right, he and Roger Evans. He listened carefully. With Evans was the girl who was getting her Master's in Physics. Everybody kidded Evans about the money his wife was going to make with atoms. He heard the Brimmers' shrieks and laughter again, the congratulations repeated, and he found with surprise he had drunk the whole bottle of beer.

Dorothy Brimmer came in with two more sacks and put them in the icebox. "Ed and Roger are here. Come on in. We're going to play the records."

"You go ahead. I'll be right in," Eggleston said.

If he stayed out in the kitchen all through the two albums of the *Brandenburg Concertos* he would gain that much time and he doubted if anyone would miss him. He leaned against the sink, drinking beer steadily and trying to follow the music, which he had never heard before. Once he tiptoed to the kitchen door and peeked through the crack. He could see Car-

gill and the atom girl sitting there, rapt, devout, and he knew
no one would be coming to the kitchen for beer until all the
concertos had been played. He hoped that his six bottles
might give him the courage and suavity to walk in and congratulate Cargill. He knew even this, that the moment he did
it, his suspicions would probably disappear. He finished the
sixth bottle eventually but he did not move. He would have to
be drunker than this.

He did a bold and nasty thing. He called it that while he
was doing it. He opened one cupboard, then another, and
found, as he had expected, half a bottle of whisky on a shelf.
He drank it all in twenty-five minutes with cold-water chas-
ers. The whisky apparently put some distance between himself and his state of mind. He appraised the latter and
concluded that he still lacked the necessary confidence. He
opened the door to the back stairs, sneaked down them, and
walked home in the mild evening, swearing at himself. Just
before he reached his apartment house, he stepped behind a
tree and was sick.

The next day he went conscientiously to the library but he
could not work; he just fiddled around. He did not want to go
back to the Brimmers' to pick up his hat because he had
stolen their whisky and that was a serious thing. At noon he
went home and lay on his bed the rest of the afternoon. That
night he took his temperature but he had no fever.

On Monday morning he considered the notion of cutting
his classes and staying in bed. He certainly felt bad enough
but he knew it would solve nothing. On his way to the campus
he rather hoped for a street accident so he could be carried
off to the hospital, where, secure in his injuries, he could receive Cargill and congratulate him quite lightly and easily.
He arrived at his office safe. He knew that if he did not meet

Cargill for lunch today after missing him Friday and dodging
him at the Brimmers' party, Cargill would be sure to come to
his office to ask why. He would probably come anyway. He
often stopped in before lunch and they walked to the lunchroom together.

Suddenly he thought he ought to talk to someone about it.
He had an hour between classes. He telephoned Mattson in
Psychology and Drew in History but one was out and the
other teaching.

At last he looked around at Overman. Overman was one of
the three men who shared the office. He was only a graduate
student teaching one class and to talk so intimately to an in-
ferior was repugnant but Eggleston felt it was his last chance
to talk to anyone before noon and Overman was better than
nobody.

"You hear about Ed Cargill?" he asked.

Overman looked up from the stack of papers he was cor-
recting. "No. What's happened?"

"He got a raise. Seventy-five bucks a year."

"That's good. Isn't it?" His answer was barely interrogatory.
It could be taken either as a confirmation of the goodness or
a doubt of it. Overman was not committing himself to anything. He was being careful. Eggleston recognized the signs.

Smiling weakly as if this sudden intimacy were comical, he
hurried on. "You know, it's curious. Ed's a friend of mine. We
roomed together as undergraduates. I've known him all this
time but, by God, I'm jealous as the devil about it. If he got
boosted, I should have, too."

"It does seem strange," Overman said blandly.

"You bet it does. I'm supposed to eat lunch with him today
and I can hardly bear to face him. What do you think of that?"

Overman shook his head and clucked twice.

"I've got to congratulate him but it's the most difficult thing I've ever had to do. I know what's the matter. It's just envy but if there were only some way I could hide it or stifle it . . ."

"Try philosophy," Overman said. It was almost an open sneer.

"But I don't know anyone in Philosophy." It slipped out. His mind had been on the seventy-five dollars really. But as he watched Overman try to control the grin, Eggleston realized with horror what he had become. The pencil he was holding broke in his hands and as Overman at last snorted into laughter, Eggleston sat there looking down at the desk in humiliation. He remembered, as he remembered the brightness of childhood, that once he had intended to be a scholar, concerned with things of the mind.

# Berkshire Comedy

THE COURTSHIP began in the spring, the night after Skinner fell in the ditch. Every evening at six, George, the landlord, opened the door of the pub and stood in the doorway, his permit above his head, *George Faulkner, Licensed to sell on these premises beer, ale, wine, spirits, and tobacco*, and one foot thrown over the other, he watched the workmen pass. They were men in caps with scarves around their necks, riding slowly by on bicycles, waving at George as they went. In the fields across the road, the farmers were leading their big teams toward the barns. After tea and a wash, they would return to the Greyhound, so many hods carried, so many joists put up, so many furrows drawn, to rest and drink beer and gossip and play games.

Mrs. George was upstairs making herself fine, combing out the tats in her hair, putting on a layer of powder, and lastly, inserting her teeth. In her youth, she had been a dancing teacher at Tooting, with small feet and ankles, and, as the fading photo in the parlor showed, a little beauty. Her memory of those days was tough and hardy, and sometimes in the dusk at opening time, she would see her face as it had been then, if her teeth were in, and she would hold out her arms, the little finger crooked like the genteel at tea, and she would waltz lightly around the room. All day she worked around the pub, sweeping and scrubbing, waxing the lino in the bar—a brown room with benches and a table, and four barrels behind the counter, two marked XX for bitter beer, two marked X for ale, and a fireplace with a shining steel fender—all day she worked without her teeth, her mouth drawn in and empty. At night when she heard the voices of the first-comers, she descended, a string of bogus pearls around her neck, her bobbed hair combed and shining, and, firm on her gums, the teeth. Some people do not show their teeth when they smile but Mrs. George did and she knew it. She lifted her upper lip high, and the teeth almost exploded in her face, white as a bathtub and glittering. Pretty, they were, she thought. She and George were over sixty. Skinner was over sixty.

A little after six, Skinner would come up the road, limping slightly if the weather were damp. It was her legs—bad, they were, with verikus veins. She chewed on nothing as she walked. She wore a big, black, bell-shaped hat and a tattered black coat. When she came into the drive by the pub sign, George would say, "Hello, artful," and Mrs. George, "And how's the rabbits, Skinner?"

"Them'll fetch sixpence apiece, them young 'uns, when they're a month old," she said. And then with a bright smile which showed no teeth but in the corners of her mouth, "You know what I'd do if I had a fortune? A hundred quid, maybe?"

"Buy yerself a Paris gown," George said.

"Shut up, you old fool you," said his wife.

Skinner folded her arms and settled them under her bosom in the comfortable way old women do. "You know what I'd do? I'd buy me a little cottage and raise chickens and rabbits, and I'd keep a pig, and sometimes, do you know what I'd do, I'd go out and sleep with 'em where they was in the fields. I likes animals."

Ten rabbits at sixpence, when they're a month old, are five shillings, and five shillings was a week's rent on the thatched cottage where Skinner lived. A few hens gave her eggs, and in the summer, she dug in a garden patch behind and grew green onions and radishes. When the hop season came, she would go away each morning in a big van that stopped by the village green to pick hops all day and chat with the pickers from London. She made five bob a day when she picked fast. She got the Old Age Pension, and with her job at the Greyhound, she lived as well as a wife and saved money in the post office against her old age. As well as a wife but that she had no man now. Her husband had been a Black-and-Tan and had died in an alley in Dublin.

By six-thirty, the farmers and laborers had come and Skinner had lit the lamps and poked up the fire. The men sat at the table, each with his dominoes in his hands, wrists bent so he could see all nine at once and he only. Others sat on benches before the bar, always saving the warm end by the fire for Old Caleb and shouting at him in the broadest Berkshire. "Oi, 'ee've od a drop a beer summat in 'ee toime, ain't 'ee, Caaleb?"

A battered bowler, tinged with the green of age, on his head, two buff waistcoats under his jacket, and his old loose face propped on his hand on his stick, Old Caleb would look up and smile blissfully at the memory of all the full pint pots his ninety years had put before him—a bloody great line of them off over the horizon, past the war, past the Queen's death, past even the time Dizzy came through the village in an open carriage, and he would answer, "Oi. Thot I av, thyousands ond thyousands of gollons."

And Skinner would lean chattily over the bar, smiling broadly and showing her empty gums. "Why, Caleb, I've had thousands of gallons meself, and I'm young enough to be your daughter." She squeaked with laughter. "Mebbe I am."

"Ay, Skinner, we knows yer a boozer."

"Well, yer better off dead when ye gits to be my age without ye can get a good booze-up once in while." And she would draw herself a half-pint carefully and drink.

Then one of the dart players would stop short in the midst of a throw and say, "Psst! Here he comes."

The noise of a stick could be heard tapping against the cobbles outside, then against the steps, and the bar door would open and the talk would stop. Every night he came for his pint, Chris, the cuckold. Feeling his way with his stick, he would get to a place on the bench and sit down. The farmers called him the "Lord Mayor" and chaffed him about his gout, his deafness, and his little eye which hardly saw. And they knew that while Chris sat, shouting as deaf men shout in answer, Creepy Terry was in his bed getting another child. They chaffed him because his wife was unfaithful, though he was too deaf and blind to know, but their jibes were never about her. They seldom mentioned women before Chris, out of delicacy. They were polite.

"How's yer hands, Chris?"

"Eh?"

"How's yer hands, I say?"

"Bad, bad. I can't bend 'em over me stick."

"Have another pint and worsen 'em."

If one of the younger men were so bold as to ask in feigned politeness, "And how's Mrs. Chris?" he would be nudged sharply in the ribs as if he had said something indecent. Mrs. Chris was thirty, tall and ruddy, and when she walked to the shops by the green, men in the fields stopped their horses to say good-day and watch her; and the little group of unemployed under the big tree on the green would pull themselves up and stand straight as if they, too, were men on whom her smile might light without waste. All the men thought she was beautiful, and as far as they ever dreamed of women, it was of her, walking slowly down by the pollards in a tattered skirt with her two-fathered children. Creepy Terry they condemned or envied, condemned if they were thinking practically of the crops, the taxes, the vicar, or the government; or, drunk, they staggered under a big moon through the shadows remembering courage and the war, and the stages of their youth, or perhaps, taking a bath in a tin tub on a Saturday, they saw the muscles of their bodies nude and thought of the uses they were put to, then they envied Creepy.

When Chris, who sat long over his beer, had finished and stumped out, Mrs. George, to avoid the coarse talk which followed, would go genteelly into the parlor to sit with the wives.

The men would say, "Now you watch. It won't take him five minutes to git here." And one of them might even pull out a watch to time Creepy.

In the parlor the black hats of the women would nod together; the whispers would come up and the titters; then the hats would part and glasses go up to mouths.

". . . and the other night when Chris was coming down the road, knocking with that stick, there was her youngest boy standing watch in the orchard, and when Chris come by, he ran into the house, calling out, 'Uncle Terry, Uncle Terry, here comes Father.' And out come Creepy through the orchard a-buttoning up his clothes."

"No, Chris never heard him. He can't hear."

"Just like a guard to watch over his own mother's sin, he was."

"And his own father's. That youngest boy ain't Chris's. He's the image of Creepy."

The wives were bitter, for even at thirty, they were faded, and the gout was coming in their hands, while Mrs. Chris remained fresh and pretty, even with poverty and six children to manage, smiling happily, a rival, and wicked.

While the men waited for Creepy to come into the bar, Skinner, bending grunting over the spigot, said contemptuously, "Gertcha, Creepy's got more guts than any of ye. All of ye thinking of Mrs. Chris when yer a-lying by yer wives." And then, giggling, "Why don't none of ye think of me? I have a willing heart and I've slept alone fifteen years now." She looked in the mirror which had *Alsopp's Ale* across the face in gilt letters, and pulled in a lock of her hair, and stroked her cheeks, which were still red under the glaze of dirt, primping and giggling. The men laughed and turned to their darts and dominoes, when Creepy came in.

"Evening, all."

"Evening, Creepy. Damp out tonight, ain't it?"

"Ay. Draw me a pint of bitter, Skinner."

He was a mean-faced red little man, who had never been respected because he was the kind of man women like instinctively. No one said much to him except in the arguments over dominoes.

At ten o'clock, George would get up from the domino table and call, "Time, gentlemen, please. Ten o'clock. Come along, please." But the players would finish their game because they knew George kept the clock five minutes fast. And in a worried voice, he would call, "Time, gentlemen, please. Come along, *please*. The policeman's waiting out there." Perhaps one or two drunks would start a song, and slowly, reluctantly, the customers would leave. "Good night, George. Good night. Pleasant evening. Good night."

When George had barred the door with a heavy bolt and closed all the shutters, the residents of the Greyhound would go into the parlor, and Mrs. George would lay the table with bread, eight-penny rat cheese, brown pickled onions, and they would sit down to eat, calling to Skinner, who was washing up the pint cups in the bar, "Skinner, bring four ales and a glass of stout." Down the road the farmers would be singing, and lamps would be lighted in the cottages. Skinner would bring in the drink and Dobbin, the plasterer, would turn on the wireless—"That's Roy Fox's band, playing in London"—and they would all eat and talk about the evening's trade, sometimes three pounds, sometimes five, and when Skinner had polished the last cup and dried her hands, she would come in.

"Git yer big feet outa the road, Jack!"

Jack had two corners where he sat—one in the bar evenings and Sundays, and one by the door of the parlor at suppertime.

His feet were big and they hurt him most of the time. He would move them out of the way without speaking.

He seldom spoke. And three summers ago when that young artist gentleman stopped here the night, Jack's was the head he picked out to sketch. Jack was sixty-five years old and he looked like a king. To keep him till his span was done, he fed the hens at the Greyhound and on Sunday mornings he swept the cobbles clean before the door with a besom, and pruned the ivy on the west side of the house so that Mrs. George might have a clear view of the road that led to the sea and watch for the cars of the gentry. As pay, he was given his bread and cheese and beer, and a small pallet in the shed behind. What he remembered, sitting in his corners, no one asked, and as he seldom spoke, no one knew.

At midnight they would all go to bed, and Skinner, after a last gulp of beer, would go home. Mrs. George let her out each night by the kitchen door, and she would stagger off into the dark cursing mildly when she tripped. The night before the courtship started, she had slipped and fallen on her back in six inches of muddy water in the ditch by the policeman's house. The whole of the next day, she told about it to all who came to the pub. It was an adventure, difficult of belief in a village where nothing happened but birth, marriage, death, and the seasons, and these common enough, and it was worth the repetition. "And there I was a-lyin' on me back as if I was a baby."

The next night when Mrs. George let her out, Jack came with her. Skinner started off in the moonlight, lurching over the cobbles and singing in a cracked voice about "The Guardsman and Poor Mary," and Jack followed her less recklessly and silent. A little way past the pub sign, standing creaking on its

pole in the breeze, Skinner stopped and turned round, calling
kindly, "Come up here, Jack, and I'll sing to ye."

Mrs. George said to her husband that night, "Now what's
come over Jack? He's seeing Skinner home. 'Twould be a
funny thing if them two hit it off and made a match."

Every night through the summer, Jack would accompany
Skinner, never speaking except to warn her away from the
edge of the road and to say good night under the eaves of the
thatched cottage.

And it was accepted by everyone that Jack was courting,
although he never spoke to her as she bobbed around serving
and joking in the bar. The domino players often turned to him
where he sat grave and silent, drawing slowly on his pipe with
his pint on the bar beside him and asked, "When you going to
see the vicar, Jack?"

But it was no sport; Jack never took the bait, and they would
leave Jack to twit Chris if he were there.

One night in midsummer, Skinner felt that Jack had squired
her long enough. She said openly that as soon as the damp set
in, it would be cold sleeping alone, and when she would tell
over what she would do with a fortune, a hundred quid maybe,
the dart players would ask, "Where you going to get a hundred
quid given you, Skinner?" She would answer, "Jack's going to
give it me, ain't you, Jack?" Then she would wink and put her
hand over her mouth like a child to hide her laughter. Jack
would merely look over at her soberly.

Jack had seen her home every night, and he had never de-
nied it when she told the bar they were made for each other,
and hinted that, if Jack jilted her, perhaps old Chris would
like her for his fancy lady, poor old Chris. She wanted Jack to
propose formally and he seemed unwilling, so she spoke out.

"Now, Jack, we shall play darts. And if you wins, you shall have me."

Jack showed no surprise. He did not smile. He only pulled his mustaches. Skinner repeated the offer and at last Jack said, "Well."

The dart players drew fresh chalk lines on the floor and got out the new darts. They put up a lamp by the dart board on the wall, laughing with excitement.

When Jack toed the chalk mark to throw his first dart, he was trembling with shyness. It was a very poor game and Jack could not even hit the board; all his darts stuck in the wall beside it and he lost. Everybody laughed hard.

"He can't play darts, not even for a wife."

"He don't want a wife, that's what."

Skinner turned on them angrily. "Shut up, all of ye. Jack never was much of a hand at darts, was you, Jack? We shall play dominoes and if you wins"—here she grinned—"you shall have me."

It is easier to lose deliberately at dominoes than at darts. Skinner lost and Jack won, and the whole pub shouted and stood them drinks. The banns would be cried first next Sunday and the wedding would be the day after Feast, Skinner said promptly. Jack went back and sat down again in his corner, studying his great sore feet.

When Feast Day came at the end of harvest, a little holiday, and Caleb could remember when they brought the last cut sheaf from the fields with a wreath around it, singing, a small fair was set up on the village green with coconut shies where you could pay tuppence for three wooden balls to throw at coconuts standing on posts ten feet away, keeping all you knocked off, and penny-rolling booths, and tents full of sweets, and gypsies selling things from baskets, and an old man with a talking parrot. All day Skinner drank in the kitchen of the Greyhound with the money she won rolling pennies, and she led Jack around through the crowd, silent in a rusty black suit that was too small for him. That night everyone stood them port and sherry, and Skinner danced in the bar, holding out her skirt, and after she teased him, Jack stood up once and kicked one foot out lamely, and then subsided in the corner.

At midnight, they were let out of the Greyhound after a gala supper, and they went staggering off down the road. There was a full harvest moon shedding a yellow light. People stood in the doorway shouting congratulations after them, and when the two were a little way down the road, Skinner shouted back, "Maybe he'll tumble me in the harvest field."

Jack put his arm around her to steady her. When they came to the corner, they went into the harvest field, walking over the fresh stubble among the sheaves.

"What you so quiet about, Jack? Think it was yer funeral. Give us a kiss."

Jack kissed her gloomily. Then he drew back and said, "Skinner, I can't go through with this."

"What yer mean 'can't go through with this'? It's all done but the vicar's words tomorrow and getting bedded together like proper married folk."

Looking at his toe, Jack said, "You makes too free with the menfolk in the bar. Talking wickedness. All the men eying you. What if you was to turn out like Mrs. Chris?"

Skinner drew herself up, lifting her chin first one side, then the other, angrily. "Me a harlot, Jack Belcher? Me what was an honest woman twelve years 'fore I ever see you? I don't take that from no man, I don't."

She marched off, holding herself very stiff and putting her feet down almost where she wished.

Without moving, Jack watched her go. Then he sighed and limped slowly back to the pub. When he saw a rook's nest in the top of an elm, he reflected that it would be a cold winter, for when rooks build in the tops of elms, it's always a cold winter coming.

Skinner let herself into her cottage with a clatter, jerking the door and kicking chairs around. She lit a candle preparing to be sorrowful when her anger went away. She sat down at the table, with the candlelight making a humped shadow of her back against the wall, and she thought about the wickedness of men, chafing her hands. Her, an honester woman he never saw, what would have made him a good wife, and him thinking she would turn out a whore because she was cheerful with the menfolk and loved a bit of fun, a whore like that great strapping Mrs. Chris, a great lout of a girl that all the men eyed and wished to be in bed with—not that she blamed the men, for Mrs. Chris was a lovely bit, strong as a man, strong as a tiger. And Jack thought she would turn out like her, did he, a great, lovely harlot? Lovely. And her sixty-three next Michaelmas, with no teeth in her head and there was her legs all covered with verikus veins and Jack thought she was lovely and all the men wanted her like Mrs. Chris.

Suddenly in the candlelight, Skinner began to laugh, rocking back and forth, hugging herself, laughing.

# All Problems Are Simple

THE DOOR of the closet was stuck. It was a sliding panel and it stuck because it was new. The newness of the whole place struck Dr. Holloway's nostrils as he tugged at the handle, an acrid smell of fresh paint and, curiously, mothballs. The door opened a foot. Dr. Holloway shoved his hat through the opening and laid it on the shelf of the closet. There were even three naked black wire hangers in the closet, and, turning, he saw a single fresh daffodil in a glass tube on his desk. Somebody had thought of everything. In the old building his office had been a little slot beneath a staircase with a desk, two chairs, no windows, and an electric bulb dangling from a cord over his head. Painted on the frosted glass of the door that he always had to keep open if he wanted any air were the words, *Student Counselor, A. E. Holloway.* On the door of his new office, there was only a gray aluminum number and a student had to look him up on the building directory in the lobby as if he were an executive of a large corporation. The University Counseling Service was at last amounting to something.

Dr. Holloway sat down at his desk, a small *moderne* article in the shape of a kidney. He had an appointment at eleven and the long hand of the electric clock covered the stud that indicated five minutes past. All students were late; it was an axiom. He reached into a drawer and took out the student's dossier. A sophomore, Miss Ottilie Schroeder. Inside were several folders containing all the relevant information: the application from high school with grades and reasons for applying, Psychological Tests A, B, and C given on entrance as a freshman, Aptitude Test, Rorschach Test, a Physical Examination report, data from Health Service showing illnesses, psychic and physical, incurred during residence as a student, and, of course, the semester grade sheets. There was also a folder intended for notes taken by the Counselor during previous consultations but it was blank.

While Dr. Holloway officially and publicly had great respect for the University Agencies who had got up this mass of forms and the high, tense pitch of organization they showed, he knew that in practice he did not need them. As he thumbed through the papers all he was looking for was the photograph and the note from the Assistant Dean. The rest of the stuff was not important.

He found the picture, a blond girl with freshly curled bobbed hair, smiling in a frantic amiability. She had buck teeth and blotches of acne barely hidden by rouge and powder. The Assistant Dean's note said that she was flunking German 31 according to the mid-semester grade reports. This was all the information Dr. Holloway needed, this and her home town. It made students feel good if he could mention their home towns. He looked up Miss Schroeder's. It was Manchester. He tossed the dossier back into the drawer, looked at the clock, and lit a cigarette.

The mothball smell, he decided, came from the new window drapes. They were the color of plug tobacco. The carpeting was beige and the chairs were upholstered in turquoise blue. The chairs had tapering legs and the laminated framework of the back and seat looked like the jawbone of an ass. On the wall hung a reproduction of a John Marin watercolor but Dr. Holloway thought it was only a lot of smudges. Still, the office was done up very smartly. If only counseling weren't such a bore.

Behind him the door opened a little, then closed. It was the student he was waiting for, Miss Schroeder. She was wretched and afraid and she had not yet been able to find courage to knock and come in.

Holloway was by the window irritably picking at a spot of paint left on the glass. Counseling was a bore, a part-time bore; teaching was a supreme bore; and certainly the research papers on Thomas Traherne and Sir Thomas Browne he whacked out in his carrell at the library were a bore. He was a seventeenth-century man and whenever he thought of Traherne and Browne, he felt warm and clever because he could remember that night in his senior year, fourteen years before, banging on a bar in Scollay Square when he had said, "I'm going out for the two-mile run. Nobody goes out for that." It was true then; the literature of the seventeenth-century had no special popularity with scholars at the time. But he, Art, later, of course, Arthur Holloway, had prowled through them early, a mess of dusty quartos. He had got a head start in the two-mile and now he had only to wait for a couple of the old guys to die off and he would be head man in the field. But it was still a bore. He hated to read.

Where he shone was at faculty meetings, club luncheons, and, above all, at the great conventions of his caste, the annual meetings of the learned societies. Thanks to a memory course he had taken, he never forgot a name. He was civil to all, and, beneath a disguise of manly camaraderie, obsequious to all who could do him any good. For, hidden under the ennui of his daily round, Art Holloway entertained a vision. He wanted to be a Dean. He was a little like a businessman who wants to be a millionaire—he did not know exactly what he would do when he became one but it was his deepest ambition, and he had an oblique, unacknowledged belief that a Deanship would offset his wife's money. You could take a few drops of iodine every day in a glass of water, he had heard, and in the vision he saw himself walking across the campus, his hair and mustache still its pristine brown (from the iodine), and people would say, "Good morning, Dean," and they would think how young and vigorous he looked for a man so high up. Also, when his wife shooed him upstairs and into his tail coat on nights when Milstein or Horowitz was playing in town, he would be able to say to her coarsely, vigorously, "The hell with that. I'm going to bed." He had never liked music.

At last there was a knock. He turned around, shouting,

"Come in, Miss Schroeder!" The door opened and she came in, glancing miserably up at him once, then back at the floor. "Sit down. It's swell of you to come in so promptly." She missed the irony completely and sat down on the blue chair with her feet close together, her head bowed, picking at a fingernail. The blond hair hung in stringy unwound spirals. She wore a sweater and skirt, both black and covered with wisps of white fuzz. She certainly had a rough case of acne. There was no sorority pin on her bosom, he noticed.

"Well, how do you like our new offices, Miss Schroeder? The old building was never like this, eh?" he said loudly.

She looked up smiling with her lip pulled down over her buck teeth and shook her head.

"How are things going? You're looking well, better than the last time I saw you," he said, leaning back in his chair with his hands clasped behind his head (Informality of Pose). "How are things at home in Manchester?" (Note of Personal Solicitude.)

"All right," she said without looking up.

"Your work seems to be quite satisfactory. Three C's on the mid-semester exams. There's only German 31. What happened there?"

She shook her head again, gulping and swallowing.

"Is everything all right? Health good? You like your roommate? Feel perfectly free to tell me everything." She did not say a word but her fingers wreathed and wove themselves together constantly in her lap. "Perhaps you feel some resistance to the language because the Germans were our enemies. We must forget our enmity to them; the war is over. Germany is a beautiful country. I traveled there before the war. Nuremberg, Rothenburg, Munich. *München war damals eine schöne Stadt.*" Munich had been a beautiful city. He recalled eagerly

all the *Ausschänker* where you could sit at a little table and
buy the potato salad and the beer radishes and *Hofbräu,
Löwenbräu, Tomasbräu, Augustinerbräu,* all those wonderful
beers. "You mustn't scorn the language. The Germans have
been a great people."

"I know," she said. "My people were German. My grandfather was born in Essen."

"Well, then. It's part of your inheritance. How does it come
you are flunking it?"

She threw up her head and spoke very rapidly in a high,
choking voice, "'*ch kann nicht studieren. 'ch habe keine
Freunde. 'ch stehe ganz allein, immer ganz allein.*"

This was a little too fast for Dr. Holloway's German. He
stood up. "I'm sorry. You're hysterical. I didn't catch . . ."

The angry defiance was gone. She was sniffling and sobbing.
"I can't study. I can't do any work. I haven't any friends. I
haven't had a date since I came to college."

Dr. Holloway looked down at the top of her head as it
bobbed up and down with her sobs, the limp yellowish hair
swaying a little. It was sex again, the old story. About every
third babe had some gripe about her sex life.

"I'll tell you what you do," he said in a warm friendly voice.
"You start going to church. There are a lot of social activities
around a church. You'll meet somebody there as sure as the
world. You mustn't be shy. You have to go halfway in your
social life, you know." With that face she'll have to go seven-
eighths, he thought. He waited a moment until she had finished blowing her nose. "Will you do that, Miss Schroeder?"

She looked at him and nodded.

"And we'll get that German up by the end of the term, won't
we? As well as you seem to know it, it shouldn't be . . ."

"May I go now, Dr. Holloway?"

"Why, that's about all I had to say. You know how it is—a flunk's a flunk. . . ." She interrupted him by starting for the door. "Glad you came in, Miss Schroeder. Stop in any time." The door closed after her.

It was just eleven-thirty by the electric clock. He had polished that one off in fifteen minutes. There was one more to go before lunch. He took out a second dossier labeled "Raymond Burch." Burch, he discovered, was a junior and a veteran, a former infantry sergeant, twenty-five years old. Holloway felt a tingle of annoyance. Veterans did not handle easily. Other students you had to treat like bright children but veterans somehow you had to treat as men and it bothered him. He glanced through the dossier. Burch, it seemed, was an orphan with no place of residence but the university; his service was spent in the ETO; and the Assistant Dean's note said that Burch was flunking every course because he seldom visited his classes. The Assistant Dean thought Burch was drinking heavily. Burch's photograph showed a thin coffin-shaped face with light eyes and another glance at the service record told him that Burch had a Purple Heart and a Silver Star.

Holloway had somehow expected that Burch's wound scars would be on his legs or torso, some place that would be decently covered. Instead there was a half-inch of shiny pink wrist showing below the left sleeve of Burch's coat; there was no hand. Holloway could not take his eyes off it for a moment.

"Shot off in the Battle of the Huertgen Forest, sir," Burch said, holding up the stump impassively. "Shrapnel."

"You—you're going to have a prosthetic device, aren't you?" The photograph had been a good likeness. Burch's eyes were red as if he had perhaps been crying. Otherwise he was the same as his picture.

"One of these fake hands with a glove on it? No, sir."

"Sit down, Mr. Burch. Sit down," Holloway said nervously, standing up himself (Psychological Dominance of Height). Burch sat down and Holloway walked up and down with the Assistant Dean's note in his hand.

"Mr. Burch . . ." he began.

"Yes, sir?" Burch interposed. When the veterans had first returned from the war, Holloway had been flattered to be addressed like an officer but he had learned to detect the bogus civility of these emphasized "sirs."

"The Dean's Office say you are flunking every subject. They say you don't come to class."

"No, sir."

"Why? How is that?"

"Drink, sir."

This stopped Holloway but he did not like to seem at a loss. He said, "Uh—you mean—"

"Just whisky, sir."

An intimation that Burch was playing him for and like a fish struck Holloway. He said sharply, "Well, what are you going to do about it? You keep on this way and you'll be out of school in June. What are you going to do?"

"Stop drinking. Study hard. Go to class every day. Sir." Burch rattled this off with insulting promptness.

Holloway stopped walking and looked at Burch. Burch looked back. They both knew that, theoretically, since Burch had given the right answer, the interview should end but Holloway could not let him go yet. He glanced at the clock.

"Cigarette, Mr. Burch?" Holloway held out a pack.

"Thank you, sir."

Holloway snapped open his lighter. "I don't think you believe it but we're here to try and help you. You're spending

your time and the government's money. It seems to me that
you ought not to waste either one by turning into a rummy.
What's the matter? What's on your mind?"

Burch had been sitting with his hand on his knee looking
straight ahead, waiting, it seemed, with patience. Now he
looked up at Holloway with his light eyes, paused a moment
thoughtfully, made a wrong judgment, and said, "Suppose I
tell you? What then?"

"If it's combat fatigue, we . . ."

"It's not combat fatigue," Burch said with a soft scorn.

"Whatever it is, if something's riding you, we've got some
good men over at Health Service, doctors who . . ."

"Psychiatrists."

"Yes. Why? Don't you like psychiatrists? They can discover . . ."

"I *know* what's the matter with me."

"Do you want to talk about it? I don't want to pry into your
personal . . ." (Ostensible Kindness).

"Sure. I'll talk about it." For the next few minutes Burch
sat with his hand on his knee, the ash growing longer on his
cigarette, staring straight ahead of him, talking. "I was stationed in Munich after the war. I knew a girl. She was a Polish
DP. She had been in the camp at Dachau. She was one beautiful dame and the only scars she had were on her back where
they didn't show in the daytime. She said there was a girl in
the camp with her and this girl was pregnant. They waited
until her time came and the pains had started and then they
tied her feet together and hung her head down from the limb
of a tree. My girl saw this from a window." There was a pause.
The ash fell off Burch's cigarette onto the beige carpet. Burch
looked up at Holloway, took a heavy breath, and said, "That's
what's the matter with me." He looked back into whatever

distances lay before him and said, "I keep thinking about it."

"I'm sure your sympathy for that poor girl does you every credit but . . ."

"Oh, I don't think about her much any more. It's the guys that did it I think about."

Holloway, a Doctor of Philosophy, was honestly puzzled. "How? In what way?"

Burch said patiently, "Why, I'm a man. They're men. I figure a man has more in common with any other man than he has differences."

"Yes. Certainly."

"But what I want to know is, have I got *that* in common? I went through the camp at Dachau. I saw the limb of that tree. I used to drive a big semi for Interstate Transport before the war. Now I'm a college boy and that's why. Maybe I find out here, huh?"

"This is a philosophical question, Burch. You can't answer it all of a sudden like this. I'll tell you what you do. Why don't you duck over to Health Service and have a talk with them. And try to stay off the sauce until sundown every day at least, will you?"

Burch sat perfectly still, saying nothing.

Across the street from the Hofbräuhaus in Munich, Holloway remembered, there had been a little open-air stage for street vaudeville. It was called the Dachauerl Platzl and the men had worn *Lederhosen* and little green hats with shaving brushes, happy fat men, smiling plump women, dancing and singing, and right across the street for only eighteen pfennigs a liter that wonderful beer. In a spasm of exasperation, Holloway said, "But you have to accept the fact that people are cruel."

Burch stood up. "Jesus, I thought maybe you guys knew

something." He spun violently around on one heel and walked out. The door was slowed down by an automatic device or it would have slammed.

Dr. Holloway glanced at the clock as he swept Burch's papers into the drawer of his desk. He had wound it all up by five minutes to twelve. He went to the closet, jerked the door open, and took his hat. In the pleasant sunshine he walked leisurely toward the Faculty Club. By arriving promptly at twelve he might just get in a word or two with the Vice-President of the university, who usually lunched there. He might even suggest that they lunch together. It would be noticed.

# The Old Man
# of the Mountain

## PART ONE

**O**LD Hank Childreth was sitting in the shade by the edge
of the road with a ten-gauge shotgun across his knees.
The road ran along a creek-bank and across the creek
rose a long narrow hill wooded with young oak and hickory.
Hank did not look at the creek or the beautiful curve of the
hill. They were familiar. Hank had lived in and around and off
them, catfish, goggle-eye, quail, and strawberries, all his life.
It was hot. Even in the shade of the dusty oak trees, it was

hot enough to make his beard prickle, and his only movement was to raise his chin every few minutes and wipe his old loose throat with a red bandanna handkerchief. With a bedsheet and without the gun, he might have been Moses resting half-way down the Mount, solemn, bearded, dignified. He was waiting for the right people to come around the bend in the road. When he was sure they were the right people, maybe he would shoot at them.

He heard the noise of a car coming but it was a Ford, a local car, and he did not stand up or get ready. It slewed around the curve, bouncing in the gravel, an old Model-T with the top down. It stopped and Luther McCarthy, the sheriff, got out. He had a tin star pinned to the left strap of his suspenders.

"So they finally sent you out here, did they, Luther?"

"You can't do this, Hank. You can't just set here with a gun like this."

"You going to arrest me for it? I ain't coming with you if you do."

"You're ruining all the tourist trade doing this."

"Let her ruin."

"What good's it going to do us, what good's it going to do now we got Hollywood to come here to make a movie and we get more tourist trade'n we ever hoped to have and you set here with a gun driving it away? You're losing friends, Hank. People that was your friends ain't got a kind word for you now."

"I'm an old man, Luther. My friends are long gone."

"Just when we gitten her started up good you take a notion to bust the tourist trade all up."

"Don't whine, Luther. You make a better sheriff when you don't whine."

"I ain't whining. I'm stating facts."

"All right. Now I'll state some. This is my land, ain't it? Own it free and clear, don't I?"

"It ain't a question if it's your land or not."

"But it is my land and I aim to see there ain't any trespassing on it."

"You got a gun. The law says to prevent trespass you can't use only reasonable force. A gun ain't reasonable."

"A gun works."

"But it's against the law."

"Luther, I ain't studying about the law. If people don't stop when I tell 'em to stop, I'm going to shoot 'em. And if you and your Chamber of Commerce all want to form a posse and come out here and haul me off to jail, I'll go if hauled. I ain't talking about the law. I'm talking about what's mine."

"Now, Hank, listen. You can't commit a murder. Just because the Jesse James Hide-Away Cave is on your property, you ain't going to shoot some little girl that wants to see it. You can't do it. You don't want to do it. You ain't that kind of man."

"That's right where you started, Luther. I ain't committed any murder." The old man raised his gun. "But I'm a-going to if you don't git into that Modern-T and drive back to town. And tell that Chamber of Commerce to quit sending envoys out here to see me. Go on, Luther."

"You God-damned old fool, you're crazy. You'll git a stroke setting there in this heat."

"It'll be a real stroke then and not a picture of one."

Hank was not crazy. He was sitting there with the shotgun because he was one angry man. At first this surprised him. He had thought himself too old to be angry any more. At eighty-six most people are not angry, only peevish. They are beginning to founder. They ask only their own continuance. And if they are surprised, it is by the last betrayal of the eye, the mere failure of the back or knee. But Hank was eighty-four and he was sore enough to have sat fifteen days all day every day with a parcel of his own biscuit and cold bacon beside him, watching the road, mildly astonished at the passion that kept him there. At his age, he thought all battles were over, all the conflicts resolved.

He was tall and the years had not bent him. Since he still worked enough land to feed himself and his two big mules, his muscles had not fallen. His beard was white because he did not chew scrap or plug like his neighbors. He had a deep voice; it was bass when he was thirty and it was bass now. Occasionally when he was alone on the creek-bank after some perch, he would sing a little, letting her out loud because he had never, like his neighbors, believed that fish could hear a damned thing.

His wife had borne him five boys but each one had died punctually his second summer and neither Hank's prayers nor the newspaper flyflaps over the crib nor the scraped apple they fed him did any good. They all died and his wife with the last one. He had never married again. He sometimes liked to talk to children. They would come out to see him and he would whittle them something.

Every morning while the mist lay over the creek and the dew spattered down from the trees like rain, Hank got up, did his chores, washed, and ate. Then he would take his loaded shotgun and sit beside the road where a path branched off up the hill behind him to the Jesse James Hide-Away Cave. Once comfortable, he had nothing to do all day and he tried hard to think, to thrust aside the drift of memory: the other men he had known who, for various private reasons, had sat waiting with guns, the other angry men, to name the sources of his own anger.

But he could not quite reach them. He could remember scenes clearly, the death of the horses, how the barber's daughter ran away, the insults given him, all this was easy to recall, but he was not sure why they had fused into this persistence. He was not educated. Abstractions, beyond a few he had tested, were not easy to deal with. He could tell over, fondling the hot gun barrel, all the events that had enraged him but the meaning of them taken all together eluded him. At night he left the roadside and went to his cabin across the creek. There he would fry bacon for his supper and the next day's lunch, make up a pan of biscuit, and lie down, still trying to identify what was happening to him. The hollering of the saw-whet owls would send him to sleep early, still perplexed.

Before Hank was born, his mother was once own neighbor to U. S. Grant up in Illinois. One time her oldest son, Mark, got into a shooting scrape. He killed a man and they shut him up in Jefferson City. When Old Lady Childreth got the straight of it, she didn't even bother about a lawyer. Instead she wrote Mark to be patient and she took some cornmeal, a piece of side-meat, and a skillet, and loaded them on a mule. Then she got on the mule herself and rode cross-lots all the way to Washington—Grant was President then—a thousand miles or better, alone on the road with peddlers, veterans going West, timber buyers, lawyers, circuit riders, wool merchants, scalawags of all kinds, across the White River, the Eleven Point, the Current, the St. Francis, the Black, laughed at by the ferrymen at Cairo, across Kentucky and the mountains to ride up the streets of the capital on a sore-backed mule.

They tried to stop her at the door of the White House but thin, small, grim, and dusty, she marched on past the soldiers and into Grant's office. When she saw him, she said, "Sam, they got Mark locked up in Jeff City and I want you to git him out." Grant was right neighborly about it, she said later, and he wrote out the necessary papers. Then she rode home again on the mule and went to bed where she stayed till the end of her days making her children wait on her hand and foot because she had seen the President.

His nine uncles and their wives had always said Hank was like his mother. When they were praising him, they said he was persistent; when they were getting ready to belt him one with a hame strap, they said he was stubborn. He had a widow's peak like hers and the same black eyes. She had whipped a thousand miles of rough country. She had left traces of her journey there and on a President—the shoe cast by the mule, long buried and rusty; the blown ashes left by the fire where she made the johnnycake every night; the worn, perhaps still-used silver dollar she paid for a new cinch-strap at a store in Kentucky, and maybe Grant himself remembered her visit, sodden in a red-plush parlor dully marking the waggle of Jay Cooke's beard.

Whatever it was he was doing, he was not going to give up. As he watched the road day after day, bitter but confused, he knew he was protecting something. He was warding something else away. That was enough. He could figure it out before the cold weather came probably.

## II

ONE DAY early in the summer Hank was sitting on the curb-stone by the courthouse square in town. He had driven in to pass the time of day. He had got all his hay up and there was nothing to do then on his little farm. Wilbur Antrim, the fat barber, sat beside him. Crops were poor as usual; the weather was fair and hot; and since they agreed on their politics, they said nothing. Other loafers sat in front of the general store, the beer joint, and the law offices. They spat once in a while but they did not talk much, either.

A new Buick car with an Oklahoma license drove slowly around the square and parked by the hitching rack. There were two rickety farm wagons and a gray horse with a Mc-Clellan saddle tied up there and beside them two Model-T Fords. The Oklahoma Buick looked very shiny, new, and urban as it pulled up and stopped. Hank and the barber watched it.

"Tourists, you reckon?" the barber asked.

"It's early for them," Hank said. The summers there were hot but there was gentle mountain scenery and fish in the creeks. People from Kansas or the Oklahoma plateau where temperatures of 120 in the sun are not uncommon thought the air fresh and cool, and every summer they came there to fish, not yet by the thousands, but quite a few.

Two men got out of the car.

"Fellow's got a shaving brush tied to his hat," Hank said. "You're a barber. Ain't that a shaving brush?"

"Yep. They're tourists."

The bareheaded one was bald and fat though young. The

other in the Tyroler hat was tall with thick black hair and a black mustache. They wore expensive sports shirts open at the throat, trousers of the same material creased from riding, and *huaraches* on their feet, leather *huaraches,* not rawhide. One of them carried a miniature camera in a brown leather case slung from his shoulder.

"You watch. They'll go to the liquor store and git a bottle and then they'll go across the street and git some canned goods and some bacon and then they'll come inquiring if they's a place where five-pound bass'll jump right out in their laps." The barber spat. "Tulsa people, more'n likely."

The strangers did none of these things. They loitered, staring and pointing at the buildings. The bald man took photographs of the bank, the general store, and one of the law offices. He took two photographs of the lunchroom and then they walked slowly around the square, looking at the court-house. They acted almost as if they were getting ready to buy it.

The courthouse had been built in 1846. It was red brick, square, with no porches or façades. Until the WPA started up in the county, there had been nine beautiful big elm trees on the lawn around the building but the WPA workers found that several of them were rotten inside and they had cut them down. Now there were only four trees. The two strangers walked all around the courthouse taking pictures, obviously much interested.

The barber stood up. "I'm going to talk to them fellows."

"They're just tourists," Hank said.

The barber waddled slowly across the lawn until he came to the two men. He weighed three hundred and five pounds and his back shirttail was out.

"Taking pictures, huh?" Wilbur had seen few cameras of

any kind. He spoke as if they had been concealing a mysterious action and he had intelligently identified it.

The tall one answered, "That's right, taking pictures."

"That there's the courthouse," Wilbur said hospitably.

"Go on," the tall one said. "Don't tell me that's the courthouse, big boy."

"Yeah. It's pretty old. Built in 1846."

"That's what it says on the stone over the door, am I right?" the tall one said in the tone you use with drunks or children.

"You fellows collect pictures?"

"That's what we do, collect pictures all the time," the tall one said.

"You git back to Tulsa and you're going to have some nice pictures for your album, historical old building like this. Many's the man been hung for murder out of this court here."

"I'll bet," the tall one said. "Enough sun for a filter on this one, Harry?" The bald man moved away and sighted his camera again.

Wilbur felt he was losing them. "You say Tulsa's your home?"

"Hollywood, big boy."

"Is that Hollywood, Oklahoma?"

"Californ-eye-ay."

"Hollywood out with the movie stars, huh?"

"We're movie stars ourselves."

The bald man overheard this and called, "Take it easy, jerk."

"*It's* easy, Harry. We are movie stars, ain't we?"

"Take it easy. We're supposed to create good will."

This meant nothing to Wilbur but he did not want to seem ignorant. "That's right. The motion pictures couldn't git along without the good will of the public."

"Christ, yes. We got to have good will. It's meat and drink

to us. How you feel, big boy, good? No? Well, you *will*." The tall man said this laughing loudly and patting Wilbur on the arm. He looked over his shoulder. "Hear that, Harry? A nifty. How's the light now?"

Wilbur had lost them again. He said, "Now you take that Hedy Lamarr . . ."

In mock panic the tall one said, "Boy, will I take her! Where is she? You got her?"

The bald man put his camera in the leather case and came over to where Wilbur and the tall man were standing. "This'll do it, Charlie." He turned politely to Wilbur. "You don't want to pay attention to what he says. He's a great ribber. We're out of Hollywood to take some pictures of your fair city and if Production likes 'em, maybe you got a movie being made here, see, podner?"

"A movie being made here, huh?" Wilbur did not believe this.

"Sure. So we take pictures of your courthouse and all the tall buildings to see if they're suitable for the production of a motion picture drama and, say, you got a railroad coming in here?"

"No," Wilbur said. "Kansas City Southern's the nearest."

"Elegant. No railroad, Charlie, he says. Looks like we're in."

"You fellows going to make a movie here, huh?" Wilbur asked.

"But stupendous, big boy. They'll budget us two million."

"What's the movie going to be about?"

"The life of Jesse James," the bald man said. "This is practically his home town, ain't it?"

"No. He was from over in Clay County."

"This'll be his home town when we get through with him, the bum."

"When's all this going to start?"

"A week, ten days. You'll know when it starts all right."

"Well," the barber said blandly, "if you're going to be making a movie here about Jesse James, I'll be seeing you gentlemen again. Here's my card: *Wilbur Antrim, Shaves, Haircuts, Soft Water Shampoos, Experienced Beauty Operator . . .*"

"O.K. Be seeing you, chum. I need an experienced beauty to operate on me."

Wilbur giggled and lingered. "I reckon these movie stars git quite a big salary. Maybe you can tell me how much that Hedy Lamarr makes."

"You know people at M-G-M, Harry. How much Lamarr make?"

"Three thousand, thirty-five hundred. Miss Lamarr is very high paid."

"Thirty-five hundred dollars, huh? She gits as much as the president of the bank there." Wilbur nodded toward the bank across the square.

"Thirty-five hundred skins a *week,* big boy. Every Thursday."

"Oh," Wilbur said. "Well, I got to be gitting back. Glad to've met you gentlemen."

Wilbur carried his paunch across the lawn to the curb where Hank was sitting.

Hank looked up. "What they say?"

"The biggest God-damn pack of lies I ever heard in my life. These tourists, they think they can say anything."

"What they say?"

"First off, they say they're from Hollywood. Then they say they're movie stars, and then, by God, they say they're going to make a motion picture drama on the life of Jesse James right here in this town, but the *biggest* God-damn lie they told is that Hedy Lamarr makes thirty-five hundred dollars a week."

"Who is this Eddie Lamarr?"

"Gret God, don't you know who she is, Hedy Lamarr?"

"Wilbur, it's fourteen miles from my place to Anderson to the movie theayter. Do you think I'm going to hitch up and drive fourteen one way and fourteen back just to see a picture even if it does move?"

"Ain't you never seen a movie, Hank?"

"No."

"Well, there's just one thing I'd like to ask them movie stars. Just one thing. If they come from Hollywood like they say, how come they got Oklahoma license plates on that Buick? That's all I want to know."

### III

To THE village people, the negotiations, what there were of them, seemed to take a long time. At first they said somebody had been kidding Wilbur again. He was so fat he was a natural butt for jokes of all kinds and when, blowing on his shears in the barbershop, he told about the two men who had taken photographs of the courthouse, who said they were movie stars, who stated that a movie was to be made right there in the village, who had given him the incredible report of the Lamarr salary, who, insisting they were from Hollywood, had not had sense enough to take the Oklahoma plates off their Buick, everyone agreed with Wilbur that they were liars. They were just having some fun with the fat man.

Then the mayor got a letter from Hollywood. He was an unimportant official who spent most of his time in his shirtsleeves sprinkling the courthouse lawn with a hose. When he read the letter, a formal request to use the town as a setting for the production of a gigantic movie, the scale of the request was so vast (he did not know that whole towns could be rented) that he hurriedly turned the letter over to the lawyer, the storekeeper, and the banker who really ran the town.

The letter made them uncomfortable. They were old—one had already had his stroke. They were cautious and distrustful. They had been full-grown men before movies became popular and to them a business deal with a movie company was still as unstable a proposition as fitting out a rocket ship to go to the moon. The Chamber of Commerce held meetings every night, some official, some unofficial, the old men talking and wrangling irritably in the evening in the courthouse square. They were afraid they would somehow find themselves putting money into the scheme and somehow, surely, losing it—fly-by-nights, gold-brickers, strangers.

The news of the legitimate offer swept through the younger businessmen with a single movement like fear in a herd of colts. To their minds, the town, Pop. 548, ought to have been the very navel of the world and each of them had a plan to make it so. In concert they had organized a strawberry festival the year before. They had chosen a Queen, crowned her with a crown of gilt pasteboard, imported a silver cornet band, and adorned the square with pennants and gonfalons of red bunting, hand-painted with the enthusiastic legend, WELCOME TO THE WORLD'S STRAWBERRY CAPITAL, and when the Joplin papers sent news photographers, the young men posed, proud, severe, their hands hanging folded together in front, conscious of Progress and Work Well Done. If they had controlled the town, they would have accepted the movie offer at once. They had heard the word "publicity" and one or two of them almost knew what it meant. But the young men held back because they owed the old men money.

For ten days there was an impasse. Nobody could decide. No one wrote to Hollywood to ask for details because this would have seemed unsophisticated. A telegram was not sent. No one ever sent telegrams; they received them when faraway relatives died. In his cubbyhole office at the courthouse, the mayor fingered the Hollywood letter wistfully, wishing he had the power to make the decision. If he sent an acceptance and the town was wrecked or grew famous by it (he did not care much which) he would never be forgotten. He was tempted but he did not dare defy his bosses.

The town never had a chance of resisting the offer, really: "Look, Chief, they got a courthouse like you said, square red brick, but ancient, believe me. And grass all around the courthouse. Certainly with trees, four, five, maybe. And old false-front stores built up high with printing on the front, old-fashioned printing, really beautiful, am I right, Harry? And, honest to God, Chief, the horses. Yeah, they *ride* 'em. No, no big hats, not Western. They ride these hay-burners right into this village naturally and tie 'em up when they get off 'em like in Civil War times. And you should see the people, Chief. Harry, did you ever in your puff see real characters better than those village people? They sit around like with tapeworm. O.K., hookworm, but really idle, some with whiskers. And the best part is that Jesse James, the meat guy, the historical robber, was actually there coupla times. A natural, I tell Harry. Didn't I tell you it was a natural, Harry. No, no railroad to gum up the sound. With labor? Not a chance. A buck a day to these type people is like a manhole cover. I'm leveling with you, Chief, it's a perfect site for a very successful production."

The movie company was used to invading the supine California towns, paying them a rental fee, and beginning production at once. Any hesitancy was puzzling, unexpected. To dissolve it, they sent the director and a bevy of assistants to the town.

The director gave a banquet for the whole town at a restaurant in a cave, choice of chicken or fried trout. The cave was damp. The salt stuck in the shakers and the guests had to dodge drops of cold water that fell from the limestone ceiling but they ate heartily because the food was free. After dinner the director made a speech, pausing cleverly at times to permit his assistants to lead the applause.

The first part of the speech was rather flat—he said the townspeople would be participants, nay creators in a sense, of a Great Artistic Event in the History of the Motion Picture.

In the middle part of the speech, he told them of the changes that would be necessary to make the town look old, to make it the Liberty, Missouri, of Jesse James's day. The assistants still had to clap hard before the guests would follow.

At the end he spoke of tangible benefits. Hundreds of extras would be selected from the citizens. Hundreds of local workmen would be hired at $2.50 a day. And, since the news of the production would be spread far and wide, the town could expect to be visited by thousands of tourists from Joplin, Wichita, Fort Smith, from Muskogee, Pawhuska, and Okmulgee, even from Chicago. The town would be famous, and, if the town played its cards right, the town would be rich. The crowd cheered and clapped for ten minutes. An hour later documents giving the movie company free use of the town were signed before a notary.

It was all done in innocence. The townspeople naturally wanted to be rich and famous. The director wanted to go ahead with the picture. The carpenters who began to erect sets around the town square, to install replicas of an old newspaper office and The Dixie Belle Hotel and Saloon wanted to finish the work and collect their pay. The painters who covered the buildings on the east side of the square with dun-colored paint so that they might photograph more clearly, and the workmen who hid the fine new WPA cement pavement under a foot of dirt were guiltless as were the truck drivers who presently arrived with the costume trucks, the elaborate lights, the crated cameras, and the color film packed in ice. Certainly the stars who eventually came to town in limousines were innocent. No one wanted to injure the town, to ruin it as a place to live in. In fact, no one gave it a thought.

A movie company is different from the other agencies of change. It does not settle and take even short roots. It will rent your town or borrow it—two weeks to get in, ten weeks to make the picture (twelve if epic), and a couple of weeks to clean up and get out. The traces, however, are just as lasting as a glacier's.

## PART TWO

### I

THE CLIFF was eighty feet high. They were all waiting for Billy Spurgeon to get drunk enough. They knew no horse would take a jump like that so they had built a chute, heavy and solid, and the trough had been greased with axle grease. The shavings, chips, and sawdust lay all around the chute but it was all right because they would not show in the picture. The horse that was to go down the chute was tied to a tree, grazing and switching the flies off with his tail. The cameras were set. The men below in the boats were ready to pick up Billy. Everyone was waiting for him to finish the bottle. It was twelve-year-old Scotch. He had insisted on that. Everyone was tense and trying not to show it. The director watched the stunt man, sitting on the ground, leaning against a tree, drinking and talking angrily to the grips to prove his courage.

In the finished production, Jesse James is being pursued by Federal soldiers or maybe it is by a posse, anyhow, he is being pursued and very closely. Jesse is not afraid. He knows what he is doing. He is confident because he is brave and, although his pursuers are close and gaining on him, you can see him smile over his shoulder with cool daredeviltry. He rides very fast up the long slope of a pasture and through a clump of trees. Without turning aside or pausing, he rides his horse off an eighty-foot cliff. A very fine scene, the vista of the open river with the tree-crowned cliff at the right, the mounted man in the air against the sky, a very brave man obviously. He swims his horse to the other side of the river, a dangerous feat in itself because the soldiers or the posse are firing at him from the cliff and the bullets kick up little splashes but do not hit him and so he escapes once more.

At this time, however, only the scene of Jesse in the air, the eighty-foot drop, was being photographed. When the stunt man finished the bottle, he threw it at a rock and it broke. He got to his feet and walked over to the chute where the director was standing. The assistants, grips, and extras made way for him. There were no tourists present.

"All set, Billy?" the director asked, smiling firmly. "Ready to go?"

"What the hell you think I been doing but getting ready to go? Where's the horse?"

They led the horse up a ramp to the platform at the top of the chute. He was blindfolded and Billy was supposed to jerk the blindfold off on the way down the chute. Two men held the horse and a third held Billy's stirrup. He climbed on and, when he was settled, he looked deliberately down the chute at the swirling brown water far below. You've done this before, he kept telling himself. But the liquor wasn't holding him up. He had a strong taste of creosote in his mouth.

The director was busy. He checked the script and he checked Billy's costume with a stand-in. He gave the word to an assistant to flag the cameras below as soon as Billy started down. Then he looked at Billy sitting erect on the platform on the blindfold horse.

"Whenever you're ready, Billy."

"O.K.," Billy said.

He clucked to the horse. The horse took a step and his front feet hit the grease. With a terrible jerk of his haunches, the horse tried to stop himself but the three men on the platform shoved hard on his rump and down he went. Billy jerked the blindfold off.

In the air the horse turned over. The stunt man fell clear, head first and safely. The horse hit the water flat and broke himself wide open. Some of the guts floated up around his head before he sank. It was no good. The cameramen below signaled that it was no good.

A little later they tried it again. First there was a conference. The director, his assistants, the cameramen, the wardrobe man and Billy Spurgeon all stood around under the trees at the edge of the cliff. Irritably the director told them what had been wrong with the first take and urged them all to do better.

(The horse by this time had floated a ways and sunk out of sight.) They dressed Billy up again in dry clothes and got another bay horse.

The second time everything went well. Billy stayed with the horse. He even stuck on the horse's back when they hit and came up on the horse's back. It was a good shot. It is true that in the air there was no tension in the horse's muscles. He fell limp, not as if he had jumped but as if he had been dropped. But the director said quickly that it was a fine shot; it would do nicely; you could not expect a noble pose from a dumb horse; it was accurate; Billy was some stunt man.

Old Hank Childreth had a job working with a gang of men at the foot of the cliff. They had two big rowboats and they had been instructed to row out and pick up Billy and the horse after the fall. The first time they picked up the stunt man. They could tell there was no use going after the horse. He would fatten catfish all the way to the Arkansas River. The second time one boat picked up Billy, who began to talk and brag loudly almost as if he were drunk. Hank's boat went after the horse. Hank got hold of the reins and they guided the horse to the riverbank.

At first the horse didn't seem to want to get out. The bank was not high but it was steep and the horse wouldn't make the effort. Hank clucked and chirped and tugged on the reins and at last the horse gave a heave and climbed out. It stood there with its head hanging down low, its mouth open, and it quivered all over.

"That's two horses they killed," Hank said.

"He ain't dead," one of the men said.

Hank did not answer. He took out a big jackknife he carried. He opened the blade with his thumbnail.

"What you going to do? That horse belongs to the movie company."

"He ain't no good to the movie company now. Look at him," Hank said.

It was clear that the horse was no good to anybody. Hank pulled his ears forward so the skin was tight over his neck and stabbed him at the base of the skull. The horse fell down dead.

"Let's git the truck and go to town," Hank said.

He was not sentimental about horses. They were just animals and these were no great shakes at that. The Joplin stockyards had two kinds of horses, the seventy-five-dollar ones and the hundred-and-twenty-five-dollar ones. These had been picked up for fifty dollars from a farmer. The first one never knew what he hit and the second didn't live long. A farmer is not surprised at animals in pain. If they belong to him, they are worth more healthy and it pays him to keep them that way. But if somebody wants to buy them for cash and shove them down a greasy chute to an eighty-foot drop and smash them, well, he has paid for them and, having been smashed beyond salvage, any man would kill them.

It was not so much the horses that worried Hank. He was worried because the movie company was lying about Jesse James.

One time when he was a young boy, he had gone with his father to Southwest City to buy a big clock. The man and the boy had started out early and driven over in a buckboard behind a pair of fine roan horses. The bargaining over the clock did not take long and the jeweler had asked his father to have a drink with him. They lashed the new clock to the back of the buckboard and tied the buckboard up in front of a saloon. Hank tagged along with his father and the jeweler up the steps into the bar.

While they were drinking, Frank and Jesse James came walking into town on foot. Everybody on the main street stopped and people ran to their front windows to watch them. They sauntered down the middle of the street and when they came to the Childreths' team, they stopped and patted the horses and ran their hands over their flanks. Then they started to unhitch them.

Someone ran in and told Hank's father. He asked the bartender for the loan of a couple of .45 revolvers hanging up behind the bar and he walked out through the swinging doors and stood at the top of the steps, a gun in each hand.

"You let them horses be," his father told the James boys.

They stopped unhitching and said with a kind of pleasant arrogance, "Why, you know who we are, don't you?"

"You're Frank and Jesse James. Let them horses be."

"Now looka here, mister. We got fourteen men waiting out here by the edge of town. If we want your horses, we can git 'em."

"Maybe your men can git 'em. You can't."

There was a long sweating pause.

Jesse grinned. "I'll tell you. I like a man that stands up for his rights. Let's all go in and git a drink."

His father let the hammers down on his guns. The James boys came up the steps into the bar and Jesse laid a gold piece on the wood and the men all had drinks. Hank remembered they wore black coats and Frank James had a fancy watch fob. They were polite. They thanked his father for drinking with them and they hitched up the horses again before they left. Hank told it around to every kid in the hollow, how his father got the drop on Jesse James and made him back down.

Jesse knew when the odds were too heavy. He and Frank would no more ride a horse off an eighty-foot cliff even if the

Devil was after them than they would have tried to take a pair of horses when a man had two guns thrown on them. Hank was not trying to defend the James boys. He did not then and never had thought they were heroes in any public sense of the word. To him they were scum left when the war died down, but he knew that to be an outlaw took cunning, even in your own country where you knew the paths over and along the ridges, where you could see how deep the fords were in the dark, where you could tell where you were by the shape of the hills morning and evening, and, riding softly into a farmer's yard at night with the horses' hooves done up in croker sacks, you knew the farmer when he spoke through the door. It took bravery, good sense, and an accurate calculating of your chances to last and the James boys had lasted a long time. And they had never ridden their horses off any eighty-foot cliff either. Why did the movie company want to make them out fools?

## II

THERE WAS a cave opening out of one of the limestone ridges on Hank's farm. People said the James boys had laid up there one night but Hank did not remember it. It was long and deep and somewhere inside it held deposits of saltpeter which a friend of his father's, old Lucas Parsons, had once used in the manufacture of lead dollars. When old Lucas came to die, they asked him if he wanted to see the minister for any reason, and Lucas took the edge of the quilt out of his mouth and spat in a crock beside the bed and said, no, he guessed he didn't want no minister. "I ain't done nothin' but make a little whisky and a bucketful of lead dollars." Every time Hank saw the mouth of the cave, he thought of old Lucas saying that, and chuckled. Now the movie company had rented the cave from Hank for twenty-five silver dollars and they were making a love scene at the cave mouth.

The ground sloped away from the cave mouth and there was not much room at the right level for the camera, the lights, the reflectors, and the other necessary paraphernalia yet the scene had to be taken there because the rugged slabs of gray limestone contrasted powerfully with the figures of the stars playing Frank and Jesse James, who, although they were un-shaven and dressed in the rude clothes their parts demanded, still had profiles and jawlines that had won them thousands of fans who sent letters and many small gifts from as far away as Australia. The stars together with the limestone and the darkness of the cave mouth contrasted prettily in turn with the slight but lovely girl who was Jesse's sweetheart, faithful Zee. The whole scene, the director explained a dozen times, was a study in pictorial contrasts.

Dramatically it was quite simple: Frank and Jesse are being pursued as usual. They have hidden themselves and even their horses in this cave where no one will find them. The heroine, Zee, is related to an irascible newspaper editor. In her lovely bosom, Love and respect for convention are warring. Love conquers and Zee rides alone to the cave to plead with Jesse to give up saddle and six-gun and return to the haunts of men. All that is fine in her rebels at the thought of her sweetheart— for Jesse *is* her sweetheart—hounded by the forces of the law. She pleads. Jesse says, "No." That's all there is to it, although in saying "No" Jesse must, without going into verbal detail, convince his far-flung audience that he is by no means robbing and stealing for what there is in it but for Justice. The star was adroit and by clenching his jaw-muscles and looking past Zee into the distance, he managed to convey this on the first take.

The director, a perfectionist, was not satisfied. He had ordered with mounting emotion eleven takes and none of them had been worth printing so far. That he might collect his thoughts, he had gone to sit on a chunk of rock alone on the hillside and he had posted one of his assistants between him and the movie people to insure privacy.

For two or three days Hank had wanted to talk to the director about Jesse James. Every time he had approached him he had been told that the director was in conference or he had been obviously busy. When Hank saw him sitting alone on the rock smoking a cigarette, he started up the hill to talk to him.

The assistant had never seen Hank before. He stopped him. "Sorry, mister."

"I just wanted to talk to the director, son."

As if this were going to end it, the assistant said, "No autographs."

"I don't want his autograph."

"He ain't seeing anybody. He's busy."

"What's he so busy doing? He's just setting there smoking a cigarette."

"He's working all right. What do you want to see him about?"

"I don't want to see him but a minute."

"What about, I said. You want to see him so say what it's about."

"It's about the other day. Over on the bluffs there. When you fellows shoved the horses down. . . ."

"Oh. S.P.C.A. guy, huh?"

"What's S.P.C.A.?"

"Don't gimme that, old man. Go on, beat it. You can't come snooping around here."

"I ain't snooping. I just want to ask him how come when he has to shove horses down a greasy chute off a cliff, how come he thinks Jesse would ride off it, the real Jesse, I mean."

"We got positive proof those horses were sick before we used 'em at all. It would have been cruelty to let 'em live."

"All right."

"Well, all right, so beat it."

"Listen, bud, you and me don't seem to understand each other. Let me talk to him."

"The horses were sick. We bought sick horses for that purpose. Taking that jump was a kindness to 'em."

"Forget the horses. They're dead. I want to talk to the director. He's just a man, ain't he?"

"I gave you all the dope. You don't have to talk to him."

The director heard. He got up from the rock and came toward them quickly. "By God, Morris, you're going back on publicity. As soon as we get back to the Coast, so help me, you're punching a typewriter again. . . ."

"Now, wait a minute, Albert. . . ."

"I ask you to keep people away from me. As a personal favor. I wanted to have some peace and quiet and you could give it to me. So you get some long-haired whiskery old bastard and start screaming at him right in my ear. This is my peace and quiet, huh? You're through, Morris." Then he said to Hank in a tired, cross voice. "Get out of here, will you?"

"Don't go calling me names or I'll throw you off the place, picture or no picture," Hank said.

"Who is this man?" the director shouted. "Good God, Morris, can't you even find out who somebody is?"

"He's S.P.C.A. . . ."

"Who gave him the whiskers? If he's S.P.C.A., why does . . ."

"He's somebody the S.P.C.A. sent here. About those horses the other day. Honest, Albert."

"Oh." He said to Hank quite pleasantly, "I think you'll find our relations with the Society have always been friendly. We have a remarkably clean record."

"I told him the horses were sick. We bought sick horses especially for the jump," the assistant said.

"Certainly. They had pneumonia."

"We put 'em out of their misery."

"That's right. Those horses were doomed to a horrible death. We saved them from it quickly and cleanly. Oh, I don't think the Society will want to take action. Ours was essentially a humane act," the director said.

"I don't give a good God-damn about the horses. I didn't come from no S.P.C.A. . . ."

"Jesus, I'll kill you!" the director bellowed at his assistant. "Three days behind schedule, the light going away from me, everybody dead on their feet, and he's not from the Humane Society. Get out, get out, get OUT, all of you!"

The assistant turned away and went up the hill to the cave mouth, jerking the heads off weeds as he went.

"Get OUT! You hear me?"

"I'm not going to get out," Hank said calmly. "I've got something to ask you. I been waiting long enough."

"Who *are* you? What do you want? What are you here for?"

"I wanted to ask you how come when you have to shove a horse off it, why you think Jesse James would *ride* a horse off an eighty-foot cliff."

"What did you say? Come on, out with it, speak up!"

Hank looked at him a second. "I asked you why you think Jesse James would ride a horse off an eighty-foot cliff. He wasn't a nit-head."

"Why would he? Why ask me? How do I know why he would?"

"He never did. It would have killed him. But you show him doing it in the picture."

"Oh, my God," the director said. "It's a picture, see? It's a moving picture."

"That's what I say."

"It's art."

"Has it got to lie about it?" Hank asked.

"Yes. Hell, yes, it's got to lie about it."

"What for?"

"Why, we got to please hundreds of exhibitors and millions of public and . . . oh, please, for God's sake, you dear kind old man, *leave*, will you? Beat it. Get out."

"No. Guess not. I got a right to stay here and watch," Hank said.

"Hey, Morris, Freddie!" the director shouted. "Come here. Hurry up. Get this God-damn old ridge-runner out of here."

"This is my land," Hank said. "I'll get you outa here if you're not careful."

"Oh, my God," the director said. He scrambled up the hill away from Hank, waving his arms at his assistants. He shouted at the actors and the cameramen to get ready to shoot the scene one last time.

Hank stood alone on the hillside and watched it in the fading light. It seemed a lot of trouble to go to for a lie. They were not the kind of people he wanted to see around there, insulting and deceitful.

## III

HANK drove his big mules carefully out of the village. He was careful because he did not want them to get scared by some tourist kid and run away. Although it was two months after the Fourth of July, the local druggist was selling not only his drugs, sodas, pop, sundaes, bathing caps, magazines and little booklets on the life of Jesse James but also his hitherto un-bought stock of fireworks, and hundreds of out-of-town boys were shooting off firecrackers. Hank had gone into the village for a sack of flour and he wanted to get back into the country again without any trouble.

Once he got safely on the road that led out along the creek he let the reins slide through his fingers. He wanted to think and the mules knew the way.

After he had bought the flour, he had gone into Francine's Eate Shoppe, now resplendent with a new sign painted on the side of the building, *Where Hollywood Eats. Why? Not You!* He was flush with the money the movie company had paid him for the use of the cave. As he ate the chicken dinner, Blanche, the waitress, told him about Wilbur Antrim's daughter.

She had run away with one of the Hollywood trick riders, a man named Spurgeon. Gone right off in his car last night. She left a note saying she loved Billy, that was Spurgeon's name, and he was going to take her to Hollywood and get her a job in the movies which she was sure of getting because she had great talent, Billy said. So it was good-by to stuffy small-town life, and Romance for her from now on, the note said.

And Wilbur had come tearing in at six-thirty this morning

and drunk a cup of coffee and he had rented a Ford at the garage and gone off to bring Maybelle back. He was so upset he could hardly drink the coffee. And the funny thing was, Maybelle's note never said anything about that Spurgeon marrying her. Maybe that was what upset Wilbur so. He was always chasing her away from everything in pants.

"I can just see Wilbur. I can just see him." Here Blanche had begun to laugh boisterously at the vision. "Stopping at all the gas stations and trailer camps, 'Anybody seen my daughter?' he's saying. All the way to Oklahoma City, all the gas stations, all the cheap hotels, I'll bet the sweat's just running offa him and that big bay window's jumping up and down. 'You seen my daughter, mister? Seen her any place?'"

At an age when all young people are hard to place because they resemble their mothers or their older kin, or maybe because they are so young, Hank had always recognized Maybelle, Wilbur's daughter. Since his wife's death, Wilbur had taken pains with her upbringing and she was always polite but that was not it. It was the way she looked, the last innocence, at seventeen when even the ugly ones are pretty, the final moment of ripeness before she is handled. And now this fellow Spurgeon had his hand up her leg, the fellow who had to get drunk to kill the horses. This happening would kill Wilbur also.

Tenderness was funny in a man as fat as Wilbur. He had raised Maybelle like a lily in a pot. He had bought her toys every time he went to Joplin, and when she grew up, had asked her pitifully what she would like in the way of clothes and brought her the Monkey-Ward catalogue. He had pestered the life out of the high-school principal to find out exactly how Maybelle was doing in school, and that time in the shop when Wilbur was helping her do American history, Wilbur didn't know anything about American history—it was just a string of fellows with whiskers like the old steel engravings—but he tried to explain what he didn't know, sweating, fidgeting, hunting for words, because Maybelle had to go to college.

And when, like the other little gals, Maybelle wanted to go to the Saturday night dances at the beer joints, Wilbur kept her away and she cried and it made Wilbur so nervous he cut chunks out of three men's ears the next day in the shop. In this part of the country the men are too proud to stop by for the girls, so the girls walking barefoot in the darkness down the roads with their shoes in their hands meet the boys at the beer joints. Wilbur didn't want that or any of the laying up together in the dark. Maybelle was going to be a lady and go to college.

Wilbur might have known somebody would git to her. She was slender but she seemed to be busting right out of the Monkey-Ward gingham when she walked across the square, her little bottom and her little breasts jiggling slowly. The loafers would always whistle and go "a-*ah*-uh" as if they had been hit in the stomach, and Wilbur would run out of the shop with a razor in his hand and cuss them as if it was all their fault Maybelle was so slick. In the end, all it took was a man in stitched boots who could talk about California, that's all, and when he talked, Maybelle went right with him and Wilbur was alone.

The road ran out of the sunlight into the shade of the trees where the creek went through Hank's land, and the mules slowed down, taking it easy. Hank heard some people in swimming near the ford, shouting and splashing. Somebody shot off a firecracker and the mules began to snort and walk stiff-legged. Hank said, "Whoa, there, boys." They stopped. Hank got down carefully and tied them to a tree.

He went down the road to the edge of the ford. There were ten or a dozen people in bathing suits wading in the shallow water. Tourists.

"Excuse me," Hank called.

"Look! Who's that? What's he want?" they said.

One of the little boys said, "Mamma, is he a hillbilly?"

When they got quiet, Hank said, "Pardon me, but I got a couple of mules here that are skittish. They're apt to jump around some when they hear any sudden noise. I wonder if I could ask you folks to be a little quiet till I git across the ford."

Nobody answered him. Several of them giggled. Hank looked at them a moment. He did not expect much from strangers. He turned back to where his mules were tied. He heard the women titter and he knew that he was a hillbilly to them.

He started the mules slowly down to the ford. There was a good gravel bottom and the water flowed clear and swiftly, dappled in the shade with flecks of sunlight. The mules stopped in the middle of the creek to drink, and the water chuckled through the spokes of the wagon wheels. The tourists stood in a row on the bank, some bland-faced, some giggling.

Suddenly a man threw a firecracker. It went off right by the gee-mule's ear. They jumped in terror, neighing, stumbling, trying to gallop, heaving themselves through the water. The wagon slipped and tilted. Hank fell out as the wagon turned over. The mules, jerking and fighting the harness, dragged the wet wagon up the far side of the ford, making a trough in the gravel.

Hank wrenched his leg in the fall. For a second, he sat still on the gravel bottom, the water nearly floating him. Then he got up and limped ashore. His beard hung soaked and lank. Some of the tourists still giggled but most of them, shocked, were quiet. Hank did not look behind him. He followed the mules, found them standing in his yard, wet and still trembling. He unhitched them from the wagon and tied them to a post, speaking gently and soothingly.

Then he went into his little house and got a shotgun.

The tourists forgot about Hank as soon as he had gone. They did not think he would come back. They started playing a portable radio, and a young man and a girl in a white satin bathing suit began to dance to the music, jigging awkwardly on the flat gravel by the creek.

When they saw Hank returning, muddy, wet, limping, they commenced to giggle again. When they saw the gun, it seemed even funnier. They were from Kansas City and they were not used to being threatened by bearded men with guns. Even the papas and the mammas began to laugh, it was so comical to see the old duck staggering through the stream holding his gun up high like in war pictures.

Hank walked up to them, holding his gun ready at his hip. "Now, God damn you, git off my land," he said.

The young couple stopped dancing, and the papas, grunting, stood up to resent the outrage.

One of the women with a fat old belly and pince-nez glasses on her nose said loudly, "Some people better learn how to act like gentlemen in the presence of ladies."

The men came up close to Hank and one of them said, "Yeah, what's the idea?"

Another one said, "Looka here, friend, you better be more careful about this cussing around with ladies present."

They were city men about forty-five years of age. They wore bathing suits. Hank looked at them and snorted.

"Git offa my land," he said.

"Pop him one, Dad," a small boy cried.

"This is public property. Both sides of a stream are public property and we got a perfect right to be here."

"Aw, pop him one, Dad," the boy said again.

"Sonny, you better try to git your father to leave because if he don't and your mammy don't, I'm going to fill the lot of you with holes like a sieve. Now git."

"You can't do this. . . ."

"Certainly he can't," one of the women said.

"Go git in your car and drive away or by the Eternal I'll kill you dead!" Hank shouted.

That was enough. Those sitting stood up and those already standing turned to go, the women muttering, the small children wailing and blubbering. The men picked up the blankets and cushions and started for the car, lifting their tender feet nimbly from the harsh gravel. The girl in the satin bathing suit carried away the radio still playing. In a flock they went up the road. The jingling music faded. Hank heard their car start and the car doors slam and they drove away.

## IV

WILBUR had not found his daughter. As a fat man he had grown away from the expectation of sympathy and he had masked his fatherhood with false lecherous smiles at the red pumps of Oklahoma filling stations, asking for a young girl with a classy shape, California car with a saddle on the side? No. He did not find her at the tourist camps, Bide-a-Wee,

Restawhile, Cummon Inn, no daughter. Nor anxious at the little hotels near the Texas border.

Wilbur had always wanted to make a journey, to get out and around and look things over, but he had never gone. He had stayed in the village cutting hair, ambitious to go but bashful. He had hoped and saved that Maybelle might go away instead, unlaughed at. Under a maple tree beside his house, he had combed her chestnut hair pinked by the sunlight (it was a lovely head of hair—upswept, page-boy, pincurl, how should he do it for the journey?), shaking it, combing it, teasing out the snarls, her arms uplifted. Virtue and learning she should have as talismans and then she could escape, his flesh, no one would call her Fat Stuff, go yonder, everywhere, to see what the world was like beyond the little ridges.

She had gone away all right and he had not sent her. And he had gone away, too, to chase her, his haste reflected in the jerking of his paunch and the sweat washing his jowls, driving night and day, until all his pretenses were tired out and he asked, "Seen my daughter? Seen her anywhere?"

When he returned, it was a time for Wilbur when all the people he knew became strangers. With blank unfriendliness, they stuck their heads in the door of the shop. "Didn't find Maybelle, hey? Kept her shut up too close, that's what you done, Wilbur." If they did not laugh in his face, he could hear them cackle as they moved away. Flies buzzed on the screen door and beyond it hummed the mob of tourists' voices. The stink of his shop nauseated him, bay rum, hair tonic, eau de cologne, witch hazel, shaving soap. Fat men are funny. Fathers fooled are funny.

Suddenly he got dizzy. Leaning his belly against the shelf full of lotions, he stared into his big mirror astonished. His face swam mistily away and disappeared in a cloud that drew over his eyes, then slowly, darker, it came back again. His legs trembled. He stamped his feet and shook his head and blinked his eyes. As soon as he could trust his strength he pulled down the cracked green window shade and left the shop. He pushed his way through the crowd of tourists to the rented Ford. He climbed in, took a deep breath, turned the key and started the car. He wanted to get to where there was at least a friend.

He drove slowly out the road beside the creek and he could not seem to remember that he knew the way. It was like a strange country. The trees looked black and small. They bent away from him. The wooded ridges appeared low to him as if they were pressed down by the weight of the burning blue-gray sky. He saw trees, posts, rocks, and gullies he had never seen before. He knew what he was thinking but he did not want to think it hard enough to make it real. He slowed the car down and kept his eyes on the ruts ahead in terror.

At last he saw old Hank seated by the roadside with the gun across his knees. Wilbur stopped the car.

"Didn't find her, huh?" Hank asked.

"No. No. I looked everywhere I had the gas to go. Nobody'd seen her. Nor him neither," Wilbur said.

"They got too big a head start on you."

Wilbur wanted to say over and over, "What am I going to do? What am I going to do?" Hank was old and steady, and, with his big white beard, he resembled Wilbur's meager private idea of God, but even in the midst of his fear he could not conquer the reticence that being a fat man had imposed on him. He said, "I heard about you setting there with that gun."

"Well, I'm still a-settin'," Hank said.

Wilbur was looking straight ahead through the windshield.

"I don't blame you," he said mechanically. He saw the little grove on Hank's place where he had eaten picnic suppers. It was dark and wavering. The trees were smaller than before, stunted, threatening. It was like a jungle hiding wild beasts yet he knew it could only be the little grove where he had once sat with his daughter eating sandwiches and hard-boiled eggs.

Hank spat and rubbed it into the ground with his foot. "It's the movie. Trace it all back, it's the movie made you lose Maybelle."

"My daughter," Wilbur said, choking. "My little girl." These phrases he had been repeating for three days. They made him cry. "Did you ever see her hair? She had a fine head of hair. Chestnut." This was the sum of his remembrance, the shy look she had given him, the delicate curve of her arms uplifted as she combed and bowed her head, combed and lifted, the comb crackling faintly in her hand, spangled with light through the green leaves.

"Beautiful hair, Wilbur, just beautiful."

"I'm all alone," Wilbur said. It was the first time he had said it out loud and, with the sound of the words, old Hank and the little grove of trees faded away into this blackness and he could see, almost like a movie, his shabby empty house with the blinds drawn against the sun as at a death; the wallpaper with its abrupt green palms and scarlet birds mocking him; the overstuffed couch where she once had lain, staring him out of countenance. And, moving around in the house, just moseying through the rooms, he saw himself. He was not Maybelle's father any more. He was just the barber, just the fat man. He could hear people saying, "Wilbur? Ain't he the fattest thing you ever saw? High at both ends and belly draggin' on the ground like a hog going to war. He had a

daughter once . . ." He was afraid of the misery and wretch-
edness of this picture as he was afraid of bad dreams, a helpless suffocating terror, and if the dream didn't stop, he knew
what would happen. He had been almost thinking about it all
day, not quite pausing to think, never dwelling on it. He
would go crazy.

The trees in the picnic grove and the figure of old Hank
floated slowly, gracefully, back into his vision and Wilbur
found that he was shaking so that his feet were going tap, tap,
tap on the floorboards of the car. He had to do something.
Maybe he could get Hank to help him somehow.

The old man had been talking, was talking still, excitedly,
moving his hands.

". . . and that's why I decided to live to be a hundred."

Wilbur heard that. "What's that? What you say?"

"I say, that's why I decided to live to be a hundred."

"You're crazy, Hank."

"No, I ain't either crazy."

"How old are you now?"

"Going on eighty-seven."

"You think you can make it?"

"I'm strong. Now I got an interest in life, I'll make her.
Fellow gits to be my age, he's got to have an interest in life
or he'll pass away."

"What interest?"

"What I been telling you."

"I'm sorry, Hank. I guess . . ." Wilbur waited a second
before he spoke. The fear did not come back. ". . . I was
thinking about Maybelle." He said her name without a
twinge.

Hank straightened himself on his thin old hams. He spoke
solemnly and loudly as if he had learned what he was saying

by rote. "What do you want? Truth or lies? Maybelle or a picture of her? Everything's coming secondhand now. Somebody's got to live straight, touch what he touches, see what he sees without nobody or nothing gloving his hand or coming in front of his eye. And I'm going to be that man, and I'm going to live a long time so I can tell whoever asks me how things really were."

"Yeah. Sure. Sure thing," Wilbur said nervously. "You're going to be the one, huh?"

"Yes, sir. I been setting here trying to figure out why this whole business got me so mad and I've done it. I know, now, and now I got me a job to do, I'll round out my century. You see."

The back of his neck prickling, Wilbur watched the old man closely. His eyes were bright. He waved his hands, a thing he had never done before, and on his lap was the ten-gauge, the instrument of murder. An old, old man already.

"How you feel right now, Hank?"

"Fine as silk, Wilbur."

Wilbur jammed down the starter. He was eager to hurry away but he was a little afraid to.

"Well, I got to be gittin' back to the shop."

"Come on out again. I'll be right here."

Wilbur turned around and drove slowly until he was around the bend where Hank couldn't see him and then he stepped on her. The old man had helped him but he did not know it.

## V

As WILBUR hurried back to town, he decided Hank was crazy. Hank was his friend and he wished him well but he was honestly anxious to have him put away before he harmed someone. Everybody around the village had been saying Hank was crazy and when he heard him say firmly that he was going to live to be a hundred, Wilbur was convinced.

He went directly to the bank to see Charlie Howard, the president and the head of the Chamber of Commerce. Charlie was the richest man in town. He was sitting before a roll-top desk cleaning his nails with a paper clip. In the ordinary way, Wilbur would have knocked but now that he had a mission, he walked right in.

"Charlie, old Hank Childreth's crazier'n hell," he said.

"That's what they say, Wilbur," Howard said.

"Well, it's true. I hate to say it because I like Hank. Always have. But I just been out talking to him . . ."

"Still sore at the tourists, ain't he?"

"Yeah, but that ain't all. He's bound and determined to live a hundred years, he says, and he'll be damned if anybody's going to come on his land and . . . look here, Charlie, don't you think we ought to git one of these lunatic commissions going and have them take Hank up to Nevada to the insane asylum? He's setting there with that ten-gauge. He'll blow somebody's head off first you know."

Howard stuck one thin hand in front of him to look at his clean nails. "Wilbur, I don't think Hank's crazy." Slowly, assuming the shrewd air that was expected of him because he was rich, he said, "No. Hank's just sore, that's all."

This was a lie. Howard believed that Hank was crazy. He had believed it ever since Luther McCarthy had first told him but he was afraid to go near Hank because of the shotgun. In doing the things he had had to do to get rich, he had offended a lot of people, ruined a few, and a couple of them had cracked down on him and they had missed. People did not use guns in this part of the country as freely as they had thirty or forty years before but the banker knew that Hank was an old-timer and a gun was a natural instrument. He did not want to take any chances with this archaic method of working off anger, especially when the anger was only the whim or crotchet of a lunatic. Ever since the moonlit night when he heard a .30-.30 bullet zip past his ear, only an inch or two away, Howard had been terribly afraid of getting shot, any gun, any man, any reason. He could not stand to think about his head, the way it would look if a bullet or a handful of buckshot smacked into it. He started to clean the nails on the other hand.

"But what are you going to do? Just let him set there?" Wilbur asked.

"He won't hurt nobody," Howard said. "As soon as the cold weather comes, Hank'll forget about this. Won't be any tourists then anyhow. No, Wilbur. Hank'll be all right."

Just then the sheriff, Luther McCarthy, walked into the office. He ignored Wilbur and spoke directly to the banker. "You want us to hang around and direct traffic, don't you?"

"Hell, yes. They's a lot of tourists around town yet. What's the matter?"

"Well, there's a woman out here. She's a tourist and she says she's kin to Tom Pendergast."

"How close kin is she?" Howard asked and they all laughed.

This was when Pendergast was still powerful in the state.

"She didn't say."

"What she want?"

"A police escort, she says. She's seen all the sights, the Dixie Belle, the Jesse James home, the whole works so far, and now she wants to see that cave of Hank Childreth's. I told her he was crazy and she said she was related to Tom Pendergast and she wants a police escort to protect her. You want me to go with her or keep on directing traffic?"

"Where is she? Go git her."

It was not necessary. The woman had got tired of waiting. She had a massive bosom and, even in the heat, she was strapped into an old-fashioned corset which every man in the room identified at once. Below the corset she had perspired and it showed through her lace dress in a big damp splotch. The rouge and powder on her cheeks had been damaged by rills of sweat. She addressed them in a voice of bogus sweetness, "My name is Lewis, and I've been so happy to visit your beautiful little town and show my son the movie sets and all, and I just wondered if you couldn't let me have your nice Mr. McCarthy as an escort out to the Jesse James Hide-Away Cave. Mr. Pendergast will be delighted to hear about it all. It won't be too much trouble, will it, Mr.—"

"Howard's the name," he said and jumped to his feet. Usually he did not stand up for anyone and he was a little startled that he had been so slow this time. He scratched his ear. "The escort ain't what's the trouble, Mrs. Lewis. Be glad to have Luther take you out there but . . ."

"Mamma, we going out to the cave?" came the voice of Mrs. Lewis's son from the front of the bank.

"Yes, dear, just a minute," she called and resumed her sweet smile.

"You see, Mrs. Lewis, there's an old man sets out there by the cave with a gun and he's been acting sort of queer lately and . . ."

Wilbur spoke out. "Look, Charlie, why don't we all go out to Hank's, you and Luther and Mrs. Lewis and . . ."

"What for?" Howard asked sharply.

"Don't get sore, Charlie. Hank knows us. He wouldn't cut up just for us. But Mrs. Lewis is a tourist and tourists are what he hates. If she was to go ahead of us sort of, you could see how crazy he is. The minute he saw her he'd git to helling and damning and threatening to shoot her . . ."

"How do you know he wouldn't shoot Mamma?" Mrs. Lewis's son said. He had come to stand in the doorway, a thin pimply boy of about thirteen.

"Hank's too much of a gentleman to shoot a woman. Oh, he might stomp around and threaten and cuss at you but he wouldn't pull the trigger. You see, Mrs. Lewis, this old man's a friend of mine and I want to convince Mr. Howard he's crazy so we can get him put away where he can't hurt nobody," Wilbur said earnestly.

"Mrs. Lewis don't care who Hank's friends are or who they ain't," Howard said. "It's just a question whether she wants to be threatened and cussed out, and unless I miss my guess, Mrs. Lewis is too much of a lady to . . ."

"Mr. Howard, I brought Alvin down here to see *all* of the scenes where they made the Jesse James movie," Mrs. Lewis said firmly. Ever since she had discovered the power of her kinsman's name, Mrs. Lewis had never really been afraid of anything.

"Well, Mrs. Lewis, I just didn't want you to be offended by strong language. I think you got a good idea, Wilbur. We'll all go," Howard said. He had been quickly and delicately balancing one fear against another, and at this moment the Boss was more frightening than a shotgun.

Mrs. Lewis and her son went in one car, and they were led by Howard, Wilbur, and the sheriff in Howard's car. Mrs. Lewis was oblivious to any possible danger. She was enjoying the homage she always received at the mention of Tom Pendergast's name. He was a very distant relative actually but she contrived to announce the connection in department stores, filling stations, and Parent-Teacher meetings just for the pleasure of watching people jump. It was a purely aristocratic pleasure, and, driving along, erect with both hands tight on the wheel, she did not think about meeting a crazy man with a gun. She spoke only to tell her son to stop picking at those things on his face.

The two cars stopped before they turned the last bend in the creek road, where Hank could not see them. The banker asked Mrs. Lewis if she were certain she wanted to see the cave and she said she certainly was.

Hank heard the squeak and rattle of pebbles and he looked up suddenly. He saw Mrs. Lewis climbing the steep path that led to the cave. She pulled herself along by holding to saplings or her son's hand and occasionally she would push one hand against her fat thigh. The back and seat of her dress were wet and she was panting heavily. Hank waited until she was about halfway up. He stood up and sauntered over to the foot of the hill with his shotgun laid over his arm.

"Just where was you going, madam?" he asked.

"I'm going to see the Jesse James Hide-Away Cave," she said.

"What for?"

"Because they made the movie there."

"That's it, ain't it? You don't want to see the cave because the James boys really *did* hide out there once, do you? You want to see it because they made a *movie* of 'em hiding out there."

"It don't make any difference why I want to see the cave."

"No, it don't. Because you ain't going to see it anyhow."

"What do you mean?"

"It ain't allowed."

"Why not? Who don't allow it?" Mrs. Lewis felt that she could afford to be patient.

"I don't. It's my cave. On my property."

"We won't hurt your cave. We just want to look around."

"Madam, it ain't that I mind your seeing my cave. It's just that I ain't going to let you. Come on down, now. You, too, sonny."

Mrs. Lewis had enjoyed baiting the old fool but now was the time for triumph. She did not believe that any man in the state of Missouri was crazy enough to resist her sesame. "It might just interest you to know that I'm related to Tom Pendergast."

"Tom Pendergast, huh?"

"I just thought you might be interested," she said complacently.

"So all doors fly open at your touch, huh? Well, madam, let me tell you something: if you was to come down here all wrapped up in a pillar of fire, with a hundred angels all playing the slide trombone, and if you was to tell me you was own sister to the Twelve Apostles, you still couldn't come on my land if I didn't want you to. Now git!"

Mrs. Lewis had never had an experience like this in all her life. The old man's gun was still over his arm but she began to be frightened. She turned and called, "Oh, Mr. McCarthy, Mr. McCarthy, Mr. Howard!"

The banker and the sheriff came sheepishly around the bend. Wilbur stayed behind, unwilling to face his friend.

Hank took the gun from the crook of his arm and cocked it.

"Hank, we've had enough of this foolishness," Howard began, trying to act brave in front of Mrs. Lewis.

"You're just like all heathen, Charlie," Hank said. "Your God's the Boss and you think he's going to protect you when they ain't nothing but a dollar shirt between your naked bosom and a handful of buckshot."

"Arrest that old devil, Luther," Howard said.

"Luther, you ain't going to arrest me, now are you?" Hank said in a wheedling, menacing tone. "You know he ain't. Look at him."

Fresh sweat popped out on Luther's forehead. "I—I ain't got my gun, Charlie."

"Go on. Git out of here, all of you," Hank roared. He threw up his gun and let go with one barrel over their heads. The shot rattled among the trees, the cut twigs fell, and the echoes crackled far across the hollows.

They all ran. Luther ran because he had no gun and it wasn't a fair fight unless you both had guns. Mrs. Lewis, pale and gasping, hustled herself around the bend through fear, the more fearful because it was a new emotion. The banker ran because, at the roar of the gun, he saw a vision of his head, torn, smashed, and bloody. The boy with the acne ran because everybody else was running.

Hank watched them, laughing. "God damn 'em," he said. "The movies, the automobiles, the tourists, all of 'em." He stopped. Then he said, "God damn the whole twentieth century," and he fired the other barrel.

# Fugue for Harmonicas

EVERY AFTERNOON they came up to the village green to wait, the unemployed, a few men sagging limply against the wall of a barn, with large soft hands, caps on their heads, and their necks swathed in scarves knotted and held sometimes with brummagem pins. They spoke little, watching the vapors lift or sink above the Downs, and hearing, in front of the cottage across the road, an old man's parrot squawking

in the sun, a gray bird with a red crest. Or to escape the sudden rains they sat on the bench beneath the big elm on the
green, watching for the newsboy to bring the *Mail,* which
would tell them if their horse had won the four-thirty at New-
market and the shillings they had bet turned into five or six
or seven; or they waited until the pub, the Greyhound, should
open at six o'clock.

From the green they could just see the big cross of limestone
in the churchyard, gray against the yews, a memorial with a
graven base, bearing the legend, "For God, King, and Country." It was erected by small subscriptions in the village to
commemorate the bravery, and the deaths, of their friends
with whom they had gone out to war. Few of the unemployed
ever looked at it because there was always the mist to watch
above the distant summit of the Downs and the parrot's curses
to listen to.

Jack Haines was unemployed, living on twenty-eight shillings a week dole, and supporting his wife and his son, Cyril.
He never went to the green to wait out the day, but in fine
weather dug in a small garden patch, or if it rained, stayed in
his cottage teaching his five-year-old Cyril how to play the
mouth organ.

Out of such a dole you would not expect much of a house.
There are two old willows in front, a flagged walk, and the
garden beside it. The cottage itself has a thatched roof, and
in summer there is wistaria climbing up the side, very pretty.
There are also rats in the thatch that will face a terrier down,
and in the one room, the bricks of the floor are laid on the
earth which spurts up mud in wet weather. The pump is outside and there is a small fireplace. On the mantel are cigarette
cards with colored pictures of fish, flowers, and racehorses on
them. "I was on him when he won the Autumn Cup at New-

bury," Jack says, pointing to Loosestrife, a handsome bay horse. "Won a fiver. Coo, I didn't half have a night out."

Tea at the Haines's is bread, bacon dripping, and a poached egg, but if you are a guest Jack's wife will buy three of the baker's best little cakes—"Get down, Cyril, there's none for you. Shame on you"—with icing colored violet, red, and a brilliant malachite. After tea, Jack offers a twopenny packet of Woodbines to smoke.

When Cyril has played the newest piece he has learned on the mouth organ, Jack will tell, while his wife smiles a set and patient smile, of the high point in his life. This is not the three years he was a company runner in France and often carried sacks of Mills bombs in the open when the support trenches were blown, but the halcyon evening when he won the South Berks shove-halfpenny championship. "On the Bell board at Wantage 'twas. Landlord had it polished till it shone like glass."

The recital takes an hour, with gestures, while Cyril squeaks illicitly on the mouth organ, and, as a climax, Jack brings out from under the bed a huge photograph of himself in a dark oak frame, looking very sheepish, with a big silver cup dangling from one hand. "We had to sell it. Only fetched seven and six. Man at the jeweler's shop said it was lead."

It had been very bad with Jack before Cyril was born and while he was a baby too young to talk. There had been no work much since the war, and until Cyril began to ask questions and run about, Jack had gone every day to the village green with the rest of the workless. They had not talked against the Government nor about the war nor their officers. They simply had not talked, but leaned and sat in apathy, waiting for the day to go over their heads, sunshine or mist.

But when Cyril began to grow a little bit, Jack could see

that he was very bright and quick. If he saw the baker with the back of his wagon full of fresh loaves, he wanted to see how bread was made, and often on rainy days they watched the baker, with flour in his hair and eyebrows, molding the dough and putting it in pans for the ovens. Or when they passed a farmer working in a garden, Cyril had to know why he dug, what he planted, and how it grew.

Jack started his own garden at that time, and Cyril helped him. And once a gentleman gave Jack three big trees to cut down on his estate and told him he could have the wood to sell in return for the cutting down. Jack borrowed a long two-handed saw, and Cyril was just large enough to guide one handle and keep it from wiggling. At night Cyril walked into the cottage, struck his cap on his thigh to shake out the sawdust and shouted, "What's for tea?" in the same manner as his father.

Every evening at six Jack and Cyril came along by the row of pollards to the pub. Jack is very tall and Cyril came up to the middle of his thigh. But Jack never walked slowly so the boy could keep up and Cyril never hung on to his father's coat. He trotted breathlessly beside, gasping, "Yes, Dad," to Jack's remarks.

When they got to the doorway of the Greyhound, George, the landlord, standing with his hand on the lintel waiting for custom, would say, "Hello, artful," to Jack, and always, "Yer sprouting up like a weed," to Cyril. Jack and Cyril answered, "Evening, George," together. Then the three would go in and the landlord would draw a pint of ale for Jack and give Cyril a chocolate biscuit.

As champion of the district, it was Jack's right to take the shove-halfpenny board into the sitting room, a small chamber with piano and aspidistra, and on the wall a picture of the

landlord's son in uniform at Poona. The barroom is too small
to play in, because the bar itself and the four barrels behind it,
two of ale and two of beer, the domino table and the space
before the dart board take up the room. The sitting room is
usually reserved for occasional transient gentry and the wives
of the men in the bar, who sit in chairs around the walls, gos-
siping and drinking small bottles of stout, and when they
laugh they hold their hands genteelly up before their mouths.

If no one would play Jack at shovers, he would take on
Cyril, whose chin just reached over the tabletop. There were
no concessions. Jack was quite as polite when Cyril made a
good shot and as scornful of a bad as he was with a man. When
Jack got another partner, Cyril knelt in an armchair gravely
watching the game.

He was a fat little boy with cheeks the color of raw liver
and he kept his cap on indoors like his father. He would comment, "Well done, Dobbin," or "Bad luck, Dad," impartially.
When he thought Jack was not looking, he climbed down from
the chair and nipped a drink out of his father's pint. If Jack
caught him at it, he would shout, "Stay outa me beer, me son,
or I'll smack yer 'ead."

Often Jack would take Cyril on the bike as far as The Fox
at Steventon or The Noah's Ark, and Cyril would sit on the
bar singing while Jack played the mouth organ, with the farmers and workingmen joining in the choruses. Sometimes Cyril
got drunk from too many nips into his father's pint and the
women of the neighborhood often said that they were going
in a body to Mrs. Haines to speak sharply to her about her
dear little boy drinking in public houses.

They should have spoken, even though Jack would have
cursed them out of the place for meddling, for one day Jack
noticed that Cyril looked too fat. It was three days later that

he saw it was not fat around the boy's chin but a swelling. The backs of his hands were puffed. He put the child to bed, where he sang songs and jumped around for a week. He did not feel any sickness but the swelling grew until his legs were as big around as a quart pot. At last, with the poor man's fear of all officials, Jack called the charity nurse, who packed Cyril off to hospital in Wantage. When Jack came to see his son the first time, the matron, an old woman in a hooded cap, told him it was Cyril's kidneys and that it was very serious.

When Jack told his wife, she suggested timidly, "Perhaps you shouldn't have fed him the beer."

A bewildered man, seeing his little mainstay broken and knowing no way to answer but in anger, he said, "Don't speak to me of that. He shall have beer if he wants it. Gallons of it."

Every day for weeks that spring Jack rode his bike the five miles to Wantage, where King Alfred was born, and stopped at the confectioner's in the market place to buy chocolate biscuits to take to his son as if he would wheedle him back to life with songs and little gifts.

And every night he was in the bar at the Greyhound drinking old beer, black and musty, because it was strong and he could sleep if he drank enough.

One day the matron met him at the door of the ward and whispered, "He's very bad. He won't last the day out. I'm sorry, Mr. Haines. He was a dear little boy." And Jack, turning his cap around in his hands, could only answer, "Yes, madam."

He entered the ward softly, a long room full of bedridden old women with iron-gray braids, who began to nod and whisper when they saw him. In the corner was Cyril in a crib. When he heard his father's step, he rolled back his head so he could see under his swollen eyelids. "Hello, Dad," he said weakly.

Jack talked to him very cheerfully and rapidly a long time telling over all the things they would do together as soon as he was well again. A terrier, certainly, and perhaps a little bike of his own, and Newbury for the races. As if he were begging the child a favor, Jack spoke, and pulled out the mouth organ and wiped it on his trouser leg. "What'll it be, me son?"

" 'The Old Rustic Bridge by the Mill,' " whispered Cyril.

Jack played it, making one hand flutter at the end of the mouth organ to give expression, and some of the old women sang in cracked voices.

He asked Cyril again, and one of the women said with false encouragement, "Play 'Gandhi' so Cyril can sing it."

Jack played the tune and Cyril's lips moved with the words:

> *Gandhi, Gandhi, they're coming after you.*
> *When they catch you, they'll give you a month or two.*
> *They'll bind you up with wire*
> *And tickle your Black Maria,*
> *And you'll look sweet upon the seat*
> *Of a bicycle built for two.*

"Now what, Cyril?" Jack said.

But Cyril had closed his eyes and turned his head away.

Jack said, "Tell me a song to play fer you, son."

Cyril did not answer.

"Tell me a song, son," Jack said again and the tears ran down his cheeks.

"Tell me a song, Cyril, tell me a song."

The old women had begun to cry noisily.

"A song, son."

The day after the funeral, the little group of idle men on the green saw Jack coming toward them along the road, head down, walking hard. As he passed, one called, "Where be going, then, Jack?"

Jack stopped short, and looked up startled, "Why—nowhere, Tom. There be nowhere I'm going." He looked at the barn, plastered with advertising posters, and the line of men sagged against it in the sun, and he turned slowly with resignation and leaned against the barn.

"Too bad about the little chap," a man said.

"Aye," Jack answered.

After an hour or two of staring at the grass with the cackling of the gray, caged parrot in his ears, Jack took the mouth organ out of his pocket and threw it into the ditch.

# Game Chickens

WHEN I FINISHED high school in Memphis, Tennessee,
it was in the middle of the year. The graduation
exercises were held about the first of February and
the next day I went out to look for a job. I intended to work
for a year and a half, save all my money and go to Yale or,
if I could not get in, I was going to ship out to Hamburg,
Germany, on a cattle boat. I cannot remember now why

Hamburg seemed to be more important than Gravesend, Cherbourg, or Stockholm. I believed Yale to be a difficult college to enter so that I felt an alternate choice was necessary and I may have heard that a great many cattle boats went to Germany.

I particularly wanted a job in the office of one of the big cotton factors on Front Street facing the levee, a cobbled ramp that sloped down to the river. If you worked for a cotton factor, you wore very good clothes which meant at that time four-button, no-padding-in-the-shoulder jackets and narrow trousers with sharp creases and during working hours the suit would be covered with wisps of cotton lint. Inevitably you went to all the debutante parties and many of your colleagues were young Englishmen from Liverpool, and this seemed to be a strange romantic fact. I tried all the offices on Front Street but I didn't get a job. We were Yankees and I had no connections. I didn't get a job anywhere else either.

After looking for a week or so I began to get discouraged. I felt that I was no good. Although I had taken the platitudes of the principal address at graduation with a grain of salt, I had unconsciously accepted more of their message than I realized. I took to spending more and more of my afternoons swimming at the YMCA to bolster up my self-esteem. I was local champion at fifty and one hundred yards. It was a small sixty-foot tank in a room with a low ceiling. When I took the water my kick made a loud booming noise that made everybody stop and watch and had even drawn fat businessmen out of the barbershop and off the rubbing tables. I swam a good deal and I thought I was getting myself in shape for the outdoor racing season which began in June.

It was there that I met George L'Hommedieu. The first time he told me his name, he called it "Lommadoo" and he spelled it out immediately with a certain pride and then said it was a nuisance as a name. I saw him come out of the showers one afternoon. He was about twenty-four or five with a good enough build but I knew he could not swim because he walked gingerly over the wet tiles as if they were hot and he tried the water with his toe before he climbed down the ladder at the shallow end. The first day he stood timidly around up to his waist, patting the water. Occasionally he screwed up his face and lay down on his side in the water, straightening up immediately to cough and spit and wipe his eyes. He seemed to want to swim but he knew nothing about it. As I swam by him he seemed to admire the display, so I volunteered to teach him and in a week he could swim the length of the pool. His arms looked stiff and brittle as he did it and he always swallowed quite a lot of water when he tried to breathe but anyone could tell it was a crawl stroke he was attempting and not a nasty feminine side stroke. At the pool we became quite good friends.

He told me he was a graduate of the University of Illinois and this was a recommendation to me because any college man was not only a Bachelor of Humane Letters, or something; he also knew about liquor and women. When I saw him in his clothes, I thought at first he worked for a cotton factor; he dressed with the same elegance. I asked him but he said, no, he worked for the Illinois Board & Filler Company. It seemed to be a dull name and I did not inquire further. Although he was a Yankee like me and alone in Memphis, he got around a good deal. He mentioned the names of two or three debutantes and I was sure he led an exciting life. I was a little proud that I had taught him to swim. He became a proxy through whom I could imagine the conquest of the wild beautiful Mississippi girls who were drawn up to Memphis

from the river towns of the Delta to "come out" every winter.
Some were girls from towns with the same names as theirs: I
remember Elizabeth Banks, of Banks, Mississippi. I thought
she looked like Corinne Griffith and I hoped she was kind to
George and saved him some "no-cuts" at the dances. Actually,
I can see now he was a lonely young man who probably spent
most of his evenings at the boardinghouse reading magazines
on the bed in his room.

He got me the job I had been looking for and while working
on it, I walked out of a room three minutes before a murder,
maybe five minutes, anyhow, it was as close as I have ever
been. We were sitting on the edge of the pool one afternoon
and he asked me if I wanted a job. I told him I did and he said
I could have his. He was quitting to work for a glass company
up North and his home office had told him to find someone to
replace him. The job was nothing, he said, very simple, very
easy. I told him I was two months past my seventeenth birthday and I had never had any business experience.

"That's all right. Don't worry. There's nothing to this job.
Meet me here tomorrow and I'll take you out to look the place
over," he said.

The Memphis Branch of the Illinois Board & Filler Company was at the extreme north edge of town. Beyond it lay
river bottoms and gum-tree woods. When I first saw the place,
I was troubled and frightened. It seemed tremendous, and
George had explained on the way out that my title would be
Manager. I doubted whether I could manage all this. Something would be sure to come up that I wouldn't know how to
handle. There were several long dingy gray two-story buildings made out of corrugated iron. They were laid out almost
in the shape of a U. Between the ends of the U was a small
corrugated iron building painted a dull red. This was the

office. It sat on a small patch of gritty neat grass and there was a drooping tree. We got out of George's Ford and went in.

It was an old office. The walls were made of pine boards painted a mustard color and bulging here and there. Against one wall stood an old-fashioned high standing desk. There was also a battered oak flat-top desk with a swivel chair, a rickety adding machine, a huge black safe with a rustic scene on the door and a rusty little base-burner stove. Two rush-bottomed chairs with wire between the rungs stood in corners.

George knelt at once in front of the safe and spun the knob around the dial forward and back. I could hear the tumblers clank faintly.

"This is a hell of a safe," George said as he swung the door open. He brought out a bottle of gin from the top shelf and stood aside to let me look in. "We keep coal in there. Coal, gin, and stamps. They're the only valuables. No money comes through this office." In the main coffer of the safe was about a bushel of soft coal.

"What's the combination?" I asked. I thought it sounded businesslike.

"There isn't any. Just give it a whirl," he said.

I asked him what the Illinois Board & Filler Company made.

"Oh," he said as if he thought he had already told me. "Egg-case fillers. We sell fillers and flats and knocked-down cases."

This meant as little to me then as it does to you. George went into an adjoining room where the files and typewriter were, I learned later, and brought out, folded up and dusty, one of these crisscross cardboard things they put eggs in. Un-folded it was a large square network of three dozen little squares. A case of eggs holds thirty dozen, hence there would be ten of these networks—fillers, in fact—five on each side.

The wooden egg-case made of $\frac{3}{16}''$ gum or $\frac{7}{32}''$ cotton-
wood was sold in a bundle, the sides, the ends, and the top
and bottom all bound together, and the dealer had to make a
box out of it himself.

George passed me the gin bottle and said, "Good luck." I
thought he meant good luck with the gin but afterward I was
ashamed to realize he was toasting my fortunes on the job. I
did the genteel thing. I took as small a drink as I dared,
coughed only once and by blinking rapidly kept the tears
from running down my face. Italians made the Memphis gin,
a standard product that smelled like Hearts and Flowers perfume. I was glad it was not their "brandy," a liquid made of
corn whisky, peach flavoring, and red pepper. George took
several swallows with great ease while I watched admiringly.

He told me he had been authorized by the home office in
Illinois to pay me a hundred and ten dollars a month. This
seemed to me a large salary but he explained apologetically
that it really was small because there was so little to do most
of the time, nothing but sit there all day long and hope that
freight agents from the railroads would stop in and talk. The
reason they were freight agents was because they were affable
fellows who could tell a good story and he kept the gin in the
safe for their entertainment. I could come to work the next
day and he would stay with me two weeks to show me the
ropes. Then he was going North.

Pat as he said this, the screen door opened and a thin little
wizened man came in.

"Cathey, this is Mr. Seager. He's taking my place," George
said.

Cathey rolled a twig from one side of his mouth to the other
and said in a high voice, "Uh-huh."

He would have been about five feet eight inches long if

you had laid him out flat on a table and measured him but he was only about five feet tall as he stood there because he was all humped over into his pants pockets. He wore a large fuzzy gray fedora hat covered with grease spots and wisps of cobweb. His shirt was blue and dirty and he had on a pair of black trousers that shone down the thighs from the oily dirt that was ground into them. He was about thirty-five years old and he had a long sagging face. As he stood there, the face did not change; he did not glance up from the floor; he looked like a man alone on a street corner.

"Cathey's the foreman. He knows about everything. If you want to know anything, ask him," George explained.

It seemed to me that I ought to acknowledge the introduction in some way. At seventeen manners are not consideration for other people; they are a display you make to prove you have them. I stepped briskly forward with my hand stuck out and said, "How are you, Mr. Cathey?"

He rolled his light eyes up at me and down again. He pulled a hand slowly out of his pocket and held it three inches in front of his thigh. I could take it if I wanted to. I took it, limp, thin, and moist, and squeezed it once and let it go. He put it back in his pocket. George went on talking to me about the job. Cathey stood looking at the floor, moving the twig by hand from one corner of his mouth to the other, then spitting, and after a few minutes, he turned around and walked out of the office.

"Doesn't he ever talk?" I asked George.

"Who, Cathey? Sure he talks. He knows all about this place. He could run it all by himself. He can read and write."

After George had gone and I had settled into the work, I found that there was really very little to do just as he had said. The factory "ran" four months of the year. The rest of the

time we shipped orders out of stock and I kept bankers' hours.
I used to take a Poplar Avenue streetcar, pick up the morning
mail, and board a Thomas Street car for the factory. The
Thomas Street cars were the oldest in Memphis. They ran very
slowly, rocking backward and forward, and it was nearly
nine-thirty when I reached the office, which was at the end
of the line. It would take me about an hour to answer a letter
or two (in longhand) and write up the orders and bills of lad-
ing. Cathey came in sometimes silently, sometimes saying,
" 'Morning," picked up the orders and bills and walked out.
He and one colored man made up the orders and before noon
I would see our ratty old Ford truck taking the cases and fillers
down to the depot to be shipped. At twelve-thirty I took the
streetcar back downtown, had a malted milk and a sandwich,
picked up the afternoon mail and was trundled sedately back
again. There was another hour's work and I was finished for
the day. I had to stay there, though, because somebody might
call up on the phone. During the off season there were only
three people in this huge clump of buildings, Cathey, J. T., the
Negro, and myself.

At first I spent some time exploring the place. The factory
had made cottonseed oil during the war but none had been
made there since. The windows were thick with a gummy
dust, almost opaque, and inside the light was dim. Long fes-
toons of old ragged cobwebs hung everywhere with lint and
chips of wood caught in the loops. The floor was damp and
against the wall in heaps of dust and corners some kind of pale
weed sprouted. There were structures I took to be vats, blis-
tered and rusty, and wherever there was machinery the lines
of its curves, spokes, and joints were broken by the thick coat-
ing of grease someone had put on them to preserve them. In
some of the rooms there were metal bins full of moldy cotton-

seed hulls and it was from these that the whole factory took its rank rubbery odor. Rats lived on the hulls.

The rats were monstrous and Cathey's terrier would never go inside the factory. They had lived there battening on the greasy hulls so long unmolested that they were full of confidence and they usually moved at a slow trot shaking all over with their fat. They did not seem to see, hear, or smell very much. You could walk up within a yard of one, then at some point he would become aware of you and slash like lightning at your shoe or ankle. I did this just once and then I let them alone.

Once after a tour of these gloomy buildings I was coming out of a doorway into the sunlight when I saw a chicken yard in front of me. I had not noticed it before. Chickens were just chickens to me and I was about to pass by when I saw they were not ordinary chickens.

I walked over to the fence and looked down at them. I had never actually seen any before but I knew from pictures in the *National Geographic* that these were game chickens.

"Them are game birds." I heard Cathey's high voice and, turning, I found him at my elbow.

"What do you do with them?" I asked.

There was an accent of soft scorn in his voice. "Fight 'em."

I was young and ignorant especially with people and half-consciously but helplessly I blurted out the obvious, "It's against the law, isn't it?"

It was as if he were overlooking a breach of etiquette. "I fight 'em Sunday mornings over there in the bottoms with the niggers."

"With gaffs?"

He spat over the fence and a young cockerel jumped and fluttered. He swung his pale eyes at me deliberately and said,

"Uh-huh." Maybe he thought he could tell what kind of a damn fool I was by looking at my face. He knew he was going to have to work with me, damn fool or not, and he hunched his shoulders and leaned over with his forearms crossed on a thin little fencepost and resumed politely but without any polite inflections, "We git over there about ten o'clock Sunday morning and we fight two, three mains for ten-dollar side bets." He spat again. "Make money."

The cocks stood up high off the ground. They had long serpentine necks that gleamed in the sun. Some were a beautiful greenish black, others a reddish bronze, others a kind of dirty speckled gray. Everything had been bred off them but muscle. They stepped around stiff and alert, stopped, scratched, and stopped, the neat reptilian heads turning slowly, blinking, one claw lifted, and then ran quickly on.

"They's good blood in those birds. *Im*ported. Those gray ones are Irish Grays. You know Paul Dickson down at Rosedale?"

"No. Who's he?" I said.

"Got a big place down there. He keeps a big string of game chickens. I got 'em from him."

I would have liked to ask him more about cockfighting but I didn't want him to think I was any stupider than he did already. I said, "Well, I better be getting back to the office," and just as I said it before I had time to turn away, I saw him smile, a slow hoist of his sagging cheeks that let out his orange broken teeth. He knew I had no work to do and I had been stupid again.

As spring came and the weather got warm, I tried to find things to do. I practiced typing about an hour a day sitting on a tall three-legged stool. I was anxious to get ahead (of whom I didn't stop to think) and I considered buying a book on poultry so that I might learn the business from the egg up. I tried conscientiously to envision the industry as a whole: the farmer, the wholesaler, the salesman, the manufacturer, and the Home Offices, but I was always stopped by a sort of sneaking thought that egg-case fillers were not very important. I know now that this was not a sneaking thought. It was a conviction that I was unwilling to recognize then and it made me inefficient in the little work there was. I made mistakes steadily.

I had to keep a simple set of books on expenditures and payrolls. I knew they were simple but within two weeks of my start, I was three cents out and I never did find that three cents. Once a month I took an inventory of the stock on hand and one warm April day with a light breeze and the toad-frogs chirping and clunking in the bottoms beyond the factory, I walked right past a whole warehouse full of fillers and I showed a fifteen-hundred-case loss on my inventory. Three days later I had a special-delivery letter from the President of the company. It began conventionally enough, "Dear Mr. Seager," and opposite the salutation above the body of the letter was typed, "*In re:* Monthly Inventory." It continued: "Yours of even date received and contents noted. Would say in reply" (and here the style blew up) "just what the hell are you doing down there, Allan?" Then he explained, more formally, my mistake.

The worst came a few weeks later although I did not hear about it for a long time. A letter came in canceling an order. The letter-paper was charred brown around the edges and on it the customer said his whole establishment had burned up. I thought for half an hour about the shock and distress of having your business burn up and then I sat down on my stool to compose a consoling reply. I wanted it to be warm, humane, and sympathetic for I felt that this would help the prestige of the I. B. & F. Co. I began, "I am terribly sorry to hear about your fire. Fire is so relentless and uncaring. . . ." There was a lot more like this and it was not until six months later that Uncle Joe Thomson, the salesman, a shrewd old man with an Elk's tooth, brown vici kid shoes, and a wad of Peachy Plug always sleeping in his cheek, came in off the territory and said there was a fellow over in Marked Tree, Arkansas, thought I was crazy.

When the weather got hot in May, my attempts to improve grew more sporadic and they withered completely in the summer when the little iron office building used to take enough heat so it jumped up and down. Nobody came to visit the place then, not even the freight agents, and I sat stripped to the waist with my feet on the desk, reading *The Faerie Queene* and *The Adventures of Gargantua and Pantagruel.* The sweat used to run off my hands and forearms to my elbows and drop off to the floor. There was always a puddle under my elbows. I got through both books during the hot weather. I had picked them because they were good and thick and would last me a long time. I did not want to be lugging books back and forth on the streetcar from the library.

Cathey spent a lot of his time sitting next to the cold boilers in the factory, some of it with the game chickens and a little of it talking to me in the office. He never stayed long because it was too hot and after he saw the puddles under my chair he would urge me to come sit by the boilers with him but I thought that was the same as sitting down cellar and I had heard it would give you rheumatism. I got my name in the paper whenever I took part in a swimming race during the summer, and I think this made Cathey look more kindly on me. Anyhow, he became affable and, for him, talkative.

He had been a soldier in France during the war. I wanted to hear about his experiences. It went this way:

"Yeah, I shot a German."

"How?"

"Just shot him, that's all." And then he would stare at me again with his faint blue eyes.

Or he would answer, "Sure, I been to Paris."

"What was it like?"

"Well, it's bigger than Meffis, more spread out."

"Was it a beautiful place?"

"It was all right."

The only thing touching his war experience that he seemed willing to discuss at length was the crudity of the French. They were a barbarous, uncivilized people. He had been sent to a rest camp near some village behind the lines and he had been shocked by the privies. They were not like anything he had ever seen and they were much worse. "They ain't human, God damn it. They got these damn little old houses and they ain't nothin' in 'em but a couple of handles and . . ." He had been glad to leave France and get back to civilization.

Unlike many American soldiers, he had scorned the French women because you couldn't understand a damn word they said even when they were talking English. Yet he was a hot lover. He told me about affairs he had contrived in Mississippi with waitresses, farm girls, and married women. (He was married himself.) He was proud of the married women but I could not imagine how this ugly, scrawny little man could attract any woman because I believed you had to be handsome, vigorous, and rich for the job. I got one inkling, though. He was going on one day about a brakeman's wife in some river town. He said in a matter-of-fact tone that he had gone with her fifteen times in one night. Ordinarily I never questioned anything he said or made any comment on it but this was the kind of statistic that had been hashed over pretty thoroughly my senior year in high school and I said, "The hell you did."

As if I had pressed a button he began to shake all over and stride up and down the room, swearing in a high voice almost falsetto with rage. I just sat and shook my head.

At last he jerked off his fuzzy hat and threw it on the floor and kicked it.

"I *did*. I swear I did. I did it. *Yes*, sir," he shouted. It is the only time I ever saw him with his hat off. His forehead was a shiny greasy white and he was bald with wild uncombed strands of hair fluffed up from the sides of his head. He was uglier than ever yet his passion gave him a kind of dignity, at least you could take him seriously as a human being. He looked at me waiting for me to acknowledge him. He was not exactly angry, not at me anyhow. My doubts seemed to have tainted the memory of the night with the brakeman's wife. He was waiting for me to make it right again and the anger was the shock that his past could be tampered with.

At last I said, "O.K."

He picked up his hat without any embarrassment and went out and began to handle his game chickens.

Along about October the factory began to "run." I had very little to do with it. One morning I saw smoke coming out of one of the smaller chimneys. I went to the shop and found all the machines running, each operated by a colored woman. That afternoon Cathey led them all into the office to sign the payroll sheet.

"They git fourteen dollars a week," he said. He turned to the first one. "What's your name?" he bawled.

"Willie Sue Mawson," she said and tittered.

"Kin you write it?"

"Naw, suh," she said.

"Write down Willie Sue Mawson," he said to me. I wrote it down.

"Make your mark," he said and jerked her forward by the arm. She took the pencil and made a shaky cross after her name. There were about twenty women in all. Three or four could write their names and one printed it out in block letters. When they had all signed, they began to file out of the office. Cathey stood beside the door jocosely patting the young ones on the behind, and they cooed and giggled.

My easy days were over. I came to work at eight o'clock in the morning because there was a much larger mail every day, more bookkeeping, a constantly shifting inventory, and I had to dicker with the railroads for empty freight cars. If I got to the office a little early I would see the colored women drifting past my windows toward the shop. Few of them wore stockings although the mornings then were getting sharp. Most of them had broken men's shoes on their feet and one of them wore a man's staved-in hat. They walked beautifully, languidly, cackling and giggling in high shrill voices. I never did anything but just barely notice them and I never could tell them apart.

One morning I had to go out into the factory to get Cathey to check a shipment of strawboard with me. He was in the machine room overseeing the work of the women. I told him what I wanted and we went out to the siding and opened the freight car that had just been switched in. It was full of big yellow rolls of strawboard about four feet high. It didn't take us more than five minutes to count them. We shut the car again and Cathey returned to the machine room. I added up

my figures and started for the office. I was always in a hurry
those days and it was shorter to go through the old factory
past the huge gloomy power wheels and the bins of cottonseed hulls.

I came out of the building and was crossing the road to the
office when I noticed Cathey coming toward me. He was
walking slowly, all humped over, looking at the ground as he
usually did. He was too busy himself to come to the office unless he wanted something so I waited.

He took a match out of his mouth and spat. He looked up at
me and gave his weak yellow grin. "One of them nigger
wenches just killed another one out in the shop," he said.

"Killed her?" I suppose I said. "How?"

"Cut her." He sliced the air beside his throat with his forefinger.

I had already started walking toward the machine shop
very fast and Cathey had to hustle to keep up with me. He
resented it and took it out in the high complaining tone of his
voice. "We wasn't gone five minutes. God damn 'em."

I didn't say anything. I guess it was because I had to see the
body first.

Cathey said, "Ain't no need to hurry thisaway. She'll keep."

She lay on the floor beside a machine. There was a long
bloody gash in her neck and a big pool of blood on the floor.
Already the floating lint from the strawboard was settling on
its surface. Her eyes were open and her hands lay open by her
sides as if she expected to receive something. I don't think I
had ever seen her before in my life.

There was no one near her. The other women stood in a
group about ten feet away staring at the body. Cathey had
switched off the machines and the place was still. I could hear
a loud passionate whisper somewhere at the back of the group.

"I tole her. Didn't I tell her, Loreen? I swear I tole her a hun-
did times." It was evidently the voice of the woman who had
done the cutting.

Suddenly Cathey shouted, "Now, God damn it, all y'all git
back to work. And git her out of here." He threw the power
switch and the wheels began to turn and the belts started
flapping. The women drifted back to their machines.

I said loudly to Cathey, "What were they fighting about?"

He nodded his head toward the door and started for it. I
followed him. The day had turned out warm and bright with
a haze in front of the red gum trees across the bottoms. We
walked slowly up the bumpy cinder roadway toward the
office.

"What were they fighting about?"

"Hahda I know? They're always fightin' about somethin'."

"We ought to send for the sheriff, don't you think?"

He stopped dead and looked at me. "Sheriff?"

"To pick up the woman with the razor. It's murder."

He began to quiver, walking back and forth across the road,
cutting and slicing with his empty hands. "God damn it, don't
call no sheriff. They got enough to do. Come way out here?"
he shouted. It was hard for him to say what he meant because
he was so angry. "God damn it to hell, they're just niggers. The
law don't want iny part of a nigger killin'."

I said nothing. I was balked by the intensity of his anger
and by the stink of the cottonseed hulls and the dull red of the
gum trees. They had their own ways of doing things here and
maybe I had better not monkey with them.

"I been to ever' nigger shanty in North Meffis to git these
women. Now I gotta git one more. I don't wanta git two more.
You call the sheriff and he taken her to jail and I got to start
out again askin', askin' . . ." He stopped, and putting a hand

on a post, he jumped lightly over his chicken fence and caught one of his cocks. He began kissing it. He took its bill between his lips, cooing and clucking as he would to a child, and stroking its long black shining neck.

He turned to me with the bird in his arms, smiling. "You have to get 'em used to this. When they git hurt in a fight, you spit in their mouths. It'll put 'em right back on their feet sometimes. Why, I seen it when . . ." He went on telling about cockfights and how game birds should be handled. I stood there and I must have been listening to him because I didn't hear the car go by or if I did I thought it was our truck.

I saw the car when it came back, though. I don't know how they sent word for someone to bring it. No one had used the phone. Maybe some one of the women had run down the railroad tracks back of the factory. It was an old Model-T touring car with the top down. One of the wilted fenders flopped loosely up and down and the colored boy driving it kept slamming the front door that wouldn't shut and steering with one hand. Three women sat in the back seat. The one on the far side was old. I could see gray hair sticking out under her red head-rag. The near one was about sixteen. Her hair stuck out in stiff pigtails and I could see the neat pattern of parts on her skull like a map. The one in the middle wore a man's dirty felt hat and her throat was bound up with a piece of calico. Just as they passed me, the front wheels went over a small culvert and the head jerked to one side with a dreadful limpness. As the hind wheels struck the tile, it jerked back to the other side. I saw the old woman trying to straighten it up again and at last she put her hand up on the back of the seat and held the head erect so that it would not show when they passed down the street.

I did not think Cathey had noticed the car. He was still

talking to his game cock but when the car turned out our front gate into Thomas Street, he looked up and said slyly and cheerfully, "They'll be some sure-enough big doings now. They always have a brass band at them funerals."

# Jersey, Guernsey,
# Alderney, Sark

H E HAD spent twenty minutes in his uncle's outer office glancing over the titles of the lawbooks. He had picked one out and thumbed through it hoping to find some of the amusing legal phrases he had heard about, like the one calling a bull a "wild and mischievous beast," or the injunction against the bowling alley that complained of "the rolling of great balls by day and by night," but what he had chosen was a book on torts and it was dull.

The stenographer was busy typing but he thought she knew who he was because she looked up at him every time his head was turned. He could see her reflected in the windowpane. Maybe she was looking at the scar. It was still a purplish-blue.

"How much longer do you think he's going to be?" he asked.

"You can never tell with these clients," she said.

"I've got to get back to the office pretty soon," he said.

"Would you mind waiting a little longer? He wants to see you."

He could tell that the girl knew all about it. His uncle had dictated letters about whatever it was.

"What's he want to see me about?"

"I don't know," she said.

"Oh, come on now."

"I don't. Really I don't."

"I don't think you're telling the truth," he said, smiling.

The girl got huffy. "Mr. Lacey isn't in the habit of divulging his personal business to me."

"I just asked," he said mildly. "But I still think you know." He stood up to walk around again.

The girl suddenly cringed and looked very frightened. "Now, please, Mr. Lacey, I don't know. Honestly I don't."

"What the hell is this? I don't care whether you tell me or not. I'll find out in a minute anyhow."

"Now, Mr. Lacey, sit down. Please sit down," she said.

"All right," he said. He sat down again. "I'm sitting. Satisfied? What's the matter, am I a tiger or something?"

Just then his uncle came out, a man who could wear a pink shirt with dignity. "Hello, Charles. Come on in," he said pleasantly. And then in a lower voice which Charles was still able to catch, "If anyone calls, I'll be back in half an hour, Velma."

The client had evidently gone out the office door. The office was empty. His uncle closed the door carefully and the Venetian blind stopped clacking at the window.

"Well, how's the world using you, Charles? Sit down," he said. "I'm sorry I missed our little golf date the other day but then, you don't want to be bothered by an old duffer like me."

Charles sat down across the desk and made perfunctorily the appropriate answers. He recognized that his uncle's gabble was mere politeness, the usual businessman's approach to put the customer at ease by talking with enthusiasm about something as far removed from the subject as possible like Australia in the old joke or the warts on the moon.

His uncle, jaunty bachelor, was sitting back in his chair with his legs crossed spinning a paper knife on the ball of one finger and watching it spin. He looked up suddenly. "How are you feeling now, Charles?"

"Fine. Why?"

"No headaches since you got out?"

"No. No lights flashing. No ringing in the ears. No terrors in the night. I'm O.K."

"Hmm," he said. Then, jovially, "I understand you people are moving a lot of stuff out at the plant."

"Foreign orders," Charles said. His uncle was feeding it to him slowly.

"How do you handle them? Strictly cash, I suppose?"

"There was some talk of Italian credits but the dough has to be on the line here in the bank before we ship, and it's FOB the factory."

"That's very intelligent. Smart way to handle it. Working pretty hard? You, I mean?"

Should he try to flush the old boy out into the open now or

should he string along? Better wait, he thought. "Oh, I put in a couple of evenings a week."

With his face blank, thinking of something else, perhaps money, his uncle said, "Uh-huh. We're not going to have any depression." He took the paper knife and sprung it in a curve with both thumbs, and his face became grave and comprehensible. "Charles, I want to talk to you."

"Shoot."

"You were in this wreck . . ."

"Hell, I'm all right. I just told you. I don't have any headaches. I'm not overworking."

"You feel all right, eh?"

"It's been two months since I got out of the hospital. It's a good hospital. They wouldn't have let me out if they thought I was going to keel right over."

"I didn't know but what you . . . oh, maybe you were having some sort of hangover from the accident, headaches or something and perhaps you weren't saying anything about it to anyone. That was a terrible crack on the head, you know."

"Yes. I had a fracture. A honey," Charles said patiently. "But Carter's a good brain man, isn't he? He discharged me."

His uncle was looking out of the window. "It'd only be natural after all that time in the army . . ."

"What would only be natural?"

"Why, it was three years out of your life. You feel you're behind. You're anxious to do well. You may be just putting too much into it. Working too hard before you're ready to."

"Look, Uncle John, I'm all right, see? I'm not hiding anything. I'm doing just what they told me: I'm on the wagon. I don't eat anything but vitamins; I'm in bed by nine o'clock the nights I don't work. Hell, I don't even drive. I take the bus to work."

"I talked to Reilly yesterday. He thinks you're under a strain."

"Reilly's the one that's under a strain. He's out there every night until midnight. I see the light in his office when I'm going home."

"He's not the only one that thinks you're overdoing it. I've talked to a lot of people, Charles."

"Well, I could go to Carter and get checked over again and you could show the report around. To all these people."

His uncle missed the crack. He was looking at the paper knife in his hands. "No, I talked to Carter myself." He looked up. "I think maybe a little vacation would fix everything. Carter says it wouldn't be a bad idea."

Well, that was all right. He could take a month off and go to Nassau or the Bahamas or someplace and play a little golf.

"As I get it, you think I'm overworking. So does Reilly and this unknown host of friends. You've talked to Reilly and he's willing to give me a month off to rest up. Is that it?"

His uncle did not look at him. He got up and went to a water cooler that stood in a closet. He took a drink and came back to the desk. His face looked tired, as if it needed a hot towel and the daily massage, and after he had sat down, he bowed his head as if he were ashamed.

"You're a lot like your father, Charles. You get angry when people don't do things to suit you or explain things fast enough, just the way he did." He raised his head, his face young again, smiling the old radiant smile that for him expressed all he could still feel that did not cause him pain. "I always liked him. For brothers we were pretty good friends. A lot of people didn't, though. I guess it was his temper."

"I'm sorry. I didn't mean to get sore."

"That's all right," his uncle said. "You know the Spencer girl, don't you?"

"Caroline? I thought we were sending me away on a vacation. Yes, I know her."

"You took her out to dinner the other night, didn't you?"

Patience. Wait. He'll tell all. "Yes. Why?"

"I heard you had some trouble. With the waiter?"

"Oh, that. Yeah, I cussed him out. The food was cold and he was slower than the wrath of God."

"Caroline says you were violent."

"He got snotty and I just offered to pop him one, that's all," he said. It had been nothing. Caroline had a bosom and the waiter had stared at it. Then he had brought the asparagus ten minutes late and stone cold. His final impertinence had been to answer the complaint logically. He himself had lost his temper. He had almost forgotten it but what his uncle said made it seem ominous like the look on the stenographer's face. "Has this got anything to do with the vacation idea?"

His uncle made an indeterminate sound in his throat. "They said there was a nun came into your office the other day collecting money for China and you drove her out."

The young man blushed. "Shoo! Shoo! Getoutgetoutgetout!" he had said. Ever since he was twelve years old and the boys from Rathbun School at the first good-packing snow had marched up to St. Mary's School with a snowball hidden under each armpit, he had felt that way about nuns. They would run out of the school and stop the fighting, their habits swinging and flying like the wings of birds. They were not people; they were birds, and he had always shooed them away. Four or five times in his life he had done it, shouting, waving his arms and stamping his feet. It was one of those childhood compulsions whose indulgence will satisfy you all your life. But it is secret.

"So you think I'm crazy, huh?" he said in a tough, angry voice.

"Now, Charles . . ."

"Do you or don't you?"

"*I* don't think so, no. All I think's the matter with you is your temper. But there's been a certain amount of talk. Caroline's mother's upset . . ."

"And Reilly, huh?"

"Well . . . yes."

"The bastard. He's had in it for me ever since he took over when Dad died."

"Put yourself in my place, Charles. I'm just trying to do the best I can for you. Here you go and break yourself all up in an auto wreck and you lie unconscious for two weeks, and now you start doing things people think are strange. They may not actually *be* strange things but people think they are when you do them. They see that scar and they remember your accident and, well, you see how it is."

"Did Reilly put you up to this?"

"Nobody put me up to it. I talked it over with him, yes, and Doctor Carter, and you can't have Emma Spencer blabbing it all over town."

"Come on, Uncle John. Come clean. Did Reilly put you up to this?"

"Charles, for God's sake . . ."

"God damn it, I want to know."

His uncle's chin was down on his chest and the roll of flesh nearly hid the knot in his tie. "I have a letter here from the state psychiatric hospital. Your admission is all arranged for. They will give you a month's observation and if you are all right, they will give you a clean bill of health and let you go, and Reilly says your job will be waiting for you."

"And if I don't?"

"Your job is gone and with gossip at the normal rate of flow, you'll be crazy as far as this town is concerned." He had spoken slowly, looking Charles in the eye.

"Do you think I'm sane?"

"Of course I think you're sane."

"Tell me one more thing. This is just Reilly, isn't it? Isn't Reilly taking a little revenge on Dad through me?"

"Charles, I'm attorney for the plant and I'm sixty-four years old."

"You are also my father's brother. But I get it. You've said enough." The young man pursed his lips and looked out of the window. "I thought that girl of yours was acting funny while I waited. Seemed scared." He stood up. "O.K. Thanks, Uncle John. I'll come in and see you in the morning. I've got one or two things to finish up. . . ."

"The state hospital is expecting you this evening. You can get that five o'clock train."

"Oh, everybody's in a hurry, aren't they? I suppose Reilly's got a guy with a butterfly net right here in the closet. I can go alone, can't I? Or do I have to have an attendant to watch my reason totter? The brain that just missed Phi Bete, the brain that gets me up and feeds me and ties my tie and gets me to work . . ." He stopped. He was talking too much.

His uncle stood up and walked around the desk. He took Charles's hand in both of his. "I'm sorry, Charles. Awfully sorry. But there's nothing I can do."

Relaxed now but contemptuous, the young man said, "No, there is nothing you can do, is there?" As he turned away, he saw two lines appear between his uncle's brows and the smooth, pink, tended cheeks bulge up under the eye pouches. It was his other expression, the one of pain.

He reached the station half an hour before train time. He had misjudged the time and come too early because, after leaving his uncle's office, there had been nothing to do with the afternoon except to pack his clothes, which he had done with unusual neatness and care.

As he folded his shirts and even ran his fingers into the toes of his socks looking for holes he could not mend, he had been thinking of Reilly. The bastard. Reilly was with him almost as actually as if he had been sitting there, squat, black-haired with a large diamond in a claw setting on one fat hand.

He bought his ticket, and as he looked at the clock, he realized he was ahead of time. Abruptly he sat down on a bench in the waiting room. He was, he believed, still thinking of Reilly, but what he was really doing was looking at things, identifying and describing them to himself with as much precision as he could, as if his departure would be taking him away from all the simple things he had known. "That is a railroad waiting-room bench. It is oak. It is strong and many travelers have sat on it waiting for trains. There is a drinking fountain of white enamel, perpetual flow. It has been placed there to quench the thirst of people who come to the station." He looked carefully at the newsstand, named over the magazines, and painstakingly enumerated the tasks of the clerk. He examined the brilliantly colored travel posters that called him to California, New York, Bermuda (where he was not going on his vacation), Sante Fe, and other interesting places. A vague regret came over him that he had forgotten to describe and list the furniture of his apartment, the familiar chair, the convenient bookcase. Then it occurred to him—it alarmed him—that if he wished to retain it whole as he remembered it, he ought to examine the entire town and the country around it where he had grown up. But there was not time.

His alarm made him catch himself. He recognized that he had not been thinking of Reilly at all. He had been trying to fix the waiting room in his mind, and the waiting room or any of these things was not important. He had been silly and it annoyed him. As the train came in, he was buying cigarettes, a magazine, and a newspaper at the newsstand.

He went into the smoking car. He had no more than sat down and opened his newspaper when an old-fashioned commercial traveler sat down beside him. You could tell. He wore the UCT button in his lapel and a pencil was clipped in his outside breast pocket. He was not high-pressure but Charles knew that conversation would soon take place.

Nodding toward the newspaper, the traveling man said, "Looks like this Stalin wants the whole damn continent of Europe."

"It does at that."

"Yeah. Grabbing this, grabbing that. But he'll run into the U.S. Army one of these days. That'll put the kibosh on him. You going far?"

With the air of one who makes an absurd statement, Charles said, "I am on my way to the state psychiatric hospital to have my head examined."

"Go on. What do you mean, have your head examined?"

"There is a man who hated my father. Until his death, my father owned the tool-and-die company here, and this man, Reilly's his name, worked for him. When my father died, there was not as much money as we expected and Reilly took the factory over and I went to work there. Do you follow all this?"

"Yes. Sure."

"Not long ago I had a wreck with my car. I hit a freight train on a foggy night. I was in the hospital unconscious for a long time. You may notice the scar. Now Reilly says I act strangely and I had better go and get myself examined."

"How do you act strangely? What do you do?"

"I don't. Am I acting strangely now?"

"Hell, no. You look all right to me."

"He hated my father and he's taking it out on me. Anything to make me look bad. Revenge is the idea."

"It'll be a tough thing to live down, going to an asylum. Afterward, I mean."

"It's just revenge, you see."

"It's a hell of a thing to do."

"My father was actually a very nice guy."

"Oh, you'll be all right if you don't let it get to you, being shut up there with the nuts."

"Sure. I'll be all right."

"Excuse me a minute." The salesman got up and swayed down the aisle to the washroom. He did not come out right away. Charles wanted very much to have him come back and sit down. The salesman was a very important man. But he didn't. He stayed in there.

Charles looked out at the fields through the window and almost at once he began silently, "Those animals are sheep. They are cropping grass although sheep have no upper teeth. Man gets wool from the sheep." He broke off in disgust. It was like a child's encyclopedia.

The traveling man did not come out of the washroom.

"That is a cow, a Guernsey. The breed originated on the island of Guernsey, which is one of a group in the English Channel, Jersey, Guernsey, Alderney, and one that is always hard to remember. Sark. Jersey, Guernsey, Alderney, Sark. The cow gives milk. . . ." He burst into tears.

# The Conqueror

**T**HE YOUNG SOLDIER paused after he shut the glass door and then came timidly forward to the bar. It was early and there were only two men drinking. They were war workers; he could tell by the metal tags that held their photographs at their lapels. The bartender was down at the far end of the bar showing them his false teeth. It was an upper plate and the hand in which he held it was gloved fastidiously

with a dirty handkerchief as he pointed out the color, light-
ness, and delicacy of its structure. One of the workmen poked
him on the arm, nodding his head toward the soldier. The
barkeep thrust the teeth back into his mouth, drew up his lips
in an exaggerated smile to show the excellence of the fit, and
approached the soldier, stuffing the handkerchief into his hip
pocket.

"Beer or what?" he said.

"Beer," the soldier answered.

Sucking loudly at his teeth, the barkeep drew the beer and
set it up on the wood. He took the soldier's dime, rang it up,
and went back to the end of the bar again and began pushing
his plate upward with his thumbs. The soldier watched the
seething foam settle upward in his glass into a neat white
collar. Then he took up the glass with deliberation and drank
half the beer.

At one end of the room stood a black upright piano, shut,
and on it lay a piano accordion. The tables were all empty.
Lettered in white on the mirror behind the bar was BINGO!
*Thursday Eves, Elks Hall.* The soldier straightened his neck-
tie and lifted his chest as if he did not want people to come
into the bar and find him slouched and unkempt.

Behind the bar as setting for the mirrors was a series of
Ionic columns, richly carved in dark red wood. They supported a pediment which curved upward just over the cash
register into a broken baroque arch ornamented with a car-
touche. The wood held the reflections of the lights and seemed
to the soldier luxurious, satiny, and rare. Above the bar was
an oil painting in bright colors. It depicted a struggle between
a mounted Arab and a man on foot. The horse was white,
rearing and frightened, and his eyes bugged out like billiard
balls. (Foreign horses have big eyes maybe.) The Arab was

dressed in flowing bed sheets and he was swinging a curved sword. The man on foot was taking aim with a gun that had a thin, graceful stock. Although he had seen the picture before, he had always felt sullen and discontented after looking at it, and now he was a little surprised to discover that he could take a tactical interest in the fight. In the next instant of time the scimitar would miss its aim because the horse was reared too high and the barefooted man, if he was any shot at all, would get the Arab between the eyes. Also they had Arabs in North Africa. Norm Dudley had seen them in a town called Marrakech.

In a loud confident voice he called to the barkeep, "Hey, gimme another beer." He glanced around the barroom to see if any more people had come in. The tables were still empty and he wondered if there was a circus in town or a big fire. Maybe nobody would show up, nothing would happen at all; maybe he had gone through all this trouble for nothing. The war workers were joined by two more war workers. Later, after another beer or two, he would speak to them. He would call their hands. He felt seriously that he ought to assert himself tonight. Especially tonight. Yet, while it seemed to be almost a duty to remonstrate with the war workers, the striking bastards, it was not what he had planned to do, and as he drank his beer he began to take wooden matches from the box stuck on the ash tray and pinch them in two and make little designs with the pieces. It was a nice place to drink, all right. A man wants shining wood and a hand-painted picture on the wall. (Now that I am a man, a drinker.) But to prove these things takes more than a triangle, then a square, then a little row of broken matchsticks. He swept them over the bar into his hand and dumped them into the ash tray, and rapped the ash tray loudly on the bar two or three times.

The bartender looked around at him. "Beer?"

"Let me catch this, soldier."

He turned around. It was a girl beside him, an older girl, a woman, you could call her.

"Let me buy you a beer, huh?" As he stared at her, she continued earnestly, nervously, "Look, you're alone. I'm alone. Why don't we talk? You're a soldier fighting the war. I got money. Why can't I buy you a beer? All right? You don't think I'm fresh, huh?" She smiled brightly. "Two beers, Louie." She pushed a new bill folded across the bar.

"I ain't fought anybody yet."

"No, but you will." She took one of the beers, raised it, saying, "Here's luck!" and drank. "You going to drink that?"

"Why don't I buy my own beer?"

"This is government money, same as yours. I work up at Burns Stamping. We make end connectors for tanks."

"I know."

"You come from around here or are you a stranger? You never know with soldiers. I mean maybe I went to school with you but the uniform changes them. They look different in uniform."

"I'm a stranger here in town but I live out near Devil's Lake. I went to Addison High School." He decided it would not impress her to tell her he had played on the basketball team.

"Last year?" She looked at him sideways. "You've got pretty pink cheeks. What's your name?"

"Arch Brady."

"Well, now that we're acquainted, are you going to drink that beer or are you just going to let it stand there and evaporate?"

He took a drink of the beer, smiling at her over the rim of the glass. She was pretty but she was a lot older than he was, and he tried to guess how much older. This was one of the events he had planned to celebrate the evening, to find a girl, a new girl, different from Gladys, to find her in a strange place and pick her up instead of growing up with her and remembering all about her, a placid train of Halloween parties, picnics near the summer lakes, giggling in the school bus, shouting at basketball games. None of these things was dangerous and he was changed now and ready for danger, but he was wary of older women, and if this girl was thirty she would be too old. She would know too much for him and he could not be the boss. Yet he did not know how he could find out if she was thirty.

"Where you stationed?" she asked.

"I don't know. I just finished basic at Custer. When I go back I'll get sent somewhere else."

"Then this is your first trip home. What's it like? Fun?"

"It's shrunk." He grinned in embarrassment because he had spoken the truth.

"Shrunk, how do you mean?"

"Everything seems smaller, the house, the barn, the trees. They all look little."

"It always looks like that after you've been traveling," she said. She looked at him kindly. "You've been away from home before, haven't you?"

"Oh, sure. I went up to Mackinac with the senior class, high school, but everything was the same size when I got back then."

"Your girl the same size?"

"No. She's put on weight."

"It's just fat, I hope."

"And how! It's malted milks. Every afternoon she drinks a couple of them when she's waiting for the school bus to take

her home and it's making her skin all break out and she's getting a double chin. . . ."

"And you're just having a hell of a time, huh?"

"I told them. I told them tonight. That's why I got here so
early. They had me all lined up for another chicken dinner.
So when they said they were going over to Uncle Roy's and
eat chicken and then I was to have a date with Gladys again,
I just told 'em and walked out. I was valedictorian and last
night it was the twelfth-grade teachers and chicken fricassee
and Gladys, and the night before it was fried chicken at
Gladys's house and I couldn't get away. But I got away tonight. I told 'em I was going to do as I pleased and I walked
right out of the house and thumbed my way in here."

"Why, you just drink up that beer and we'll have some
more. You got one good time coming to you."

She had big dark eyes. She was good-looking, but telling
him to drink up his beer that way, her tone was an echo of his
mother's. His mother thought she could give him a good time
by feeding him white meat of chicken and making him stay
late in bed mornings, by urging him to do as he pleased and
then making dates for him until he had no time to do as he
pleased, like the dinner (chicken) at Uncle Roy's; the dinner
(chicken) at Gladys's; and complaining that his high-school
teachers missed him until he had to go visit them at the school
and get hooked into another chicken dinner. He did not want
women to run him any more; yet she was pretty, even if the
tone of her voice did remind him of his mother and without
looking, hardly, you could see the breastworks filling out her
sweater tight and after Lights Out in the PX the other guys
were always saying that all kinds of people would buy you
drinks on furlough and you were lucky if they were dames,
especially good-looking ones, and he had never looked up at

all during the last mile of the hike; he had watched the legs of the man in front of him and the sergeants and the officers had counted cadence all the way in "HUT, hoo, hree, hore, HUT, hoo, hree, hore."

"Hey, I'm here," she sang.

"I'm sorry. My feet are sore." He shook his head, blushing, as if he could shake away his error. "What I mean is, just before I came on furlough, they had a thirty-mile hike and all this other stuff happening, you say I got a good time coming, well, I guess I have."

Then he tried something. He winked.

He saw her face stiffen. "So we're all set, huh?" she sneered. "Well, I don't have to go forcing my attentions on anybody."

"No. No. Sure you don't. No," he said in panic.

"And if I come in here and see you sitting here all alone and I want to be patriotic, you needn't think I'm the kind of a girl that . . ."

"I don't. Honest, I don't. I didn't mean to look at you funny. I just did it. And I'd like to pay for my own beer." He stopped, perplexed. "Look, what's your name?"

In the center of an intense calm, she took out her compact, stretched her lower lip over her teeth, and touched it with the scarlet of her little finger. "Marie," she said and snapped the compact shut. She turned on her stool and looked at him. There was no life in her face.

"Look, Marie, I don't know how we got to fighting this way. It don't make any difference who pays for the beer. I don't want you to get sore. I . . ." He could not think of anything else to say except she was the first strange girl he had ever known and she was pretty. By talking to her (and maybe later something else) he was defying, he was leaving something, he was breaking some tie that had to be broken, and if he could go on talking (and later kissing her, maybe touching her) he could forget all the chicken dinners and Gladys's tears and the little barn and the farmhouse where he lived and instead he could look forward, cheerful and unburdened, to the Arabs and the battles. It would have embarrassed him too much to say any of this. He was nineteen years old.

Her face did not change but she reached over and patted his hand. "It's all right, Arch. Forget it."

He took a drink of his beer and offered her a cigarette. "Say, where do you live?" he asked eagerly.

"In a house."

"Aw, come on, Marie. With your folks?"

"What if I do?"

"Do they stay up late Saturday nights?"

"What difference does it make how late they stay up?"

"Oh, I'd just kind of like to see where you live."

"You think I'm cute, huh, Arch? Kind of pretty, huh?"

"Sure do." He gulped. "And I'd like to turn your bed down for you."

"I can do it. It's not hard to do." She inhaled the smoke of her cigarette, bowed her head, and let it drift slowly out of her mouth. "Aw, Christ, I hate to unload this stuff with a shovel."

"What? What did you say?"

She looked up and smiled at him frankly. "You want to turn that bed down, don't you, Arch? That's what all this giggling around is about, isn't it?" She patted his cheek. "Well, you can. Tonight. Just as soon as we've had a few beers we'll go." She inhaled again and looked absently a little way above his head and let the smoke out as she talked. "And it won't cost you a nickel," she said in a low voice. She looked at him. "That's the hard thing to say. That last."

He was blushing down to his collar. This was not what he had expected. He had wanted it to be more difficult, to talk her into it, break her down, make her give in, but now that she had failed him, he wanted to be nonchalant and accept it graciously. "Gosh, that's swell, Marie. But don't get the idea I thought you were . . ."

"Save it, Arch. I'm married, see? I've got a two-room apartment."

"But . . ."

"He's in the Southwest Pacific. Been gone two years. Catch on?"

"Oh." This was making him think very fast. "You don't have to do this for me, Marie. I don't want to cheat a guy that . . ."

"Do you have to talk so much, buster? Can't you just take it and keep still?"

"But he's a soldier and . . ."

"He's a Marine."

"That's what I say. I . . ."

"You want to back out, Arch? You afraid to step in behind a brother in arms, is that it? Don't be scared, Arch. It's my fault. It would be my fault if we had played cute all the evening and led up to it that way. This saves time and I don't have to be cute. You've got to let me look good just a little, Arch."

Sage, now the possessor, he nodded. He saw how it was. "You want to get out of here now, Marie?" he said with eager tingling deference.

She looked at him a minute, beginning to smile. "Not yet, Arch. Order some more beer."

Just as he was about to call the bartender, the bartender appeared in front of them and swung up two glasses of beer, dripping foam, and set them on the bar.

"You got two coming." He spoke to Marie. "Uncle Mart sent 'em to your boy friend."

"He did?" She turned around on her stool and searched the crowd behind her at the tables.

"Who's Uncle Mart?" Arch asked.

"Wait a minute. There, there by the hatrack, see? The old man?"

He saw a thin old man with white hair getting up slowly from the table. At last erect, the old man looked straight at him, smiling, and said something Arch could not hear above the noise and the music. Then he bowed from the waist and sat down again carefully. The bow was astonishing. Arch had never seen anyone bow like that except in the movies. He did not think ordinary people, people he might run into, ever did it.

"You know what he said?" Marie asked him. "He was saying, 'My compliments.' He says that every time. He buys a beer for every serviceman that comes in here."

Arch lifted his beer, nodded to the old man, and drank. The old man waved back at him.

"Who is he?"

"I don't know his last name but he comes in here every night. How old do you think he is?"

"I don't know."

"Well, look at him. Look at his hair, how it's combed, and he always wears a starched shirt and his pants are pressed and his shoes are shined. How old do you think he is? Go on. Make a guess."

"Oh, seventy. Seventy-five."

"He was a soldier in the Civil War. He's a hundred years old."

Arch whistled softly. He looked at the old man again and saw him delicately lifting a shell of beer to his lips. "He's the old guy I read about in the papers. He made a speech, didn't he?"

"He's been in the papers a lot. He's always making speeches. He led the Decoration Day parade on foot, through downtown here and then out to Monument Park and then way out to the cemetery. It was over two miles, the paper said, and he walked every step of the way. And when you get to be a hundred years old, that's something. You ought to talk to him. He's real cute."

The only old man, the only really old man Arch had ever seen before was Charlie Eccles. They said he was ninety-two. His daughter led him tottering up to the bench in front of the Red & White Store in the village every morning. There he sat as long as the sun was on him, holding the crook of an olivewood cane and his chin propped on his hands. Helpless tears trickled down his cheeks and he never answered the cheerful shouts of the passers-by. If the cane slipped out from under his chin he fell off the bench and everybody ran to set him up again like a dirty old rag doll. Charlie Eccles was old age, and Arch had never wanted any part of it until he saw this courtly old soldier. Now he felt as if he had been given a present. Uncle Mart had given him ten or fifteen good years, for although he was now a man, he was still young enough to believe that what any man could do he could do. He wanted to touch the old man for luck.

"Let's go over to his table," he said to Marie.

"All right," she said, setting her foot down at once off the rung of the stool.

Arch looked at her, suddenly fearing in her readiness some

change, a shift in her intention, as if she might forget what she had promised. "Sure you want to, Marie? I don't want you to go if you don't want to."

"It's early. There's the whole evening yet and he likes to meet servicemen."

"O.K. Let's go."

"Louie," she called. "Send us four wines. Over there, will you?" She took another bill out of her purse. Arch felt silly watching her do it but he did not try to stop her.

Walking sideways, Marie holding her purse high, they slid between the backs of people's chairs to the old man's table. Marie bent down, put one arm around the old man's neck, and kissed him on the cheek. "Hi, there, Uncle Mart."

"Why, hello there, little lady," he said. He got to his feet and took her hand. Bowing and still holding it, he seated her in an empty chair. "And this young gentleman? Sit down, sit down, sit down."

"Brady, sir. Archer Brady," he said, making sure he clasped the other's hand.

The old man laughed in a high windy cackle. "Don't *sir* me, boy. I wa'n't nothing but a sergeant. You don't *sir* them, you God-damn 'em, don't you?"

Everybody laughed. Arch pulled up a chair from the next table and sat down. Uncle Mart introduced him to his lady friend, a heavy woman about his mother's age with ruby rings on her fingers. She smiled imperturbably and said, "Hello, Marie."

The waitress came up with the wines slipslopping on a tray. She set them down one at a time. "What's this? What's this?" the old man said.

"We wanted to thank you for the beer, Uncle Mart."

Uncle Mart lifted one of the sticky wineglasses. "Ladies, I'd like to propose a toast . . ." As Arch sat there, a little beered up, slouched comfortable in his chair, entranced by the point of light shining red through the wine and the gleam of the old man's starched white shirt-cuff showing at the end of his sleeve, and mingled with the drifting smoke a trace of Marie's perfume, he decided that this was the way he would live from now on, throughout his hundred years, in luxury and the graces of behavior. When he noticed that the old man had turned to him and was speaking about him, he shook his head as if to clear it.

". . . to this young soldier, may he come through his war as safe as I did mine, not a scar nor a scratch, never wounded, never taken, sound as a dollar." Just as he said "dollar" the old man stooped and somehow nimbly started a silver dollar spinning on the table, and as they drank it clattered flat to a stop.

The old man braced himself in a chair in a formal attitude, erect, his thin chest out, turning the stem of the wineglass between a thumb and forefinger, and when he saw he had the attention of all of them he took a deep breath and began in a rich, rasping, orotund voice, "Yes sir, I took part in that furious struggle for the four whole years marching and counter-marching, eating hardtack one day and sucking pig the next, and one night I'd be singing songs around the campfire with a friend of my boyhood days and the next night, in the light of a split-pine torch, I'd be turning up the sod to bury him under. And now when I see the youth of our glorious Union going out to fight for freedom, I fear for you and I hope for you. My fears and hopes sit on your banners. Why, I was at the Bloody Angle and it was terrible, terrible. They was a log breastworks with us on one side, the Rebels on t'other, and we fit them light and pitch dark sixteen hours on end and they wasn't no place you could lay a hoe full length between us. The dead and dying lay all around and we heaved guns with bayonets on 'em over the parapet like spears. They was whole trees cut down by minnie balls and . . ." He twisted around in his chair and called in a loud everyday voice, "Ella, oh, you Ella there, bring some more wine."

He turned back to them and hunched himself over the table, his bright blue eyes narrowed by his slack lids, chafing his knobby old hands and peering sharply at them out of his bowed head. Arch saw the middle-aged woman wink at Marie but he could not protest without spoiling everything. Uncle Mart went on. "And my advice to a young man going into battle is this, and I've give it three times since it was give to me, three times, three wars, three generations. I say, my advice is this: Keep a clean-washed pair of socks in your hip pocket and conquer your fear. The fear is what they don't tell you about, the drill sergeants, the friends, and the relations. They send you out like a little lamb apurpose not to scare you with it, pretend it don't exist. But no man that's ever been shot at don't know what it feels like. The dead'll give it to you —eyes open, mouth gapping, looking surprised. Or you'll see your comrades stumbling to the rear with an arm swinging wrong or a foot shot off, or maybe the grapeshot or the canister have taken 'em in the eyes, and all you see left there is the bloody sockets, someone guiding 'em." Arch could tell that the old man was not advising him. He was remembering, proud that he had such a long tail of history and still was here to wag it. Yet Arch was uneasy and he hoped that Uncle Mart would go on talking about the Civil War and not specially to him.

". . . or maybe your first sight of the enemy acrost a corn-field, giving them screeches they always give, maybe they'll

make you feel it first. Then you can fight it and lick both it
and the enemy all to once. Then you're lucky because the
average man is scared beforehand and has to lick the fear
first and the enemy after, double duty and damned hard work.
You know already, don't you, boy? You've had it already when
it's like two hearts in your chest and you want to run, ain't
you? Oh, don't wiggle in your chair, sonny. I'm right, ain't I?"

Arch did not answer but he knew it was true. He recognized
now what had begun in memory. The hot dusty field with
only burdocks growing in it and runnels in the dust left by the
men of the company who had preceded them, and the line of
sumacs red at the edge of the field. The sergeant said, "All you
got to do is keep your tails down. You got twenty-four inches."
They had all got down and started across the field on their
bellies and he could hear the dreadful air split by the slugs
going over their heads. The machine guns were shooting live
ammunition. He had suffered then, prone, wriggling, dusty,
with two hearts pumping in his chest, and since that day it
had always been there, slight, a tingle, but ready to get worse.
It had not occurred to him to put a name to it because he was
not afraid. He was fearless as he was strong, honest, and some
day to be rich. But now he knew he had a fear to lick and he
could not tell whether to be angry or grateful to the old man
for dragging it out and showing it to him.

Uncle Mart had been telling about the surrender, both his
palms around a fresh glass of wine, his head high, and his eyes
gazing off into space. Arch picked up his glass of wine, drank
a sip, and began to listen again.

". . . the finest-looking man I ever saw, the flower of the
Confederacy." Uncle Mart could still roll out the words but
his voice had dropped and was no longer sonorous. "He stood
there on the porch of that fellow McLean's house looking out

over Virginia. Then he smacked his hands together and come
down the steps and called for his horse, beautiful white horse,
rode all through the campaigns. And he did something then.
Let me see." Uncle Mart paused and looked upward at the
ceiling. "Something about the bridle or the headstall. It wasn't
right. I dunno. Then he got on and rode away, Gen'l Lee on
his white horse. And how we hollered and cheered as soon as
he was gone. We was polite. I'm always polite." He stopped,
turning the wineglass around by its stem. "The war was over
and we could git to our homes, all the agony and suffering
done. And that poor lonely man, Gen'l Lee on his white horse,
and then come Gen'l Grant on his white horse and old Cump,
and Meade and Halleck and all the rest down Pennsylvany
Avenue." The old man stopped. He was crying and he
trembled a little. He was getting confused and he seemed to
know it.

He pressed his hands on the table and pushed himself upright slowly. Arch heard him mutter, "Give you the Address,"
and then more loudly as he stood up straight, "I say, I'll give
you the Address." He drank another glass of wine at a gulp
and wiped his mouth on his handkerchief with a graceful
flourish. A few people at nearby tables stopped talking to look
at him. He began in a high unsteady voice, "Fourscore and
seven years ago . . ." His voice broke upward and under
the light the tears shone on his cheeks. He cleared his throat.
"I say, 'Fourscore and seven years ago our fathers brought
forth on this continent a new nation, conceived in liberty
and dedicated to the proposition that all men are created
equal. . . .'" More people fell silent and began to listen. Arch
heard the other woman at the table whisper to Marie, "He
always renders this. Give him a few beers and away we go."

Arch, who was listening earnestly, turned away from the old man's face and said "Shh!" firmly.

"'. . . testing whether that nation or any nation so conceived and so dedicated . . .'"

Suddenly the accordion player began "Sweet Georgia Brown" loudly and briskly.

Arch scowled and called, "Shut up!" The music went on and the old man, glancing down the room toward the player, lifted his voice even higher. Arch shouted, "Hey, you, shut up!" The accordion player, busy with his own music, did not hear him. Arch jumped up.

Marie took him by the sleeve. "Hey, Arch, don't. He's blind. He can't see."

Arch jerked his arm free and, shoving his way through the tables, he said, "I don't give a damn if he is." And as he approached the accordion player he could see that the pupils of his eyes stuck out as if they had been blown out by an explosion or some terrible blow on the back of the head. They had hardly any color, a light grayish-bluish tint. His head was cocked on one side and his lightless face was smiling.

Arch grabbed him by the collar and hit him in the face.


It is a small town and the police station in the City Hall is a little room with walls of narrow varnished boards of yellow pine put in about 1890. A roll-top desk with swivel chair, a table littered with the Detroit and local papers, three or four kitchen chairs, and an old battered sofa along one wall are the only furniture. A big brass spittoon sits beside the roll-top desk and at night the only light comes from a single drop bulb with a white reflector.

The situation was one that required the opinion of the commissioner of public safety and the downtown night policeman was explaining it to him. On the couch lay Arch, the soldier, asleep with his cap over his eyes and a leg drawn up. Sitting at the table, Marie was making up her face with great care, taking as much time as she could.

". . . that old man, the Civil War veteran, Mart Carey," the policeman was saying.

"What was he doing?" asked the commissioner.

"Making a speech, she says." The policeman tipped his head sideways toward Marie.

"He was reciting Lincoln's Gettysburg Address. He always does that when he's had a little beer," Marie said. She did not look up. She rolled the scarlet-lacquered cartridge of her lipstick over and over in her hands.

"Was he drunk too? That old man?" the commissioner asked in a shocked voice. He was a man who would have liked to get back into his drug business but he ran for the office term after term because he was afraid of his wife, and now that the town was bigger than he had known it, swollen with war workers, hillbillies, Negroes, foreigners, he kept on as he had always done, trying to pass every little fist fight, drunkard, and adultery through his own hands, and the effort was a strain on him. He could not pace himself correctly—he was kind when he should have been rough, startled when he should have been bland. He knew it and it worried him.

"Nobody was drunk. I told you that. Uncle Mart always has a few beers or wines. Arch, he'd had some beer and wine too, but—"

"The soldier was drunk," the policeman said. "They don't have to be laid out unconscious before they're drunk. Louie said he'd been tossing back beer and wine all evening and he said you'd been paying for them."

"Maybe you better book her too, Dan," the commissioner said, staring at the table as if he was thinking of something else. "There's one thing sure," he began confidently.

"Book me? That's a fine thing. I come down here trying to help a soldier and you want to arrest me. What's the idea? Am I drunk or what?" Marie said angrily.

"There's too many of you babes buying soldiers drinks," the policeman said.

"Well, it don't break any law, does it? It's all right if we try to give them a good time, isn't it?"

"They's servicemen in here every week saying they been rolled by girls trying to give 'em a good time," the policeman said with his thumbs in his belt.

Marie turned the lipstick end over end in her hands on the table. "Don't you talk that way to me. I work up at Burns Stamping. I buy a bond every month. I got a husband in the Pacific. I . . ."

The policeman snorted and leered, "Oh, I catch. Lonesome, eh?"

"Well, what of it? I live in my own apartment." She turned her face to the commissioner. "Is he paid to talk that way?"

He ignored her question because he had made a small decision. The girl was an extra factor in what to him was a complicated problem and he had not known quite how to treat her but now he could tell that she was not one of the people he had grown up with in the town when it was smaller and simpler, and he spoke with authority. "It's immoral, that's what it is. And if you don't keep still I'll have you charged with—cohabitation and you can do your talking in court." Eased, he turned away from her. "Dan, get the Fort on the phone. We can't arrest this man. He's out of our jurisdiction. The M.P.s will have to take care of him."

The policeman lifted the receiver and waited for the night operator to answer. "You want me to lock him up till they get here?"

"Ask them," the commissioner said.

The policeman asked the operator for the number, and the station was quiet while the connection was being made. There was a row of maple trees outside the window and a gust of wind whined through them. The commissioner looked around at the soldier, lying on his back snoring, his tunic unbuttoned and his shirt torn in front.

"Look, Mr. Stevenson, couldn't he come up to my place? I mean instead of being locked up? I'll keep him. I won't let him leave. If the M.P.s say it's all right, let him stay with me," Marie said.

The policeman was talking to the Military Police at the Fort and the commissioner was listening. "No," he said to Marie.

The policeman said, "O.K.," for the last time and hung up the receiver. "They'll be down after him the first thing in the morning. Meanwhile, lock him up, they said."

The commissioner was relieved. He had been instructed what to do. "That covers it, Dan. I'm going home. Put him in the second cell. How early did they say?"

"They've got to drive it. It'll take them two hours anyway."

"I'll be down at eight-thirty." The commissioner took off his nose glasses and put them in a case. He buttoned up his topcoat and put on his hat. He said firmly to Marie, "Now if you'll take my advice, you'll go on home and quit hanging around beer joints buying servicemen beer. Get you into trouble."

"Yes, sir," she said. She stood up. "Mr. Stevenson, can't I say good-by to him? You're going to wake him right up, aren't you? I'd like to—you know, just say so long."

Puzzled again when he had thought it settled, the commissioner looked at the policeman. The policeman lifted one shoulder.

"All right. Good night, Dan." The commissioner went out.

"What's the matter, you got a yen for this guy?" the policeman asked.

"You've got me all figured out, haven't you, officer?" Marie said. "No, I think he's a nice kid."

"You're about the only one still awake in this town that does think so." He grabbed the soldier by the shoulder and shook him roughly. "Come on, bud, wake up, wake up."

Arch came out of sleep fighting. He seemed to be pulling himself off the couch by his head, swinging both arms. The policeman stepped back quickly and reached around at the back of his belt for his night stick. Finding no one in front of him, Arch stood still, blinking at the light and sniffing.

"Still soused," the policeman said. "Fine stuff, in a United States uniform."

"Oh, my husband wears one of them." Marie walked around the table and began to smooth Arch's tie and button up his tunic, and she spoke as if to herself, "Got yourself all messed up. There."

Arch opened his eyes wide and straightened up. "Hey, what is this?"

"You're in the police station, soldier. You socked a blind man and they were just going to beat you up when I got you out of there."

"I socked a blind man?" He looked quite sober as he said this.

"What did you do it for, Arch?" Marie said reproachfully. "Honest, that was an awful thing to do."

Slowly, with an expression of bold country shrewdness on his face, he bent one knee and swung his buttock around so they could see it and pulled his hip pocket carefully inside out. When it was all pulled out he flapped it up and down, grinning. "No socks, see?" He looked suddenly fierce and shouted hoarsely, "But I licked him, see? I oughta had clean socks but I licked him just the same. All you gotta do is tear right in and rush 'em off their feet. That's what the coach says and you'll *lick* 'em."

With a swoop he dodged past Marie and picked up a glass ashtray and balanced it on his shoulder. He faced the policeman, hitching his shoulder upward as he talked. "Go on. Knock it off. Knock it off. Knock it off."

The policeman seized him by the shoulder and one arm, swinging him around to the door that led to the two cells. The ash tray broke on the floor.

"Copper!" Marie shouted.

The policeman stopped, affronted, turning, approaching her with Arch still struggling.

Marie, watching only Arch's white set face as he pulled and tugged, said, "Wait a minute."

"Listen, you, he's drunk. . . ."

"Wait a minute. Arch, don't you know me?" she asked.

Arch immediately stood still, smiling brightly. "Sure. You're Marie. You're my girl. Let's go, Marie."

Marie stepped back a little and slapped his face twice and the second time a little rill of blood ran out of the corner of his mouth. He stared at Marie, astonished, and began licking the inside of his cheek with his tongue.

"Jesus, I thought you said he was a nice kid," the policeman said.

"He is a nice kid," Marie said. "My husband was a nice guy too when he went away and he's been away a long time and I want to know what he's going to be like when he gets back. You sober now, Arch?" she said kindly.

"What did you want to slap me like that for?" Arch said sullenly.

"Let him sit down, officer," Marie said. The officer released him and he sank down heavily on the couch. Marie sat down beside him and twisted her body so that she faced him.

"Arch. You know you hit that blind man."

He nodded his head and sucked the blood into his mouth.

"Well, what did you do it for?"

"I don't know, Marie."

"I told you he was blind. Before you left the table I said he was blind."

"I was mad, I guess."

"Do they teach you to get mad that way?"

He looked up at her. "Teach me?" He dropped his head again and spat some blood out on the floor and rubbed it slowly around with his foot. The policeman shoved the spittoon near him.

Marie put her arm around him and took his face in her other hand, lifting it until she could see his eyes. "Now, Arch," she said in a tender, wheedling voice. "Tell me why you hit him. That was a terrible thing to do."

The soldier tore himself away from her and stood up. "Lemme alone, will you?"

She rose too and stood in front of him. "Oh, now, Arch," she began, coaxing and patting his hair.

"God damn it, quit bossing me all the time," he shouted furiously. He swayed there uncertainly a moment looking around the room, seeing how strange it was to him. All at once it came to him that the Arab horses had all run away where he would never find them; that all he had done was to hit a blind man; that he was still a boy and still afraid.

# No Son, No Gun,
# No Streetcar

**H**E BEGAN to be afraid before he even left the telephone. The first thing Mr. Caldwell had said was, "William, would you like to go to the opera tonight?" and in the little time before the next words were spoken, he had been pleased, not that he knew anything about opera—he had never seen one—or that he liked music very much unless what the Mound City Blue Blowers played was music. His pleasure sprang from a sudden vision of next Sunday's "open house" where, since it was vacation, college football players would be lounging (and he could watch how they moved and listen avidly to their talk) and all the pretty girls would be home from school up North, and he could mention his visit to the opera with a proper negligence and ease. But the pleasure and the foretaste of his admirable nonchalance vanished with the next words Mr. Caldwell said: "I have two tickets for tonight. It's *Aïda*."

The fear began when he grasped that Mr. Caldwell said that he had *two* tickets. His forehead prickled and the bones of his knees seemed to melt. If Mr. Caldwell had only two tickets, it meant that only they two were going to the opera. Mr. Caldwell wanted to see him, talk to him alone, and because Mr. Caldwell was a gentleman, this was the way he would pick to tell him everything had been discovered.

"Would you like to come, William?"

"Yes. Yes, sir. I sure would," he said wretchedly, unable to summon a refusal, even sure that he could not honorably refuse after what he had done.

"I'll pick you up about a quarter past eight."

"Yes, sir. Thank you, sir."

He hung up the receiver and walked away. His tennis racket, which had been leaning against the calf of his leg, fell flat on the floor. He did not even look at it. He went into the living room and stood for a minute looking around as if he had never seen it before. He sat down precisely on the edge of an armchair and began to bounce the tennis ball he had been holding in his hand all the while he had been talking on the phone. How had Mr. Caldwell found out?

*She* wouldn't have told. She wouldn't breathe a word because she loved him. She had given herself to him. She had said it in so many words, raising herself out of his embrace, her hair shining in the hot moonlight. "All right. I'll give myself to you." It had been like a play, almost suffocatingly dramatic. And she had, sure enough, right there in the swing where they had spent so many summer evenings talking, murmuring, kissing and drinking, spiked with his gin, the lemonade the maid brought out. And when it was over and the quiet that followed it was over, she had walked up and down nervously before him on the grass asking if he believed her *now*, if there were anything he dared accuse her of *now*, did he think she loved Seton Taylor or Battle McDonough if she would do this for *him?* All in a high tense whisper. And he, stunned by a pride he could not help mistake for love, had meekly agreed until he remembered he was a man now, had seized her and pulled her back to the swing. Because he was eighteen and did not guess that she at seventeen knew much more than he did, he accepted what seemed to be the marvelous truth that they were in love, and for the first time in a year of doubts he was sure that the Betas would take him next fall and he would make the freshman football team. Remembering this evening of his initiation, he was certain she would not have betrayed him to her father. She loved him far too much. She had proved it.

But Mr. Caldwell had found out. How?

At the violence of his next guess, his stomach fluttered and got hot and he let the tennis ball bounce by itself until it dribbled away under the sofa. Perhaps she was going to have a baby and in that fear and desperation she had told her family. At once the campus of the university, its colonnades, the rotunda, and the serpentine brick walls crumbled and vanished from the place in his mind where they had been fixed ever since he was fourteen. He foresaw himself sweating over a

long table in an office above the Front Street levee, picking up
little wisps of cotton from the table and testing the length of
its fiber between his fingers, his seersuckers covered with lint,
working for a cotton broker for so much a week if a cotton
broker would have him, never learning how to drink corn licker
out of a Mason jar, never going to the Easter dances, never
dodging and butting his way for any touchdowns at all, rather
going home to a little apartment where there was not even a
servant but only *she* and his squalling son. He surmised that
this must have been what happened and, as sick and angry as
he felt, a twinge of useless pity for her crossed his mind chased
by his fear.

He could run away. He almost started from his chair at the
thought of Brazil or Australia and how he would start for them
before sundown, before the opera. He relaxed miserably. It
would be wrong, and besides, he had—he laid it out on his
palm—only three dollars and twenty-seven cents.

He lunged forward out of his chair and walked tiptoe
through the house so as not to wake his mother, who was taking her nap. He could not possibly have explained to her why
he had not gone to play tennis. From the kitchen he stepped
into a narrow pantry where on the top shelf stood a dozen
bottles of whisky, vermouth, and gin, his father's cellar, still
forbidden him.

He took down a half-full bottle of bourbon. He lit a cigarette and laid it carefully on the edge of a shelf, ready to hand.
He poured out half a water-glassful of the bourbon, looked at
it, swishing it round in his glass, and, taking a deep breath,
drank. Holding his breath, he stuck the cigarette in his mouth
and drew on it. Then he let the breath, the smoke, and the
burn of the whisky all out together. As if his little theft had
made a noise like thunder in the house, he raised his head and

listened—there was no sound. He waited a few minutes until
the saliva stopped springing in his mouth and drank the rest of
the whisky in the glass with the same ritual. He went into the
kitchen, drew half a glassful of water from the tap and poured
it into the bottle. It was as full as before. He set it back in the
same place on the top shelf, opened a can of coffee, took out a
small handful, and munching it for his breath, he returned to
the chair in the living room, feeling better. At least he had
done something to help himself, something a man might do
who was in trouble.

In the way anyone can turn his attention to his heartbeat,
hear it and count it because it is there all the time, he began
to think of what he knew he would have to do, what he had
known all along he had to do, frame his reply when Mr. Caldwell accused him. His own great-grandfather had had a troop
in Forrest's cavalry but he knew because *she* had told him that
Mr. Caldwell's grandfather had commanded a regiment in the
Army of Northern Virginia and had twice sat down to dinner
with General Lee at houses in Fauquier County. These facts
were not part of a dim traditional background. They were
touchstones burning in his mind as if he and Mr. Caldwell
bore like scars on their foreheads the devices of their fore-
bears' military rank. Undoubtedly Mr. Caldwell was his superior—that was why he was doing it all so casually, making a
social occasion out of it, taking him to the opera, in fact. It was
a crushing disadvantage to be forced to oppose a man who
kept the ghost of Lee behind him but he knew by all the im-
peratives of his upbringing that his answer had to match Mr.
Caldwell's question in ease and courtesy, no matter how he
suffered while he made it.

Suddenly he wanted to run away more than ever, not to any
formal goal like Australia or Brazil: just out of town. There

was a streetcar line three blocks from his house. He could take
it as far as it went, then walk. He could find something to do
whenever he got far enough away. "My name is John—John
Carter." Or, with a tightening in his throat, he wished that his
father would come home and say heartily, "It's all right, son.
I've talked to Caldwell," and magically, as it had been long ago
in his childhood, it would be all right. But if he was young
enough to hope for these escapes, he was old enough to know
bitterly that they were impossible. He would have to go to the
opera with Mr. Caldwell.

At eight o'clock he was sitting in a wicker chair on his front
porch, upright, a hand on each knee, a strained and unfamiliar
posture, staring straight ahead of him. He was wearing a fresh
white linen suit and a straw sailor hat with a band in his prep-
school colors lay unregarded between his knees. At dinner-
time his mother had insisted on giving him an aspirin because
he looked sick. He still looked sick and the sweat ran down his
face in two steady rills just in front of his ears. The fear that
he would be unable to make a proper answer to Mr. Caldwell
had made him unable to form one at all. He was not thinking of
*her*—she was merely bait that had lured him prematurely into
a trap he had hardly been aware of although he had friends
who had been caught in the same one and he had laughed at
them then, but he, he had not been ready, not amply warned,
and it was unfair somehow.

The opera was a summer civic project put on by local music-
lovers. The singers wore rented, what William took to be me-
dieval, costumes. Warily he followed the plot closely enough
to be able to say something in reply to Mr. Caldwell's com-
ments when they walked in the steaming crowd in the lobby
between the acts, smoking and buying cold drinks of lemonade, but the music seemed less loud than the pulse in his ears

and the antics of the singers in the field of distant light were like dolls! If people were going to sing, he thought, why didn't they stand still and sing? If they wanted to act, why didn't they act and say what they had to say, not sing it? But his attention was only a film on the surface of his fear and anxiety. He still did not know how he was going to answer Mr. Caldwell.

It was not until the fourth act that he began to think about the .45 revolver that his father had brought in from the farm out near Somerville several years before. It lay in the top drawer of Father's bureau where it would be handy if there were prowlers at night. Twice he had been allowed to shoot it, his father handing him a bullet each time, because men did not need hand-guns in this part of the country any more and instruction in their feel and use was a paternal foible of his father's, who wanted him to know it but knew he would not need to in the way he had to know how to handle a twelve-gauge shotgun on quail. But he did not think of his own twelve-gauge standing in its case in the corner of his closet because it was for his present purpose too messy. It was rather the muzzle of the .45, the ring of bluish steel surrounding the dark nothing, the symbol of what came out when you pulled the trigger. He did not suppose it would hurt much and you could pull the trigger with your thumb. He did not plan on leaving any note of explanation, and he kept pushing away the suspicion that kept obtruding—that it was cowardly—because it was complete. People knew he was in love with her; people would know he was dead. Eventually, later, his love might become the cause of his death, and they might call him a fool but they also would acknowledge him a gentleman. Right through the forehead.

There was a roar of applause. The singers were taking their

bows and the audience was standing up to go. Mr. Caldwell was standing up to go. There was no reason to speak in the crowd leaving the auditorium but he knew the crisis was approaching and he had decided nothing. The streetcar, yellow and lumbering; the heat-sodden little apartment; and the .45 all whirled in his head like a dreadful pinwheel. They got into Mr. Caldwell's car. They drove for several blocks in silence and it was clear that Mr. Caldwell was getting ready to say something and looking for a place to say it. William's head ached and his mouth was dry. There was nothing that would save him now but luck and he had never passed three times in a crap game in his life.

Mr. Caldwell turned his car into a dark street full of homes with trees overhanging from both sides. As he had expected, Mr. Caldwell slowed down and stopped. The street light at the end of the block seemed far away and all the people who lived on the street had gone to bed. There was only the light on the dashboard and the occasional glare from a passing car. Mr. Caldwell said, "Cigarette, William?"

"Thank you, sir." He took one and lit it from the other's match.

"I've been wanting to talk to you for some time," Mr. Caldwell said.

"Yes, sir," he said. He cleared his throat.

"You've been seeing quite a lot of Emily."

"Yes, sir. I been seeing her."

"She's a pretty girl."

"She's beautiful." At least he could match him there and he thought it was true.

"I don't know what your plans are . . ." Mr. Caldwell let it fade away. In the light from the dash William could see him staring at the end of the cigarette in his hand.

He could not speak. There was nothing to say because he didn't know what his plans were, either.

Mr. Caldwell flicked the ash away. He seemed to be considering the best way to put it, consistent with his honor and the feelings of his opponent. He was about thirty-eight years old, well into middle age, and growing bald. He looked up straight ahead of him and began, "William, I married a beautiful woman."

"Yes, sir," he said, trying to give it sincerity. He could see that Mrs. Caldwell had been, once, long ago.

"I don't know whether you know the Delta. Your people come from Fayette County here in Tennessee. The Delta's a strange place, a wild, violent place, and Mrs. Caldwell was from down there, Greenville. She was very lovely. I saw her at all the dances. I still don't know how come she picked me when there were so many to pick from." Mr. Caldwell turned his head and looked at William. "There certainly was a lot to pick from. But I married her at nineteen. She was seventeen."

Mr. Caldwell stopped and William said, "Yes, sir."

"After our marriage it was necessary I go to work. I had gone to Virginia just one year, you understand, and then I had to go to work."

"Yes, sir."

"Don't do it, William."

"Don't do what, sir?"

"Don't get married now. I know you're in love with my daughter but don't marry her. Don't even try to marry her."

It was like being tipped up on a seesaw when you were a little kid, the rush of confidence. "Yes, sir?" he said.

Mr. Caldwell seemed to be scrunched down in the seat. He spoke in a cold precise voice. "Because I am now the treasurer of a wholesale grocery company. I have a fine home, a wife, and a beautiful daughter and listen, William, listen to me, boy, I would swap them all, bury them under the ground, tip 'em all into the river, if I could be an architect. That's what I wanted to be, an architect."

"Yes, sir."

"That's a terrible thing to say. I know it. It is the one last final way a man can be unfaithful, the way a woman never understands. Don't get married now. Go be an architect first. Then marry."

"Yes, sir. Thank *you*, sir. I won't ever say anything about this."

Mr. Caldwell turned and stared at him, gave a short barking laugh, flipped the key, started the car, and drove William home.

# The Unicorn

H E had begun to talk. First she had served tea and anchovy toast and he had lain silently in the armchair staring into the fire with the flames glinting off his beautiful shoes. When he had finished his tea, she had brought out the decanter and a siphon as usual. He had made himself three big warm drinks one after the other and his

face had brightened. He had noticed her. He began to talk.
It was a kind of reminiscent chant done more or less for her
pleasure but he never took his eyes off the fire.

". . . and a battle quietens down eventually, you know. I
had a bathe and a feed and one evening I went out to walk
about a little. Quite cool there after the sun goes down. I
came to the officer's cage . . ."

"Cage?" she asked.

"Misnomer. It's not a cage at all, really; barbed-wire pen
for the prisoners. They were a sad lot. Damned poor show for
them, peeping through the wire. Not peeping curiously,
though, at us or anyone, not they. They were seeing vistas,
*Deutschland*, home, and glory, that sort of thing. Stared right
through me into Germany. I had just about seen enough when
someone called out 'Antony!' and there stood old Gussy surrounded by what was left of his staff."

"Gussy?" she said punctually.

"Gussy von Stolp. Colonel-General Baron Gustav von
Stolp," he said in German. "Their commander."

"You knew him?" It made her seem stupid to ask but even
now he was incredible.

"Oh, rather. He was at Sandhurst when I was and once
upon a time he and I were at a cram school together at
Westgate-on-Sea. Had a wen or pimple on his foot. Got it
infected somehow and he spent a fortnight in some awful
nursing home—nothing to do; the doctors suspicious of the
Teuton; the sisters all plain-faced and surly. And the food,
one's gorge simply soars at the food in a nursing home. He
wrote me plaintive little post-cards, whimpering little post-
cards about the food. He was discharged at last, foot perfectly
O.K., and we went out for some golf. He felt something
softish in the bottom of his golf bag, reached in and came

out with a boiled lobster. 'Good God, Gussy, what a revolting thing to carry about with you,' I said. He cracked the shell on a rock and sat down to eat it. 'How old is that dreadful creature?' I asked. 'I cannot tell you. I haf him only since four days,' he said. 'I bought him when I leave the nursing home and I forgot him until now. All the time I am lying in bed I am dreaming about lobsters. Now I eat.' And he ate up every bit." He stopped. It was one of his little courtesies to stop before the climax of a story so that she might ask a question.

She had learned to be equally courteous and never to ask the question he expected. "Why had he put it in his golf bag?"

"It was wrapped in paper."

"But . . ."

"Gussy was already a German officer on leave from his command." He paused. "Officers are not seen carrying parcels."

"Oh," she said. "What did you say to the Baron when you saw him behind the wire?" There had never been a baron in this house or within fifty miles of it. It gave her a pleasure she recognized as faintly snobbish to ask the question as if the ghosts of her mother and grandmother were behind the plum-colored window drapes to hear.

"Say? Oh, 'How are you? How've you been?' What does one say to a friend?"

"But wasn't he a Nazi?"

"Gussy?" He barked once contemptuously. "He was a Pomeranian," he said as if that explained everything.

"I'm sorry. They're just fluffy little dogs to me."

"Really, Ellen, you don't know the very simplest things, do you? Pomerania is Prussia, don't you see?" He turned now to look at her, his face motionless, but the very fact that he had made the effort, had turned his head, expressing his mute fury, not at her, not at this strange country, rather at his own stupidity for allowing himself to be drawn into situations where he had to expound the things one took for granted as naturally as earth or sky. When he saw that she didn't see, he said, "Oh, damn it, Ellen. They were an old family. Knights. Soldiers. Served the country, the land. You follow me?" He sighed, swallowed half a drink and spoke with a gentle condescension. "The von Stolps lived in an actual castle, full of towers and steeples, moat with a draw-bridge, a great moldy old pile. I saw it once. As a matter of fact, the family of their *Jäger*, the chief huntsman, had served them for four hundred years. Any government, Hitler's or Friedrich der Grosse's, simply doesn't matter. A government is only temporary." He looked back into the fire. He was not particularly anxious that she understand; he was merely will-ing to explain.

She was charmed and irritated by this elegant figure lying almost on the back of its neck in her chair by her hearth. It was as if she alone on this Middle-Western plain had snared some strange heraldic beast like a unicorn. From him she had learned that there was more to conversation with a man than the feints and sleights preliminary to an attack. Since he was a man, he began always with himself but, encouraging her with the foreign inflections of his voice and the beckon-ings of his long, bony, graceful hands, he led her unwittingly into an empire she had hurried over as a tourist or glanced at in forgotten history books and there pointed out hundreds of fascinating things she had never heard of.

He dressed well, too. She had seen English clothes before but she had never studied them. When he saw her a little surprised at the handkerchief up his sleeve, he remarked coldly that officers kept it there. He wore a black homburg cocked on the side of his head in a town where no one wore such a hat and an old dark blue Guards overcoat with long leather-lined pockets, "for carrying whisky in," he said. It pleased her to see how conspicuous he looked among the solid lawyers, bankers, and factory owners the rare times he took her out.

Although she had noticed it briefly in other Englishmen, his confident rudeness annoyed her. No one had ever treated her like that before and she was shrewd enough to know why: she was too rich, and, although the decision before the mirror took a shade longer now that she was thirty-six, she was at the very least too handsome, perhaps too beautiful. In the right light, certainly too beautiful. He had been dropping in two or three times a week for months and she had just begun to comprehend, startled, a little dejected, that he was indifferent to her in the flesh and to her money; at least he treated it casually enough. She was beginning to be nervous about him because she did not know what he wanted.

". . . hell's own time finding one. No fishing much then because of the bombardment. I had half the Wogs in Bizerte looking for one."

"One what?"

He sighed and drank again. "A lobster."

"Oh."

"But at last I got a beauty. Broiled it. Wangled butter. Sent my batman down to the cage in a jeep with it on a covered tray. 'Major Braithwaite's compliments to General Baron von Stolp.' Absolutely wizard show. God, how I laughed."

"Did he like it?"

"Did he not! Sent a note back."

"What became of him?"

"I haven't the vaguest," he said coldly. "Dead, very likely."

She was shocked by his callousness and was about to tell him so when she heard the maid's heels in the hall. "Dinner is served," the maid said.

"You'll stay, won't you, Tony?"

"Yes, thanks," he said, boosting himself erect out of the chair.

She was alert. She had learned not only the composition of an English menu from his stories but also its peculiar *mystique*. They began with a clear soup and a glass of sherry. This was followed by what passed for fillet of sole at the local fish market. Then she had ordered a joint of beef with the blood running out of it, some riced potatoes, and a dismal little dish of Brussels sprouts. Bread lay on the table but no butter. For a sweet, they had a "trifle." She had superintended the making of it herself. It was a cake soaked in Jamaica rum and as frosting it had a layer of whipped cream ornamented with bits of colored sugar. (She had sent all the way to New York for the sugar.) She thought it loathsome to taste but he ate it up, every bit, as Gussy ate the lobster, and said to her quite warmly as he finished, "English food," which she knew she was to take as a compliment.

They returned to the living room for port and coffee. He began a tale of rock-climbing in Wales when he had watched George Mallory ascend an overhanging cliff face without a rope, without *pitons*, with his bare hands.

"I was below on a ledge. The climb was impossible. The law of gravity forbade it."

"Did he fall?"

"No bloody fear. Went up like a cat. I had known George

all my life but in places where the ground was flat. Never understood why people talked him up so. I did then, though. Understood it very well, indeed."

"Was he famous?"

"George? Oh," he let his voice fall as an acknowledgment that she did not know who he was at all. "He died on Mt. Everest in the 1934 expedition. Got to within a hundred feet of the top when a flurry of snow blotted him out. Never saw him again. May have made it, at that, though."

Her impatience, curiosity, anger at last burst out. "Tony, why don't you ever talk about yourself?" she said. By which she partly meant, "Why don't you ever talk about me?" but not entirely. She wanted to be better friends with him, to pierce his reserve somehow, and men had usually begun by talking about themselves or about her but never about third parties however courageous.

"Why? Because here I am. One talks about what is past, what is elsewhere. Bloody embarrassing to talk about one's self when here, in fact, one veritably is." Then his invariable courtesy showed itself. "But I'm boring you."

"Oh, no, you're not but I sometimes wonder why you bother to come to see me." It was true he never bored her. He was handsome in a conventional English way—she had seen men who resembled him at Cannes and Miami—but he suppressed some force or emotion, rage or disgust perhaps, that gave his talk its scintillating energy and let it out only in his sudden glances or the abrupt and graceful gestures of his long brown hands.

"Must all the men who come to see you talk about themselves? Do you exact it as a tribute?"

"*All* the men," she thought wryly. "They usually do," she said.

"Surely you ought to know why I come to see you. Can't you suspect?"

"Why do you?"

For just a second his face seemed to open, almost smiling, as if he were about to say something pleasant and sincere. Then, with hardly any change of plane or feature, it closed. He said, "Because you are a very lovely woman, as you well know. Because this is the one place I can get a proper English meal. And because you give me money."

He startled her. He had told the obvious truth, and the candor that should have lacerated him only made his statements seem dull and final.

"Have you ever thought of going back to England?" She did not know whether she "loved" him or not. She wanted to force him into a kind of emotional allegiance to her that she could recognize, and, in her exasperation, she was using the gambits of a schoolgirl: she wanted to trap him into saying, in a trembling voice, if possible, "I can't go back because I can't leave you."

What he did say was, "We're not fighting anyone now."

"Have some more port," she said in a fury.

"No, thanks."

"Can't you stay the evening?" He had never stayed the evening.

"I'm sorry. Playing poker with some chaps. Can you give me a hundred dollars?"

As she had planned the dinner, she had foreseen his question. Before he had arrived, she had gone to the kitchen when the cook was laying out the coffee tray and laid a hundred-dollar bill under the sugar bowl. Calmly, watching his face for the least twitching of shame, she lifted the bowl and handed him the money. "Will this be enough, Tony?"

He was absolutely impregnable. "Oh, quite. Thanks awfully, Ellen. Marvelous dinner." He did not pause. "Good night."

"Good night, Tony."

She heard him let himself out. She took a big gulp of port. She set the glass down and said aloud, "Now how many kinds of a damned fool am I?"

She took pride in recognizing, because no one else in the town could recognize, Tony as an almost flawless specimen of a type she had met in her interminable reading and a few times in her travels, the Englishmen of good family who had gone bad somehow. Like Tony, they wore their clothes well. They were or had been handsome in a lean way. They had mustaches. They said rude things, especially about America, with a smile. Some, like Tony, had been officers in good regiments or said they had. And for various shady reasons at which they were willing to hint portentously but never to explain, they were living very well but they were not working. Tony was unique in one respect: he never hinted at anything.

Someone had told her of his first appearance in the town. Apparently by instinct he had gone to the bar of the Shawnee Club. She wondered at the aplomb that could support a man before a bartender when, as a stranger, he was not permitted to buy drinks, yet Tony had not budged and when the bartender said, "Something?" he had answered, "I'm waiting for a friend." At that moment he knew no one in the whole town, but when the bar filled up a little, a combination of brass and charm led him into acquaintanceship and ultimately into a poker game. He had won twelve dollars.

Perhaps she could have left Tony in the pigeonhole if he

had been a good gambler, if he had shown the deftness of long practice, but she had seen him with cards. He could deal without turning them wrong side up but that was about all. And, although he played poker constantly, the word had come to her that he lost as often as he won. It seemed to be a pastime, not a living.

He did not employ another resource of the floating Englishman, opening a riding school. Not many people were wealthy enough to ride. Show riding contended with Western riding for their money. The local horse show, given late in the summer at the county fair grounds, turned out half a dozen in hard hats on English saddles and about as many on Palominos jingling with silver. Watching them from her box, Tony had thought them a sad lot and said so. She had borrowed a horse from Sally Shaw, a big chestnut brute over sixteen hands high that Sally was going to get rid of. She dared Tony to ride it. He had appeared in a tweed cap, a turtle-neck sweater, a jacket with two vents in the back, and a pair of magnificent old, old boots. Of course, as she had feared, he rode beautifully. He was calm and relaxed and Sally, who talked more horse than she rode, excitedly pointed to his hands as Tony was racking the chestnut past them and screamed, "Look! You could balance a glass of water on them."

So he was not a gambler or a riding instructor. She was not so blind as not to see that he was living very well off her nevertheless, but, since he was not making love to her or anything like it, she knew her allowance to him was a whim she could abolish at any moment. It gave her a hold over him, not that she wanted one, but it did not explain why he had come to the town in the first place. A last romantic possibility occurred to her: he might be a secret agent, but she could not for the life of her find a reason why the British or any other government should want information about her home town although she had to admit the notion that they might enhanced the town's weak importance in her eyes. However, she was a stockholder in all of the four factories. She knew what they made, springs for automobile seats, paper boxes and containers, canned soup, and gents' suspenders. None of these products could have any crucial weight with Downing Street, the Kremlin, or whatever. Tony was not a spy. But what was he? Why was he there?

She had asked him one day why he could bring himself to accept money from her. She hoped to embarrass him and make him reveal something. He had been telling a story about being hauled before an Italian magistrate for running over a pig in his car. He was very amusing about it. The point of the story was that the magistrate, a big, cynical, fat man, hated the British and was inclined to throw Tony in jail and Tony was a guest at a house party at Ventimiglia and could hardly absent himself because he was the extra man. The friend with Tony, Michael Somebody, had tried to frighten the court by alleging that Tony was a noble lord, a cousin of the King's and . . .

"You're not, are you, Tony?" she had broken in.

"God, no. I'm only a Right Honourable. . . ."

The long evenings with the mound of pillows at her back, the novel on her knees, and the nembutal at her elbow helped her out. She knew that Right Honourables were younger children of earls and marquesses. "How does it come, then, that with noble blood in . . ."

"Pip, pip, pip," he interrupted. "Only Father. He's the bloody earl, not me."

"How does it come, then, that you, an aristocrat, can accept money from me?"

He raised his head in sincere astonishment. "Why, you've got packets, haven't you?"

"And all you have to do is ask?"

"Of a friend, yes," he said as if it were obvious. There was something open and childlike about him as he said it.

Hurrying it a little because she had at last forced him into a corner, eager to have the immense satisfaction of saying something both apropos and cutting she had thought of beforehand, she said, "You sound like a peasant asking help with the plowing."

"Of course. Lords and peasants are born to it. They know who they are. Only the middle class has to have manners."

He had won again. Her wince did not show and what he said sounded vaguely true, or rather, it was a statement that once had been filled with truth but now the truth had almost all leaked out of it but not entirely. She never included herself as a member of the middle class but she knew she was in Tony's eyes and when she thought about it later, she was in her own. All she had to remember was her grandfather who chewed plug tobacco. Or her father.


Her vast brick house, built by her grandfather, still bearing the complicated wooden scrollwork of his period, was surrounded by trees, gigantic maples, whose crusted boles rose thirty or forty feet before they branched, a grove. And, as a child, she thought it was a grove for hiding in, safe from the world. Later the house and yard had changed. They became a dreadful little arena where her mother, a thrifty, kind, neighborly, small-town woman who had been stiffened and corrupted at the discovery of how much money there was, tried to make her better than other people, teaching her tricks out of the etiquette books, dressing her from pictures in the magazines, grinding into her the legend of her own superiority to the children she had known in grade school, and all with a dry, untender determination she called love.

Partly because she had been prepared in this fashion and partly because she was stifled by the preparation, she raced away from the town the first chance she got: into a second-rate Eastern school because it was the only one her mother had heard of and later into a first-rate Eastern college. She thought she wanted excitement, and aloof, now beautiful, almost consecrated to the search since she in her turn had discovered how much money there was, she nearly found it at Princeton and New Haven.

In her senior year at college she married a tall, quiet young man from Dartmouth because she had seen him at a Winter Carnival soaring a hundred feet in the air, flapping his mittened wings above all the admiring faces, and his flight seemed as daring and luminous as her hopes. Pleased to find her rich as well as beautiful, he had taken her first to the Telemark in Norway, next to Garmisch and Saint-Moritz. They skiied. And using her money like a dowser, she divined something of the richness and complexity of Europe's old life. She persuaded her husband to return in the warm weather, and after the initial disappointment every traveler suffers disembarking at Le Bourget or the Gare du Nord, she discovered Paris, *couture* and *cuisine*. Just before the war, she found she was quite happy. She had matured, only a little disappointed in her clean, single-minded, muscular husband, and the goal that had shimmered first as mere excitement, then as sophistication, at last defined itself. She felt she had been promised a vividness of life, a proof that the world did not end under the big trees of her front lawn, a trophy she could shake before the eyes of her dead mother in pride and defiance, and, staring past her tanned knees through a row of cypresses at the Mediterranean, where, far in the distance like a wound-up toy, her husband was aquaplaning, she was sure she almost had it.

But the war came and her husband, sullenly raging because he was too old to fly, got himself heroically killed on a destroyer in the Philippine Sea. They sent her the Silver Star and she kept it faithfully on her dressing table. She was living at home alone in the big house. She wore black its due season, redecorated the house, and flew off to South America, where she found the beaches of Copacabana and Mar del Plata not so very different from those at Antibes. She returned home again.

There were people there she had always "known" because, although it was growing, the town was still a small town where you knew "everybody." These people asked her to dinner, one after the other, with a cateress in the kitchen and maids hired for the occasion creeping about in the lengthening silences. She had lost touch with them. She was sure they were decent, upright, hard-working people but they were dull. She had nothing to say to them, really, except accounts of her travels and they listened so hard it was embarrassing.

So she tried Italy another summer. She found herself giving large sums to all the charities and she seemed to attract suave Italians of fifty, tall, often with blue eyes, who wanted as they had wanted for two hundred years to sell paintings by Mantegna and Perugino, "quite genuine." She noted with surprise that, except for the poor, she was much alone. She was chic, handsome, driven by her avidity for something, some person who would be flashing, wild, and beautiful, but unfortunately there were many other women like her at the Ritz Hotel level where she lived. It was then that she began to read in her bedrooms. Treasonably, she admitted Italy was unsatisfactory and she went home again.

The dust covers were hardly off the furniture when a man telephoned her and asked if he might come to see her that evening. She said yes. She remembered him from her two years in high school before she went East. She had cheered him the length of a football field as he had plunged down it, haggard and battered, six or seven yards at a time. Even over the phone she recalled an aura of heroism about him and she rather looked forward to the evening. When he came into the room she saw his hair had gone and he was wearing rimless glasses. He had primed himself with a drink or two which she could smell as he actually and awkwardly bent over her hand and kissed it. With a straight face, she began to laugh and she laughed for an hour while the fake Continental graces he had devised to impress her melted into a proud, straightforward acount of the money he was making and at last into a groveling whine, "What do you do with yourself? Aren't you lonely? Can't I come to see you?" before she got rid of him.

That night as she was reading her dilemma emerged more clearly: she did not want to go away again, because they had changed the countries on her somehow; she did not want to stay here, because she could not stand the people. She had been taught to despise them and it did not occur to her— how could it?—that these were the people she wanted to impress. She had not learned that her life was rich only as theirs was stupid and monotonous, by contrast. They provided the dark background for her to shine against. In Europe she was not unusual. Here, she was, and only one or two old ladies in the town, wealthy and shrewd, born out on farms in the country like her own grandmother, suspected the truth, that Ellen Catesby was a small-town girl.

Quite naturally, when Tony showed up, she welcomed him.

In spite of the stagnancy of their relationship, her impatience and curiosity about Tony and a long string of novels wore out the winter. She was growing more uneasy. She was still young, youngish, and she could read about things and be told about things when she was seventy. To be already stuck at one remove from life seemed a waste.

She tried very hard to break down Tony's diffidence, shyness, reserve—she did not even know what it was she was assailing—but nothing came of it. She did not dare send him away for good. She did not want to send him away at all and during the winter she reached the point where she would not dare because then she would be utterly alone. If that was going to be the only bond between them, she knew she would have to accept it.

It was now, however, spring. It had rained a lot. The trees were in full leaf, the grass was a brilliant green, and her garden (walled) was bright with the fragrance of early flowers that had shot up almost overnight. When Tony came she gave him little sandwiches of tomato and watercress with his tea instead of anchovy toast, and he sat decorously sprawled out in a white chair, talking as usual. Nothing had changed.

". . . off Oxford Street. Crown glass in the windows. You opened the door and a little bell tinkled. Mr. Brown was never actually *in* the shop, however. He was down cellar fondling and clucking to the bottles in the gloom, I suspect, and presently you heard his footsteps on the stair. Except for some white patches where he squinched up his eyes, his face was nearly the color of an old saddle, deep and rich. He said, 'Good morning, sir. Care for a glass of sherry?' And he would bring out two old-fashioned cut-glass sherry glasses. He filled them. But before you could touch a drop, he said sternly, 'Have you smoked this morning?' and he thrust a packet of what you call crackers at you and commanded, 'Eat a biscuit.' You meekly ate and only then did drink." He paused. "Incredible little place. Burnt to ashes in the fire raids." He paused again. "I say, Ellen. You are lovely." He stood up swiftly, bent over, kissed her, and did not let her go at once. It was the first time.

"Why, Antony, what came over you?" she said lightly.

"Oh, I'm terribly sorry, Ellen." There seemed to be a real regret in his voice. "I didn't mean anything by it."

"Go ahead, Tony. Mean something for once."

He seemed flustered. "Well, I mean to say, you *are* a beautiful woman. The curve of your cheek—it took my eye. And, oh, spring, perhaps. The pretty birds do sing. Flowers." He threw out his hand helplessly.

"But nothing serious, eh, Tony? Merely some vague seasonal stirring of the blood?"

"Oh, now, damn it all, Ellen. Don't try to put me in the wrong. I'm not an absolute swine, you know." He was walking up and down now, apparently with some agitation.

"But it's not serious, is it, Tony?"

He walked toward her and stood looking down with an absolutely new expression on his face. She could call it tender inquiry. "You want it to be quite serious?"

"Oh, quayte," she said. She could not resist the impulse

to devil him. He had to pay something for the long hard winter.

"Marry me, then."

She was so absorbed in remarking his change of manner that at first he did not seem to be speaking to her at all and she could say only, "Really?"

"Oh, I know there's damn all to recommend me. Be a bloody bad benedick, I daresay, but"—here his face broke into a broad smile—"we could have a couple of kids. I mean, not so young ourselves, but still. Just a couple, you know. Perhaps a piece of land. Some of these tractors for the corn. Cattle. A little shooting. Room for the children to grow. I should think I could manage the place. . . ."

"An estate," she murmured not loudly enough to break his flow.

"That's it. Wonderful prospect, really." He looked down from the sky over her shoulder. "I'm sorry. Actually, I mean you're a damned fine woman, Ellen. Awfully good and kind. It could be marvelous."

"I think so, too, Tony."

"Oh, good girl. I'm frightfully happy about it." He pulled her to her feet, kissed her mouth and throat, and muttered inexplicably into her shoulder. "Near thing, Ellen. You don't know. Very near thing."

For the next few minutes she found him almost pathetically endearing. Then she said, "Where in England would you want to buy?"

His face stiffened. "England? No. Not there. Definitely."

"But I assumed, naturally . . ." She saw she had said something really wrong.

"No!" he shouted as if he were in uniform. "England's *kaput*. Too many queues, too many things to sign. Man's not a man in England any more. He's an ugly little photo on an ugly little card. His dossier's more important than he is. No. No, no. Here."

"All right. Here. Any place you say, Tony."


She planned a small June garden wedding. She had a won-derful time giggling over the list of guests because she guessed what everyone in town had been saying about her and her pet limey. She was preparing a big reception after the ceremony with floods of champagne and she wished she could hear every single thing that would be said. When she finished all the minor arrangements, she flew to New York to buy a second trousseau. Tony saw her off and as they walked across the windy pavement of the airport, she said, "Take one of the cars while I'm gone, and go out into the country and pick out your plot of ground, will you, Tony?"

Hat and gloves in one hand, the wind ruffling his hair, he said, "Yes, darling," and except for his farewell, that was the last thing he ever said to her.

For when she returned from New York he was not at the airport, and when she opened the front door of her house, the maid came running up, her eyes big, and said hoarsely, "There's a woman wants to see you, Mrs. Catesby. In there," and she pointed to the larger drawing room.

Ellen thought, "Oh, God," and she stopped to do her mouth very carefully before the mirror in the hall.

The woman was American, about sixty years old, bare-headed and shabby. She wore a black winter coat with a ratty brown fur collar thrown over a blue gingham dress. She came limping and shuffling across the floor, greatly ex-cited. "Mrs. Catesby? Don't sit down. Don't even take off

your coat and hat. You got to come with me. Right away.
You . . ."

"Why must I?"

"Major Braithwaite's dead." Her voice soared up to a high
wheeze and she began to pant. "Shot himself right through
the forehead and . . ."

"Tony?" The old woman was hustling her toward the front
door. "How do you know? Who are you?"

"He boarded with me. My name's Williams. He had my
front room, the one with the fireplace." By this time they were
down the front steps.

"But what happened? How did he do it? Are you sure
he's . . ."

"You'll see. You'll see."

Ellen drove very slowly and fussily, the old woman telling
her the way because she had never known where Tony lived;
she had never even asked. She knew why she felt weak and
cold—that was shock. The pounding headache that began
was shock also, and the pepper that seemed to burn inside
her nose. She did not know why all the big green maples in
the streets should start to fall inward upon her, lunging at
the car and barely missing it, or why flashes of sunlight on
windows and windshields should stab her eyes like a pin. She
heard Mrs. Williams' rapturous garrulity in spurts and flashes,
such a handsome man, kind of like that Ronald Colman in the
movies, a real gentleman, him behindhand? No, sir, always
on the dot, ever notice his hands, really beautiful long thin
hands, a third cousin in South Bend ran a photograph gallery,
hands just like his . . .

It seemed unimportant, merely a blemish like a birthmark,
the small neat dark-red hole in his forehead. He had lain
down on his bed and the revolver had not slipped from his

stiff hand. A coronal of dark blood stained the pillow around his head. A piece of note paper lay folded on his chest.

"That's for you," Mrs. Williams said. "I read about you and him in the papers. That's how I knew you was Ellen."

Ellen unfolded it and read, *I'm sorry, Ellen.* It was the first time she had ever seen his handwriting, small, spiny letters, almost unreadable.

She came back to his room once more before the funeral to see if she could find the name and address of anyone she should notify, friend or kin, but she found nothing. At least fifteen members of the Shawnee Club volunteered as pall-bearers and there were more flowers that she expected, all from men he had played poker with. She buried him just outside her own family plot and when she ordered a head-stone, a plain slab of gray granite, she wrote out the name, *Antony Braithwaite,* on a card for the stonecutter.

He said, "Year of birth?"

She had to guess. That was the first time she cried and they called her house for the maid and chauffeur to take her home from the monument works because no one knew who her friends were.

The summer was a horror. It did not rain and she could hear like the faint swish of a whip the automatic sprinklers turning on her lawn to keep the grass from shriveling. The heat seeped in through the thick walls, under the high ceilings of her house, and she carried an old palm-leaf fan she found one day in the attic.

Her usual consignments of books arrived but she could not read them, a few pages and the type would blur and she would get up and start to walk again. She walked slowly up and down through all the darkened rooms of her house, wearing only a negligee, her naked feet thrust into high-heeled mules that sometimes caught on the carpets, and, when they did, she stepped out of them absently and walked barefooted, fanning herself languidly. A dozen times a day she passed the massive sideboard in her dining room. There were the decanters, heavy, cut-glass, with little silver plaques hanging from chains around their necks, Scotch, Bourbon, Rye, Irish. She sometimes stopped and looked at them speculatively, picked them up and jiggled the liquor around inside, and once or twice she drew the stopper and smelled of it, but she shuddered and put it back in its row. She took quite a lot of nembutal, not that it was less vicious but that it was less traditional, and she could tell herself she did have to sleep a little after all—the heat— But sometimes she woke up at night just the same.

The worst time came in August. The heat was drier and worse. She could hear the streets were nearly empty in the middle of the day and she could not shut out the scraping cheep of the cicadas in the trees around the house. Although she did not walk so much any more, she was thinner. She lay on one sofa or another or on her bed, smoking, her legs crossed, in her negligee, her blank gaze stopped by the ornate moldings around the ceiling, and when she inhaled, the cage of her ribs shone dully beneath her breasts.

In August the women started coming to call. She had the maid turn the first two away with "Mrs. Catesby is ill" but when they kept coming, she decided to let them in. She did not value their condolences but she wanted to see somebody, anybody because she was beginning to be frightened. She had read about grief. When her husband had been killed, she thought she had suffered it but she had, as she saw it now, blandly endured a little sadness, some regret. Nothing in her life, the life she wanted so intense and vivid, had prepared her for a shock like the blow of a club which erased all memory of Tony as if her skull had been broken, left her weak and listless as if she had lost blood. All day and most of the night her head ached and the joints of her wrists, knees, shoulders, and elbows were sore. She could touch the places with her fingers. And it did not get any better. That was what frightened her.

She dressed and received her callers, with her head on one hand, barely listening. Slowly she spotted the false innocence of their questions. They wondered too many times why Major Braithwaite should have made away with himself, and their smiles were not sympathetic but openly snotty and triumphant. When old Mrs. Danvers came, a woman she had known all her life who used to give her cinnamon cookies as a little girl, and asked the same question with a concern too sorrowful not to be genuine, Ellen shut up the house again and ordered any others turned away. They had all been talking about her and she had not thought about it once.

That night she did not take any nembutal. She lay on her bed with the light out, two long hot bars of moonlight striping her body. She tried to make herself sleepy by planning a trip but she found it hard to imagine going anywhere, and she deliberately turned to the past as a more trustworthy period but she found her memories sparse and colorless as if someone had photographed paintings in black and white. Yet it passed the time better than any contemplation of the future because the future was nothing at all.

After a while she switched on the light by the bed and picked up the nembutal. She shook one capsule out in her hand, then she tipped up the bottle. She looked at the little heap of yellow capsules. She was holding her death in her hand. "Why not?" she thought.

At some moment or other, Tony had picked up the gun and he must have thought the same thing. Was it because an empty future might as well be extinguished neatly as wandered into? A chill ran down her spine and she shuddered. For the first time she seemed to be near an answer to the questions that had throbbed so long like the ache in her head, perhaps were the ache in her head, "Why had he come? Why had he killed himself?"

Like her, he believed only the images of the past to be proof of life. The present was something merely to be got through until the silliness of the process grew obvious and you ended it. Now that she thought of it, he had never mentioned anyone who was not dead. The places and the times he had been happy were elsewhere and long ago. When she had searched his room for a relative's name, she had gone through the pockets of his suits. There were only three of them; they were all made in Savile Row but they were threadbare, almost worn out. The shoes she had always admired she had never seen up close. Held in her hand they were neatly treed up and shining but cracked into a myriad of tiny lines.

The pigeonholes of a rather nice little escritoire had contained a Distinguished Service Order in a leather case, an ordnance map of Gloucestershire, and one symbol of the present, the box of bullets for the gun he had shot himself with. As if he had forgotten or broken with everyone, there were no letters.

One wall of his room was covered with photographs: Tony in flannels and a striped blazer with a group captioned *The Oxford University Tennis Club;* a polo team, Tony with a mallet under one arm, a splendid silver cup on the ground before them, and syces in turbans holding the ponies at the rear. There was a muscular Tony in a black clout lying beside the pool at Eden Roc talking to Marlene Dietrich. There were several groups of British officers standing in mud and in sand and Tony was in every one. One picture showed only a vast unidentified explosion. The most interesting was a family group on a broad lawn in front of a country house. Tony was in the center, young, thin, almost in the act of ducking his head with shyness. On a table in front of him shone an ornate silver service and in a clump at the side stood the servants, butler, footman, first maid, second maid, and all. Across one corner of the picture Tony had scrawled "Twenty-firster." It was his coming-of-age party and the servants had just presented him with the silver. Tony's father looked hard-bit and military with what Tony had once distinguished as a colonel's mustache, a drooper, and his mother was a handsome tall woman with one of those brick-red outdoor complexions, a shapeless print dress, and flat-heeled shoes with a strap across the arch. Whether the other young people were his brothers or sisters, she could not tell.

There it all was, the only world intelligible, the happy past he had moved in so easily with such grace and courage, carrying with him lightly the freight of so much history, and now all worn away, blown up in vast unidentified explosions.

Now she could see what had killed him since she felt something like it working in herself. It was exhaustion. He had been worn out. She had a vision of him landing in New York, suave, correct, and gentle, his box full of his old shoes and threadbare clothes, and the stack of photographs. Perhaps he cherished then unrotted some bare fragment of hope and it had led him to this town, a strange and unfamiliar place, which he had attacked with the only means he knew, by making friends. He might even have loved her a long time before he asked her to marry him. Certainly his proposal was the last dying flicker of his strength and, once accepted, he could not make the effort to begin again to gain the archaic riches of family and estate because he was by then too weak to take one single step into a future however sure.

"Poor Tony," she thought.

She looked down at the capsules in her hand. She was too young for them. The republic was not old enough. Her grandfather had plowed with oxen, tramping in his own furrow, while Tony's had sat drinking brandy at the Café Anglais in the red tunic of a military observer attached to the French Army during the siege of Paris. And if she and Tony had reached the same point, she was not as tired as he. She dumped the capsules back into the bottle, turned out the light, and went to sleep.

# About the Author

*Allan Seager was born in Adrian, Michigan. He moved to Memphis, Tennessee, when he was eleven years old. He lived there until he went to college at the University of Michigan and, later, at Oriel College, Oxford. On his return from England, he was one of the editors of* Vanity Fair *magazine for a year and a half, and is the author of two novels,* Equinox *and* The Inheritance. *He has traveled in Europe and South America. He has a wife and two daughters and he now teaches at the University of Michigan.*

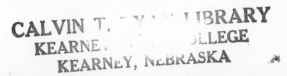